CHASING PANCHO VILLA

A Story of Mystery, Romance, and Adventure

R.L. Tecklenburg

HISTRIA FICTION

Chasing Pancho Villa: A Story of Mystery, Romance, and Adventure
By R.L. Tecklenburg

ISBN-13: 978-1-94544-740-2 (softbound)

Also available in ebook format.

Published in the USA by

Histria Books
7181 N. Hualapai Way, Ste. 130-86
Las Vegas, NV 89166 USA
www.histriabooks.com

Printed in the United States of America.

Publisher's Note

This is a work of fiction. Names, characters, places, and incidents either are the product of the author's imagination or are used fictitiously, and any resemblance to actual persons, living or dead, business establishments, events, or locales is entirely coincidental.

The publisher does not have any control over and does not assume any responsibility for author or third-party websites or their content.

For Rebecca, my friend and love

Acknowledgments

To Gabriela and those who believe Pancho Villa is a hero; for George who believes in justice for all.

I want to acknowledge my debt to Chris Pendleton, for taking the time to read and edit the manuscript. Billy Joe Cox, Bruce Richey, and Mike Reddan for their insightful comments. Without their excellent suggestions this book would not have been possible.

Either he is talking, or he is pursuing,
Or he is in a journey, or peradventure,
He Sleepeth, and must be awaked.

The First Book of Kings 18:27

CHAPTER ONE

Northern Mexico, 0830 hours, July 23, 1916

"Rápido! Rápido, muchachos," General Villa urged in a low voice. "Los invasores vienen." He sat astride his favorite horse, Siete Leguas, with the morning sun at his back.

A lone rider on a great dark stallion navigated expertly through the column of armed men to move up beside the General. The rider greeted him with a simple nod and he reciprocated, also without speaking. With a weapon strapped tightly to her narrow waist, sombrero pulled low over her eyes, the tall, slim figure, sitting ramrod straight in the saddle, made an unforgettable impression on the war-weary soldiers.

The woman—considered very beautiful by both friend and foe—was dressed in a riding habit that reflected her eclectic tastes and free spirit—a low cut cotton blouse tight against her bosom, dark wool jacket and denim jeans with U.S. Cavalry boots reaching almost to her knees. Like Villa, she rode comfortably in a Mexican saddle.

Maria Washington watched carefully without expression while Villa's men deployed along the rocks. Although just an observer here, still her dark eyes burned with the passion of a revolutionary.

To Villa's peasant soldiers, the young woman mounted on the great stallion seemed fearless and invulnerable. Believing that only good fortune would come from her presence, they smiled, touching the stallion gently on its flank or hind quarter as they walked by.

"Today, the Americans will pay for their arrogance, señorita," the General finally said in English. "And you will see how you have aided our great cause."

"Good," the woman replied, still watching his soldiers take their positions. She was not concerned for her own life, but she knew it would take more than new rifles to stop the American invasion.

Pancho Villa was doing what he knew best. Powerful enemies had pursued him for more than 20 years, since he was 16. Yet he always managed to slip away, proving himself to be a very capable field commander. That had surprised everyone but him.

He understood clearly that this was his chance to hurt the Americans but he had to be quick—hit them and escape. Silently he pointed and one of his soldiers, dressed in home-spun cotton and sandals, wearing a sombrero hanging from his neck and carrying an American Springfield rifle, quietly crawled up the rock embankment. He grasped a bandolier of .30 caliber rounds in his right hand.

Villa consciously masked the adrenalin surging through his body as he carefully supervised the placement of his soldiers, each one a hand-picked sharpshooter. They were deep in Chihuahua Province, and no one knew more about warring here than he. The terrain was rocky, dusty, and bleak.

Perfecto, he thought.

Villa looked to the woman and smiled—one side of his mouth turned up slightly, cracking the leathery, sun-baked skin—as he prepared his ambush for the great General Pershing. Dressed like his men, he sat stiff-legged and straight, comfortable in the saddle. A dark, bushy mustache on the well-creased and weathered face hung over his upper lip, concealing a mouthful of stained teeth.

"Los carretones, muchachos," he called, his dark brown eyes intently studying each man's position. Hidden beneath severely lined and half-closed lids, his eyes flashed when he spoke.

He had about 100 men with him, all that remained of the force of 500 who had crossed the border to attack Columbus, New Mexico back in March. But armed now with the American Springfield rifles he had received from the woman only days earlier, he knew he could inflict damage on General Pershing's army.

They had been riding for days under cover of darkness to avoid the Americans' aeroplanes that sometimes accompanied their troop movements, searching for him and his men. Villa had received complete information on General Pershing's line of march, enabling him to elude the Americans and remain undiscovered. He had received that information from the many patriots who remained along the border to watch the enemy.

Villa had chosen this place, west of Torreón in the foothills of the Sierra Madres, for his ambush. The horses were hidden in a narrow, tree-shrouded ravine that led deep into the mountains. The American supply trucks had to travel long distances through country that belonged to him, and the Americans always had to protect those routes.

I, Doroteo Arango, son of Agustin Arango, will again demonstrate just how vulnerable their army is in my land—the land of my father, and of his father before him, Villa thought.

Villa planned to strike hard at their trucks, destroying transport and creating havoc. Then, he would retreat once again into secure mountain lairs where his army was safe. Confronted with a force of 10,000 American soldiers moving south from the Rio Grande and Carranza's army surging into Chihuahua from Mexico City, he had no choice but to hit and run. As usual, the Sierra Madres were his escape when heavily outnumbered by his enemies.

The deployment of his men was complete.

*

Out of the corner of his eye, First Sergeant Juan Parilla of the United States 24th Infantry noticed a puff of dust from just above the ridgeline. He knew immediately and turned to locate the company commander.

"Captain! Captain!" he called to the younger soldier marching on the other side of the column. "Mire." He pointed to the ridge. But the dust had dissipated and was no longer visible.

The two men belonged to Company L of the 2nd Battalion, part of a long column of soldiers and vehicles that stretched almost two miles. For two days, the infantry troopers had been eating dust from ten Model T trucks grinding away immediately in front of them.

The reddish dust covered their skin and uniforms. Many of the men had tied bandanas around their faces and wrapped socks and other pieces of cloth from their bedrolls over their rifles for protection.

The captain looked, but saw nothing. Still, he knew after four months in Mexico to trust his first sergeant's instincts. He whispered to his Negro orderly, who ran to another officer in the first platoon. That man called to a squad leader.

"First squad, fall out," the lieutenant ordered over the truck noise. "Follow me." They ran in the direction of the ridge, meeting with the convoy's flanking force—a mounted unit of Negro troopers from the 10th U.S. Cavalry. Three horsemen turned and headed off toward the south. The infantry squad spread out and assumed flanking duties.

The Model T trucks loaded down with fuel and supplies continued on, slowly creeping across the dusty brown plateau. At the head of the long column were mounted soldiers from Troops A and B of the Negro 10th Cavalry—Buffalo Soldiers. An older man led the formation, riding ramrod straight in the saddle of a great black stallion, his eyes focused on the trail ahead. His aides rode close behind.

General John J. "Black Jack" Pershing, on orders from President Woodrow Wilson, commanded this expeditionary force tasked with finding the elusive bandit, Pancho Villa. They had been chasing him across northern Mexico since March without much success.

*

A volley of shots suddenly rang out from across the ridge. At first, the firing went unnoticed over the loud growls of the truck engines. Using the most modern American weapons, not even puffs of smoke could be detected from the rifle barrels. A soldier fell from his horse.

"Villaistes! Villaistes?" A flanking soldier from L Company finally called out upon seeing the horseman fall and then hearing a bullet snap overhead.

The ambushers found their range, and bullets began to strike cans of fuel packed into the trucks. Suddenly, an explosion and a great ball of flame rose from the rear of the lead Model T. Following too close to the first, the second truck was engulfed in flames. Both driver and passenger bailed out to escape being incinerated in the gasoline blaze.

"Keep moving forward," an officer yelled to keep the trucks from bunching together. But the inferno ahead effectively halted the convoy, trapping the trucks on the narrow, rutted wagon track. The transport soldiers escaped their vehicles, running for cover away from the shooting. The trucks were left stationary, easy targets for the sharpshooters still firing from the rocks above.

General Pershing reacted immediately. An experienced horseman, he galloped back to the infantry formations and gave an order to the L Company commander. He then wheeled to join the main body of cavalry units more than 40 yards forward in the column. All the while, his aides stayed close.

"Fall out! Form a skirmish line!" the officers of L Company yelled. Their well-disciplined troopers immediately responded. They dropped their packs, unslung their Springfields. Quickly they lined up in ranks facing the ridge. "Lock and load," the officers called out in unison. Bullets snapped and whined as the ambushers still focused on destroying the supply trucks.

One troop of cavalry was lined up perpendicular to the infantry company, but still well out of their way. General Pershing, who as a young captain led Black troops in combat in Cuba, drew his saber and joined them. They prepared to charge toward the ridge, but waited for the infantry company to begin the engagement.

The command was given, "Move forward!" The infantry marched at quick step up the slope, squad following squad in a long formation that stretched for 50 yards. Each man held his rifle tightly at port arms. No one fired.

"Stay together. Faster," First Sergeant Parilla called to his men.

"Halt and prepare to fire, first squad," Captain Bartlett James called. "Fire!" he ordered. James was excited about finally seeing action. He hoped that after four months they would at last come face to face with the notorious Pancho Villa.

His troopers fired. "Reload!" James ordered. "Fire!" Again, the troopers let loose with a volley all along the line. The bullets kicked up dust and pieces of stone. There was no return fire.

Now in position to attack, with the general himself in the lead, the cavalry swept forward at a full gallop. The mounted Negro soldiers yelled and fired their .45 caliber automatics as they charged up and across the ridgeline.

"Cease fire!" Captain James called to his L Company men upon seeing the horsemen assault the ridge. They watched the troopers reach the top. The mounted troopers continued to shoot and yell as they disappeared over the crest. But the Villaistas were gone. Only brass shell casings in the dust remained to tell the story of Pancho Villa's ambush.

When the Americans realized the Mexicans had escaped into the mountains, silence descended from the ridge down to the men remaining in the convoy. Their enemy had deserted them, denying the Americans their chance at battle and victory. From general to private, all sensed disappointment and frustration.

Later that evening in camp, Captain James was called to General Pershing's tent. No one else was present. "Captain, please sit down," the General said. "I want a word with you."

James, a tall, thin man with thick blond hair cut almost to the scalp, removed his campaign hat and sat down in one of the folding wooden chairs. "Yes, sir. Thank you sir," he said, feeling a little apprehensive. Pershing could display a temper.

"Captain, you're probably wondering why I want to talk with you," the General said directly. The first thing that James always noticed about the general was his steel grey eyes. They now watched him closely. He felt them examining and measuring.

"Yes sir, I am," the younger man responded finally. James stared at Pershing's hair. He suddenly realized he had never seen the general without his hat on, having only spoken with him in the field. The general had a full head of hair that was completely gray.

"Something wrong, Captain?" The general asked abruptly. He was sitting, legs crossed, relaxed with his tunic off. James saw that he was trim and appeared in good shape for an older man.

"No sir, "James said, quickly.

"You have an exemplary record, Captain," Pershing continued, "and that's why I requested that you be given assignment to this expedition." He looked away briefly, as if distracted by an idea that had suddenly presented itself. "Yes, well, to the point. I have a new mission for you."

"General?"

Pershing looked down at something on his desk and then smiled. "Top of your class at West Point. Good family. Yes, and I've had the great honor to meet your mother. Charming," he said, looking up again to the captain. He smiled again. "Yes, I remember her well."

"My mother usually makes a lasting impression, sir."

"So she did, Captain James. So she did." For a second the young captain sensed a softening of that stern character. But it was fleeting. Pershing returned to the brown file. He opened it and pretended to review it. "With your intelligence background and flare for languages...," he said. "Yes... fluent in Spanish and German, I see. Four years of intelligence work in Washington."

James waited, confused, knowing well that he had not been ordered here to discuss his mother or his prospects for promotion.

"Captain, we need to have better information on what the hell is going on down here."

"Yes sir." James' steady blue eyes fixed on the General without blinking. He waited patiently, knowing the answer was coming.

"They ambushed us again today," Pershing said. Anger suddenly flashed across the stern features, turning them crimson. "How the hell does that happen? He's just an illiterate bandit, and yet he successfully ambushes the United States Army, even with our aeroplanes flying overhead. We lost four soldiers, three trucks and a week's worth of fuel and supplies. Now we are forced to camp here until those lost supplies and fuel can be replenished from a base camp more than fifty miles away. I have the entire 10th Cav out searching through those mountains looking for him. Do you think we'll catch him?"

"Perhaps not, sir," James replied slowly. "He knows the mountains well. He'll just disappear again."

"I agree," Pershing said, taking a deep breath to calm himself. "We've been chasing Villa since March without success, and without much prospect of success. Not the way we're doing it now." He looked directly at James, holding his gaze. "I've been thinking."

"Sir?" Captain James asked. Whatever this commanding officer had in mind was going to involve him.

"How did Villa know our route of travel? He knew exactly where we'd be at a specific time. He chose that ridgeline, and he knew the sun would be directly in our faces at that time of day. It was damn near perfect for an ambush."

"I don't know how he did it," James responded, thinking. "Good reconnaissance?"

"Probably that and more," Pershing said, a hint of frustration coloring his words. "But if his intelligence is that good, where does that leave us?"

"What do you mean, sir?" James asked, intrigued.

"Between the Pacific Ocean and the Gulf of Mexico we have hundreds of miles of open border with Mexico. If Villa can cross it at will with five hundred men to lay waste to our towns, what would happen if President Carranza with his general, Obregón, tried it with say fifty thousand?" Pershing asked. He let the question hang there for the young captain to consider. "I don't know, I don't know. I want you, captain, to find out if there is such a plan. We must know."

"Then my mission, sir?" James asked. Is it counter-espionage?"

"Yes captain. But the President and I are most concerned about the Germans." Pershing said, looking hard at the younger man.

"The Germans, sir?" James repeated.

"Yes, I suspect strongly that they are supplying Villa and others like President Carranza with important information they get from their spies operating across the Rio Grande. Remember, they'll do anything to stir things up for us."

"Yes, sir," James agreed. "My mission, then, is to watch the Germans?"

"More than that, Captain James," Pershing said. "Our border is threatened. Villa has already proven how vulnerable we are to attack."

"I don't expect you to watch every German in Mexico, Captain," Pershing continued, as if reading his mind. "Just one—a very dangerous soldier by the name of Von Moltke. Colonel Hermann Von Moltke. Currently, he is working with the Mexican general, Obregón. We believe he operates a very sophisticated spy ring. Your mission, Captain James, is to break it."

CHAPTER TWO

Paris, France, 1100 hours, July 23, 1916

Artillery fire rumbled somewhere off in the distance just north of the city. On the busy stone Parisian streets, military vehicles loaded with supplies and replacements for the front passed others packed with returning dead and wounded. The motor vehicles made growling noises that echoed in the narrow tree lined streets and mixed with the clop, clop of draft horses' hooves. Voices of soldiers and vendors were occasionally heard above the din of civilian traffic.

Honking, then a loud crash of metal on metal followed by yelling, was heard when a motor truck laden with ammunition swerved out of control and crashed into the front of a speeding taxi. Steam from two radiators shot high into the warm humid air, sending pigeons roosting in the Oak trees upward like an explosion of feathers. The accident happened directly in front of an elegantly built 19th Century brick building, so close that it forced the old doorman to run deep into the marble-lined lobby.

The street noise penetrated the old window panes in the building's largest office, located four floors above, but it didn't disturb the room's only occupant, a youthful looking man dressed impeccably in a dark wool suit. He sat unmoving in the wood desk chair, staring out the window. Indifferent to the riot of sounds below, he looked north across the gray Parisian skyline toward the maelstrom less than fifty miles from the old city.

Harrison James had long grown accustomed to the sounds of war, but they were strikingly different and implacably ugly compared to the pleasant sounds of prewar Paris. During the first months of the war there had been a general fear that the Kaiser's army would reach and lay siege to the city, not unlike the war of more than 40 years earlier. The French evacuated most of the government, but the siege had not happened. On the Marne River, the French Army finally halted the overextended German advance.

Now entering its third year, the war had evolved into a stalemate of trenches—bloody, horrible gashes in the earth—that weaved their way across northern France, just north of the capital from the English Channel all the way east to Switzerland. The entire area became a battlefield for the contending armies known as the Western Front. Harrison sometimes wondered if it would have been better if the Germans had taken the city in 1914, possibly ending the war—and the suffering—quickly.

The summer of 1916 was devastating for the French and British armies. The allied offensive along the Somme River failed miserably to break the stalemate, with the casualty lists growing into the tens of thousands. The French nation threw everything it had into holding Verdun against repeated German attacks, exclaiming that "they shall not pass." But the fighting continued to rage unabated. Many thousands of French and German boys fighting at Verdun were already dead. Harrison calmly considered how many more would be killed before that battered old fortress would be held or abandoned.

Like millions of Europeans, Harrison feared that the slaughter and destruction would just go on until all of Europe, from Western Russia to the English Channel, became a gigantic tomb of men and ruins. He was relieved that the United States was still neutral, remaining an observer only in this tragic and futile struggle.

Yet business was good, damn good. Harrison James was a businessman, an American neutral trading with the French Government. And he was making a fortune from this war, selling American commodities to the French—everything from grain, lumber, oil, steel, and even tooth powder.

He casually unfolded a week old copy of the *Chicago Herald* and began to read. Again, noises from the street reverberated across the room, causing him to look up and out the double window. He heard the shriek of a whistle, more honking and shouting. The old city was trying hard to accommodate soldiers, wounded, and civilian life itself, Harrison knew. Still, Paris was not the same city he remembered and perhaps it never would be again.

As one of the most sought after foreigners in France, Harrison had taken a suite of offices in the most exclusive neighborhood of the city to be nearer the government. It was an older building, full of history and unique Parisian charm. Even if he had wanted to make modest improvements, he knew it was impossible to find anyone to do the work. Every man under 40 fit enough to carry a rifle was in the army. Those deemed unfit for the army worked in the war production industries.

Relaxing his tall, lean frame into the chair, Harrison resumed reading. An article on the first page captured his interest. The *Herald* was reporting on Pershing's foray deep into Mexico to chase Pancho Villa. That was Wilson's revenge for Villa's raid into New Mexico. Harrison didn't need to be reminded that his brother Bart was part of that expedition. He commanded a company of Negro troops and he was damn proud of them. Harrison recalled how hard his younger brother had fought to get a command—anything to get him out of Washington.

There was a knock on the door. "Oui," Harrison called informally. The door opened and his young female secretary entered. With the war taking all available young men into the army, he had been forced to hire a woman to do his clerical work.

"Monsieur," she said with a curtsy. "Monsieur Butcher." She indicated the man standing behind her.

"Oui, Mr. Butcher. Come in, please," Harrison said, standing to extend his hand. "This is a great pleasure. I've been expecting you. I hoped the commotion out there wouldn't delay your visit." Both men shook hands across the desk. "Sit down, please."

"Mr. James, I've been hearing much about you and your company," Butcher said. He remained standing in front of the large desk. His face revealed no expression, not even a muscle twitch, Harrison noticed. Butcher waited for him to sit, and then followed.

"I'm afraid I've come on official business. As you know, I represent the President of the United States."

"Your letter of introduction informed me of your position, Mr. Butcher," Harrison said carefully. "How may I be of service to the President?"

Although Butcher easily had 10 years on James, both men were considered handsome. They possessed distinctive Anglo-Saxon features—piercing, cold blue eyes, noses that were neither too large nor too small, and firm, well-shaped chins. Both were tall men, broad across the shoulders, narrow at the waist. But, as Harrison quickly learned, Butcher was different from the men he conducted business with on a daily basis. The diplomat sat stiff and straight in the chair with his knees pinched together, feet firmly planted on the floor, and hands resting on his thighs, palms down. He seemed to fit Harrison's image of a career civil servant—formal and rigid. A know-it-all, he thought, who is now going to lecture me on the war, I suppose.

Harrison James, on the other hand, projected an image of supreme confidence and success. He appeared relaxed and interested, even though expecting a long monologue from the diplomat. Harrison had heard it before from others, but he maintained a conscious smile. Butcher immediately took that as condescension.

"Well, Mr. James, it is more a matter of how we can assist you. Your company received approval to do business with the belligerents because you—you personally, Mr. James—have sworn not to sell munitions or any other products on the list of contraband materials to the warring parties, their representatives, or intermediaries."

"That is correct, Mr. Butcher," Harrison agreed, rocking back in his chair. "And I have honored that agreement, sir."

"Mr. James, President Wilson is fighting to maintain strict neutrality. That struggle has been very difficult, as you are certainly aware." Harrison nodded.

"Tell me: What are you currently selling to the French?"

"Grain mostly—corn and wheat. Several shipments of lumber came into Marseilles from the Northwest last month. Steel and oil are currently much in demand. I am negotiating with Standard Oil to import the oil, and with several Pittsburgh firms for a good price on steel. But trade is becoming more difficult and dangerous with German subs operating in the Atlantic," Harrison said. "How may I help you, Mr. Butcher?" he repeated.

"We suspect that Randolph James Commodity Brokers is transacting with the French Government for munitions—large bore gun barrels and explosives, mostly," Butcher told him. "As a matter of fact, the German Government has recently lodged a formal protest. They charge that your company in Chicago negotiated an agreement with a representative of the French Government one month ago to ship those items in volume. They demand that your license be revoked immediately."

"You take the word of German spies, Mr. Butcher?"

Butcher ignored the question. "Mr. James, federal agents tracked a shipment of those items belonging to Randolph James to the port of Galveston. The entire shipment has been temporarily quarantined until we can sort it all out."

"What does my mother say to these charges?" Harrison asked.

"She stated, and I might add, not under oath, that the particular shipment traced was meant for the naval depot in New Orleans. But the commandant there had no knowledge of it." Butcher watched James' reaction. "At present, the United States Government cannot prove otherwise because there don't appear to be any papers with the cargo, and no Europe-bound freighter was designated to ship it. That could change, of course. Our investigation has just gotten underway."

Harrison, who knew Butcher was watching him, nodded, and gave the diplomat a simple look of interest.

"We are hoping that you can clear this matter up, as you are the company's principle contact here in Europe," Butcher finished.

"I have no idea what you're talking about, nor have I been briefed by my mother. I have not at any time contacted or been contacted by the French or the English, or my home office for that matter, regarding their purchase of American munitions."

Butcher never took his eyes from James, obviously still gauging the young businessman's reactions.

"You say you are selling wheat. The Germans say explosives. Please understand: If their accusations are true, the United States is in direct violation of the Neutrality laws. Such business transactions could easily be considered acts of war. I am here to discover the facts of the situation, not to charge or threaten you in any way. I want to inform you, Mr. James, of what is at stake here."

"I understand," Harrison responded as sincerely as possible. "I will wire Chicago immediately with your concerns. But again, Mr. Butcher, I must state that I know nothing of this."

"And again, I must caution you. There is an official investigation underway and, if we determine that the German allegations are true, your company's license will be revoked immediately. There could also be criminal charges."

"I think you've been misinformed Mr. Butcher. Randolph James Commodity Brokers has, since the beginning of hostilities here, complied with all laws—American and French." Harrison thought he understood Butcher's type. He was driven by one thing and one thing only—his mission—and he would not lose focus until guilt was established or innocence proven.

Butcher stood and offered his hand. "Good day, sir. Thank you for your time." He turned and marched for the door.

Harrison stood behind his desk, his mind elsewhere. Dear mother, so greedy and obsessed with power. He was deeply troubled and confused by Butcher's accusations. He slowly massaged the muscles in the back of his neck.

When the James' father died quite unexpectedly, mother, Bart, and Harrison inherited equal shares in the company. Following 12 months of acrimonious in-fighting between Harrison and their mother over control of the company, Bart announced that he would vote for Harrison to run the company if his brother allowed their mother a free hand with her personal business interests. In return, she had to accept Harrison's leadership. They agreed, and Bart signed over his proxy to his brother.

That decision was proving to be a great mistake—if Harrison's only mistake. But Bart was devoted to his mother, and Harrison was not prepared to destroy his younger brother's relationship with her—or with him—by using Bart's shares that he controlled to throw her out of the company.

But attempting to circumvent the American munitions embargo? He was amazed at the audacity of it.

CHAPTER THREE

Columbus, New Mexico, 1000 hours, October 5, 1917

The muscular-looking, well-dressed man stood, waiting impatiently, in an interior corner of the Hotel Hoover's lobby. A hot desert smell blew in through the open windows and hung in the air, dusting everything and everyone with a thin red coat. The weather was unusually hot and dry for this late in the season. He had seen smoke rising from the Portillo Mountains just to the north on his train trip from El Paso. Probably a brush fire, he was told by the conductor

The man, not used to the heat and grit of southwest New Mexico, wiped the perspiration and dust from his face with a silk handkerchief. Until several years ago, he had lived and worked in Chicago. He decided that was a much more civilized place. Opportunities for making fast money had brought him to El Paso. But he had not anticipated the dangers and the endless intrigue with all the competing armies. Their spies and agents had begun to threaten his business.

Trying to appear occupied, he retrieved a newspaper from under his arm and pretended to read the front page. The war news didn't interest him, but a short article on the bottom of the page caught his eye. "Rioting Negro Soldiers from New Mexico to be court-martialed in November," he read. He wondered how many soldiers remained to patrol the border, and the state of their morale.

Then he heard a name called. It wasn't his name, but rather an agreed upon signal.

"MISTER BARNES FROM DENVER?" a heavily accented voice said. It sounded melodious to the ear. "MISTER BARNES," the voice repeated, coming closer to where the man stood.

He nodded to the young, Hispanic-looking bellboy. "Here," he said, loud enough to catch the bellboy's attention, but not loud enough to call attention from others.

"Someone looks for you, señor," the bellboy said. "I will get him?"

"Yes, bring him here," the man said. He handed the young man a dime.

*

"You're late," the man hissed to a shorter, younger, darker skinned man who had approached and was now standing only inches from him. "Were you lost?"

"Sorry, señor. Crossing the border es dangerous now," the man responded with a shrug. His thick coarse hair was black, short, and crudely cropped off. He was dressed like a local—cotton shirt open at the neck, no jacket. The young man was noticeably out of place in the Hoover lobby, filled mostly with well-dressed white men parading around with great self-importance. The white men were mostly from Denver, Houston, or Santa Fe, conducting business with the army, local ranchers, and miners, or with Mexicans who had come up from Chihuahua Province to purchase needed supplies. Everyone had something to sell, and could always find a buyer willing to pay top dollar for scarce merchandise.

"This business is muy importante, eh señor?" The shorter man's dark, cold eyes studied the taller man, whom he had recognized immediately as his contact. They both held copies of the *Houston Post*, another recognition signal that had been arranged in advance. American? European maybe, he thought. It was difficult to tell with gringos.

"That is not your concern," the white man responded crisply.

"Why do you call for me, eh?"

"It is a mission specially suited to your skills. You did very well with the last assignment," the white man said quietly, looking casually around the lobby to ensure no one was listening. The white man felt uncomfortable here. He worried that he would be remembered meeting with a man like this one. But he was putting out a fire that, if allowed to burn, could eventually destroy the entire operation. Hiring this dangerous animal was a necessary part of his plan.

"The money?"

"The usual way. Half now and half when the job is done. It will be waiting for you as before, in Juarez." The white man pulled a brown envelope from his coat pocket and slipped it to the shorter man beneath his newspaper. He scanned the lobby again. "Further instructions are inside, with the money. They're in Spanish. You can read, I assume."

Ignoring the comment, the younger man opened the envelope and looked inside. With his thumb and forefinger, he carefully touched each bill to ensure the amount was what they had agreed to earlier. Smiling, he pulled out a single sheet of paper before stuffing the money in his shirt.

The white man watched the young Indian quickly read the note, refold it, and stick it inside his shirt. "The brother must die, too," he continued. "Together, in some type of altercation—ah, confrontation—that I'm sure you can arrange." He disliked the idea of being involved with killing, but knew he had no other choice. "This must be done in January."

Today, I will help Standard Oil because they want Villa to win, he thought. In January, I sell to Carranza when he has money to pay me. A quick smile of contentment creased the otherwise expressionless face.

The young man stared at him, but said nothing.

"Everyone must wait until El Presidente has the money," the white man said, a hint of contempt in his voice.

The Indian nodded, well aware of what the gringo was talking about. His people had been smuggling for years along the white man's border. After all, it was their border and had nothing to do with his people.

"Why do you want to kill this hombre? Did he insult your family?"

"That's none of your business."

"I usually kill Mexicans. I hate them and nobody cares, eh? But don't worry. I will do this for you."

"That's good. If you have problems, you know how to contact us." The white man knew it was time to leave. His eyes moved constantly about the lobby, searching out enemies. "Oh, one more thing," he said to quickly wrap things up.

"Amigo?"

"When you complete your job you must disappear again. In Mexico. No one must ever know that you worked for us. Is that clear?"

"I understand this. But what about his people? And your own Federales? Will they not investigate? Look for me, maybe?"

"His knowledge will die with him," he replied. "Remember. The rest of the money will be waiting for you in Juarez after the job is completed. At the same place." The man turned away to signal the meeting was at an end.

He walked across the lobby, mingling with other white men from out of town in their dark wool suits with starched collars.

The Indian had no interest in following the gringo—it might be dangerous. And he had what he wanted—his money and a mission.

CHAPTER FOUR

The train racketed on into the night. The rhythmic sound of the wheels rolling over ribbons of steel echoed in the darkness, hour after hour. Its mind-numbing rhythm was mixed with the snores and coughing of passengers asleep or dozing in the coach.

Unable to sleep, the smell of perspiration and body odors from the overdressed and unbathed packed into the railcar began to overwhelm his senses. Having lived in France among the wealthy, Harrison James had forgotten how others were forced to live. Tobacco smoke hung in the stale air, clinging to other odors. He knew if he opened the window, smoke and cinders from the firebox funnel would drift in. The train's frequent stops had been helpful, but they were still an inadequate relief from what he considered to be almost insufferable conditions. Suffocating in the old wooden coach, he now wished he had waited for better accommodations in El Paso.

No babies cried. Harrison thought that seemed strange, but he was grateful for the fact. Leaving Chicago 36 hours earlier, he had fought his way through throngs of women and small children. Now, his car was filled with sleeping men in brown wool uniforms. The impeccably cut gray suit he wore seemed completely inappropriate. He tried again to sleep, leaning back against the headrest of his seat. But sleep was impossible.

The steel beast hammered its way through the western corner of Texas and into New Mexico. Day turned to night, light into darkness and then back again. James had already seen 1200 miles of America pass by his grimy couch window.

For most of the last eight hours he had watched the grassland turn into barren and empty plain. Looking out the dust-covered window at the gathering darkness, James couldn't tell if the horizon was five or fifty miles away. Distances became illusion as objects seemed to shimmer and move about. But in the moonlight, he thought he could see faint outlines of mountains far to the north.

Harrison's thoughts returned to the darkness of his car as the train chugged across the arid scrub land. Irritated, he opened the window slightly to allow the cigarette smoke to escape from the stuffy carriage.

Harrison struggled against his own deep sense of loss. He would never see Bart again, and, to make matters even worse, the meeting with his mother hadn't gone well. They never did.

He considered his brief stay with her. He remembered walking up the wide marble steps, somberly observing the acres of neatly trimmed lawn and well-manicured gardens surrounding the great mansion. Its three stories seemed to lean over him threateningly, their blank windows reflecting the emptiness he felt inside.

As children, Bart and he had only limited contact with their parents. They had been raised by servants, under the supervision of Jonathan, mother's most trusted servant and confidant. The love Harrison had for his brother was the only nurturing experience inside those great walls. For his mother he felt nothing. She had given him nothing that he could love.

Harrison also knew that it had been different for Bart. His brother, younger by five years, had always strived to please his mother, and she had responded by lavishing her attention on him. Bart was everything she had wanted in a son. But Harrison was never jealous of his little brother. He understood.

Thinking about his mother, Harrison sighed long and hard. He tried not to blame her. That was always difficult and now that Bart had died—perhaps by his own hand—it had become impossible.

It had been four years since he was home. He had returned on that occasion only to bury his father. He was not surprised that his mother had not changed during his long absence in Europe. She remained slim, her silver hair piled high on her head, beautifully coifed and jeweled. When he arrived, she greeted him in a formal gown of deep blue. She came down the stairway slowly. Like a queen, he thought, a true blueblood. Her eyes were the first things he always noticed about her. They had remained young…and very hard.

At first, like Bart, he had made excuses for her snobbishness and cold, calculating behavior. "It was because she had a childhood of poverty, growing up in the tenements of Chicago," they told their friends. The family secret—that she was a downstairs maid their father had fallen madly in love with—could never be revealed. But now, after all these years, it didn't seem to matter to anyone but her. She had with great cruelty, cunning, and spirit created her own kingdom within Midwestern high society. In her world she ruled supreme. But, Harrison knew, in her soul, mother would always be that scheming, grasping maid.

"You might have taken your hat off upon entering my home, Harrison," she said when she reached the bottom of the stairs. They were the first words she had spoken to him. "Perhaps the people you know in Europe have more unique customs."

She'll never change, Harrison thought, feeling the chill.

"Your brother is buried," she stated directly, staring into his eyes. "I laid him to rest in the family plot last week, beside his father." She stared at him with distaste. "Tonight we will talk. Rest now," she ordered and abruptly turned to walk away. "Jonathan will take your bags up." It was pointless to try to continue the conversation, so he followed the butler up the curved staircase. His old room was at the far end of the hallway, next to Bart's. The door to Bart's room was closed and, he discovered upon trying to open it, locked.

"Your mother has the only key," Jonathan stated, flatly. And that was that.

Sitting in his room that evening, he looked over the many photographs adorning the wall and dresser. Most were of him and Bart. The last photograph of the two of them together was on the nightstand next to the bed. It was taken only four years earlier at their father's funeral, just before Bart had gone to Washington to work in the War Department. He took the photo from the frame and folded it carefully into his jacket pocket.

*

In the darkness of the train, James touched his chest pocket to make sure it was there. *That's all* I have left of my brother, he thought.

*

"Harrison," his mother said later that first night, following dinner, "I have heard of your dalliances in Paris, Monte Carlo, and Madrid. Also of your gambling and fighting. Have you no shame?"

"I'm sorry, mother. Do I embarrass you?" he had asked sarcastically.

"You're a disgrace to our family," she stated coldly.

"To our family?"

"Yes. And the women you choose to associate with. Prostitutes. They're women of no class or reputation. Why couldn't you have been more like your brother?"

"Do you really think we're any better than they? Money, mother—that's what makes the world go around. You of all people understand that," he said, grinning at her.

"Harrison," Jonathan hissed from across the table. But too late.

She ignored the comment, turning to look out the large window onto her lawns. "Beautiful, aren't they, Harrison?"

"Mother, we have important matters to discuss," he said. He was determined to talk about business, knowing that was the only thing she really understood. "You remember the problems with the government, don't you? You should. Your activities nearly destroyed the company."

"You are exaggerating, as usual," she responded, finally turning her attention back to her son. "Only a simple misunderstanding. Too much trouble over nothing."

"Nothing, mother?"

"The problem resolved itself, Harrison."

"Resolved itself? You violated an international agreement on neutrality and disregarded the directives of the President of the United States. But for you it's only a minor misunderstanding," he said, suddenly white with anger.

"Eight months later we were in the war," she told him. "As it turned out, we were actually contributing to the war effort. The French needed those munitions, but never got them. And we were forced instead to do business with bandits and revolutionaries."

"Bandits and revolutionaries? What do you mean?"

"Our man in Texas—Jackson Smith. You remember him. He negotiated with buyers in El Paso willing to pay cash. They were Mexicans who worked with Standard Oil. They agreed to get our munitions to a Mexican bandit called Villa. They took everything off our hands."

James was stunned by her matter-of-fact reply. "You don't know anything about him? What does he intend to do with the munitions? Use them against our army?"

"No, Harrison. That bandit will use them against other Mexicans. Does that matter?"

"It matters," James stated, incredulous.

"Yes, of course it does." She gave him a smile of satisfaction. "We were paid in cash, Harrison."

"Where is Smith now, Mother?"

"He no longer works for us," she said, looking away.

She was lying, but James didn't press it. "Do you want to know what I do to keep you and your business associates out of jail, Mother? How much I must pay legal staff here and in France?"

"You?" She said with contempt. "I met personally with Senator Albert Fall from New Mexico. He resolved the problem for us. With no assistance from you, I might add."

"In return for what, mother? A deal with a Mexican rebel?" James asked. "You're fortunate the Germans and Butcher could come up with no proof it was our company that made the deal with the French. Mother, you were trying to circumvent international law and the President of the United States. Not even I could have gotten the company out of that mess."

"The matter was resolved," his mother said.

"I think the American declaration of war took care of it."

"That cargo would have been important to our war effort, but when the government finally released it from impoundment, the owners decided they needed to get rid of it quickly," she said. "What could I do? We are only brokers, Harrison."

"Get rid of the evidence, eh?" he asked. "Mexicans bought it, you said? "

She looked directly at him and smiled. "The consignment was not purchased by an American company, nor a French or English company either. Its destination was across the border. That is all I needed to know," she said with finality.

"You better stay on good terms with Senator Fall, mother. The problem may not be over," Harrison warned.

*

Randolph James had wanted his sons to be tough and independent like him. He believed the only way to accomplish that was to treat them accordingly. He expected his old friend from his Nevada days—Jonathan Strong—to take care of it. Jonathan followed his orders, but, not having his own sons, he tried in his own way to give the boys the love they never received from their parents. In addition, he did all that he could to teach them to be good, decent men.

Jonathan prided himself on his successful parenting, and Harrison and Bart had thought of the old man as their grandfather. He had been a member of the household for more than thirty years. But Jonathan, James had discovered, had one great distraction—he was in love with their mother.

He thought a lot about that, remembering when he had first learned of Jonathan's feelings for his mother. It was eleven years ago when Harrison had graduated from Harvard. The two came to attend the ceremony without his father. He had—quite by accident—caught them in an embrace. The two did not know of his discovery, but months later he spoke to Jonathan. Harrison had promised never to betray them and, in appreciation for his silence, Jonathan kept Harrison abreast of his mother's activities.

*

"Where is Smith now, Mother?" he asked with growing irritation. "And what is he up to?"

"You don't need to know."

Harrison sighed, knowing she would avoid answering all his questions. "Is turning a profit all that you live for?"

"Silence," she rapped out in a voice of steel. The word echoed through the large house. "Who do you think you are? We didn't make these wars, Harrison. They want wheat, so we get them wheat. They want explosives, and we find them. That is the business your father started, and it's also the one that's given you a spoiled, pampered life." Her chin was set and Harrison felt the cold from her eyes freeze into him from across the table.

He knew the conversation was at an end. "Mother, if you could only see the suffering your business affairs now cause."

"Harrison, you may leave the table."

"No. And I didn't come here to argue with you over business. I came because of Bart. Tell me what happened," he said.

"We're both distraught, Harrison. Go to bed. We'll talk in the morning. I'll answer your questions about Bart then."

"But…"

"Harrison, do as your mother asks," Jonathan said. He still stood behind James' mother. His right hand rested on her shoulder. She reached up and laid her hand on top of his.

He did as Jonathan asked, but later caught the trolley to Market Street for an evening of entertainment.

She was right, he thought. This is my beautiful, empty life.

*

"Harrison, gather your wits," his mother stated the next morning over breakfast. She spoke as if they had not clashed the previous evening. "A telegram from the Army stated that Bartlett had committed suicide. Evidently, some sort of riot among Negro soldiers in Houston—your brother's soldiers—involved him," she continued. "The Army has a Major Snow who wishes me to believe Bartlett committed suicide as a result of that riot. Read this." She gave him the telegram:

> Dear Mrs. James, Captain Bartlett James died on Saturday, September 2, 1917. Investigation concluded the captain died by a self-inflicted gunshot wound in his quarters here at Camp Furlong, New Mexico. Arrangements for transporting the body will be forthcoming. My deepest condolences, Major Kneeland Snow, Commanding, Second Battalion, 24th Infantry Regiment, United States Army.

She then handed him a newspaper clipping from the *Chicago Herald* she had retrieved from somewhere in the folds of her white silk morning dress.

He reached across the table for the clipping, already yellowing and severely lined from constant folding and unfolding. Spreading it out on the fine Irish linen tablecloth, he read through the article. He focused his attention on the second paragraph:

> Captain Bartlett James, a West Point graduate from the Chicago area, acted with courage, coolness and common sense the night of the Houston riots. As the commander of Company L of the 24th Negro Regiment, he was an important witness in the Negroes' court martial...

"...found dead in his tent with a gunshot wound to his head..." he finally read, then stared at the crumpled slip of paper. James had not even known his brother had been in Houston. The last letter he had received was from New Mexico.

His mother's eyes bored into him. He knew that look well. "I will be quite clear, Harrison. My Bartlett did not die that way. He could not possibly have done such a thing to himself, or to his family. You must expose and utterly destroy this falsehood. You will go out to the frontier and discover what happened to my son," she commanded. "For once, you will not disappoint me." Those were her last words to him. Within an hour, he had begun his journey south.

*

Resting the back of his head on the metal frame of the carriage seat, his hat over his face, Harrison closed his eyes and again tried to sleep. The coach had not cooled much with the arrival of darkness. He raised his hat and wiped the perspiration from his face with a blue cambrie handkerchief he retrieved from his coat pocket.

In that pocket also was the El Paso address of Jackson Smith and his new company, courtesy of Jonathan. He knew he could always depend on the old man. Jonathan did not always approve of his mother's activities, but could never bring himself to confront her; thus, he clandestinely worked with Harrison to prevent her excesses. And Jonathan was no fool. He knew that with Bart dead, Harrison owned almost seventy percent of Randolph James Commodity Brokers.

CHAPTER FIVE

The deep starlit night swallowed up the train and highlighted the solitude James felt. Unable to sleep, he stared aimlessly out the window again, seeing mesquite trees, sagebrush, and cactus pass by in the brilliant starlight. A giant cactus almost brushed the side of the train.

The glass in the windows rattled, his view suddenly shrouded in heavy black smoke as the engine slowed and struggled up a steep incline. Then, the speed increased again as the train returned to level ground.

Restless and still feeling lonely, Harrison wandered through the old wooden car, searching out people to speak with. He moved along the aisle, quietly observing faces in the dim coach light.

In the last seat he found someone awake—an army officer. "May I, captain?" he asked, pointing to the empty space beside him.

"Yes, do," the soldier responded, sliding over to make more room. "I'd appreciate the company."

After introducing themselves, James and the soldier talked casually to pass the time. Harrison was interested in a soldier's life along the Mexican border, and asked several questions about chasing smugglers. But the soldier was unwilling to share any information except on the weather. "Pretty dry this fall, Mr. James. Too dry. Dust everywhere. The cotton didn't do too well, I fear, sir," he said.

"Do you think the Mexicans will declare war against us?" Harrison finally asked, tiring of crop talk.

The captain laughed. "No, sir. They're too busy fighting each other."

"What about Pancho Villa, captain? My brother, who fought against him, said he was very popular around here."

"Your brother?"

"Yes. Captain James, Captain Bartlett James, 24th U.S. Infantry."

"I knew him, sir. A fine man."

"Yes, he was," Harrison said softly.

"I'm sorry. His death was a great loss to the United States Army. Even General Pershing said as much."

There was an awkward pause.

"Did you know my brother well, captain?"

"Not well, sir. Your brother and I served together briefly while the Army was in Mexico chasing Villa. We first met in Washington...." He suddenly stopped talking

"In Washington? You worked together in Washington?"

"Yes, sir, but different assignments, actually...not together at all."

Harrison was excited to meet someone who knew Bart. "What type of work did you do?"

"Staff work, Mr. James," he answered shortly.

"Were you also working in intelligence?"

"No, Mr. James. We worked in different sections. My job was mostly routine staff work. I don't know anything about your brother's work there, I'm afraid," he said, looking away. "If you will excuse me, sir, I need to stretch my legs." The captain got up and walked down the aisle. James returned to his own seat, puzzled by the captain's abruptness.

*

As children, Bart and Harrison had traveled extensively with their parents. They were as much at home in London and Paris as in Chicago. Bart spoke fluent German and Spanish, and Harrison, who was only fluent in French, had always envied his younger brother's ability to speak several languages well. Bart passed as a native speaker when they traveled in Spanish speaking countries on business with their father.

Back in his seat, Harrison reached into his coat pocket and retrieved a bundle of papers the family had received from the Department of the Army. He leafed through them until he found the citation from General Pershing, given to the 24th Infantry upon returning to New Mexico.

"Men, I am authorized by Congress to tell you that our people back in the States are mighty glad and proud at the way the soldiers have conducted themselves while in Mexico, and I, General Pershing, can say with pride that a finer body of men never stood under the flag of our nation than we find here tonight."

*

Harrison knew receiving that citation had been a proud moment in his brother's life. Bartlett had welcomed the opportunity to lead Negro troops, and believed devoutly that he was helping to prepare the U.S. Army for war in Europe.

Harrison's mind returned to the last letter he had received from his brother, written in June. Bartlett wrote that his troops were chasing bandits and smugglers along the border. Bart had seemed satisfied with his duty. He confided that it was a difficult assignment, with his men having to perform garrison duty while other units prepared to go overseas, but he did not complain. Bart never complained. Then, not more than three months later, the family received the telegram informing them of his death.

In the news article, the writer had stated that Bartlett's battalion had rioted in the streets of Houston, and that many of the Negro troops were charged with mutiny and murder. But he had also written that Bart acted courageously.

He refolded the bundle of documents, then pushed them back into his breast pocket with the photograph of Bart. Harrison considered the information: a suicidal hero? His brother was very adaptive, and handled difficult situations well, but he could be overly emotional, too. Had he become depressed over the Houston troubles? No, Harrison decided, Bart could not have committed suicide. But he was not certain. Doubt remained.

CHAPTER SIX

The old wooden El Paso and Southern railcar James was riding in suddenly hissed loudly and screeched, jerking to a stop and throwing him forward in his seat. His wide-brimmed felt hat rolled into the lap of one of the two soldiers asleep in the seat facing his.

"What?" the young soldier stammered, jerking awake.

"Sorry," James responded, reaching over and taking his hat. He wondered how long he had been daydreaming. It didn't seem more than a few minutes, but the dull ache in the back of his neck told him it was longer. Standing to rid himself of the stiffness in his legs and back, he focused on the two soldiers. "Where did you gentlemen come from?" he asked, still somewhat disoriented. He shook his head, rubbed his eyes to refocus.

"Got on in El Paso," one of the soldiers answered. He nudged his buddy. "'Bout a half hour ago, I reckon."

Still feeling a little groggy, Harrison squinted out the grimy window. Platform lights indicated that they were stopped, but where he didn't know. A faint light was forcing its way through the dirty glass. Peering across the wooden station platform, he glimpsed unpainted clapboard and adobe buildings lining a deserted street, empty except for an early morning rider and several horses tied to posts. Here and there he saw a light peeking through a window. Everything appeared to James to be the same dusty red color. Bleak and barren, he thought. He was again reminded of La Paz.

"Canutillo. Canutillo, New Mexico," the conductor announced as he marched quickly down the aisle. "All aboard," he yelled. "All aboard."

"How long to Columbus?" Harrison asked him. He blocked the aisle.

"'Bout two urs, sir," the conductor answered without looking up. Intimidated by the much taller man standing in the narrow aisle, he tried to step around him.

"Sir, do we have time to eat?" James asked, moving aside.

"Nope," the conductor responded. "Nothin' open this time a'day, noways, sir."

"Where ya headin'?" the other soldier asked, awakened by the noise. He was older than his companion. The spider webs of wrinkles around his eyes indicated he had spent a lot of time in the harsh desert sun.

"Columbus," James said, sitting down again.

"Why ya goin' there?" the older private asked. "If I didn't have ta, I know I wouldn't. It's worse'n hell."

Harrison observed him casually. "Do you gentlemen know anything about the 24th Regiment? L Company, 24th Regiment?"

"One of the nigger companies," the thin, younger private answered, rubbing the back of his hand. "What business ya got there?" He pulled a leather pouch filled with tobacco and some cigarette papers from inside his wool tunic, and carefully shook tobacco into a paper slip.

Harrison looked at him. "How long have you been in the Army?"

"Joined up 'bout a year back to fight Pancho Villa," he said, licking the crude edge of the paper. "But, time I got out here, it was all over. So they send me to Columbus to guard the niggers. Me 'n' Charlie been doin' that since September. Right, Charlie?"

"Yeah. Oughta hang 'em all, I say. Guardin' them niggers and chasin' smugglers ever' day ain't what I joined up for. Now, I want to kill them Germans," Charlie replied.

"I know some people in Columbus...at Camp Furlong. Relatives from Illinois," James said. "What's your unit?"

"We with the 13th Cavalry. Regulars," the young soldier answered. Once sealed, he popped the cigarette into his mouth. "Not infantry."

Charlie eyed the well-dressed Yankee enviously.

"What kinds of units are out there?" Harrison asked.

"They got infantry, cavalry like us. And, when they moved us in…moved us in with some nigger cavalry—Tenth Cavalry—already stationed there along the Rio Grande. We fightin' those Mexicans. Chasin' 'em all over hell. That is, Charlie here was fightin' 'em," the younger one said.

"Yeah, I been in the Army since '15. Always in the cavalry, too. Best place in the whole U.S. Army to be, I reckon," Charlie confirmed.

"You serve with the Negro soldiers then?"

"Those boys are in our camp," Charlie said. "Don't like niggers or spics, and I don't like nosey Yankees." Charlie gave him a sour grin, revealing a mouth filled with black, stumpy teeth.

"Where are you boys from?" Harrison pressed deliberately.

"I'm from Illinois," Jonesy said. He struck a match across the metal back of the seat to light another hand rolled cigarette. Smoke enveloped them as bits of tobacco sparked and fell on the floor. Charlie's from Kentucky," he said with a smile.

"Don't tell 'im nothin'," Charlie mumbled. He didn't like James. Yankees, Charlie thought, always thinkin' they's so almighty important.

"And the Negro soldiers out here? Where're they from?" Harrison asked, ignoring the older soldier.

"Everywhere. Like us, they's regulars. Even them that rioted in Houston. Right, Charlie?"

"Maybe," Charlie responded. "Most of them niggers should be shot or hung fur what they did up to Houston. We's here," he said with sudden anger, "Out here in the damn desert 'cause a what they done in Texas. 'Bout burned the damn town to the ground. We should be over in El Paso or down to Brownsville gettin' ready to move out to France. But hell no, we's here patrollin' this damn border an' watchin' them damn niggers. Ain't right. Now we's all crowded in out there at Camp Furlong, in the desert. Out in the damn desert wid the fleas and the snakes and the niggers."

"Yup," mumbled Jonesy.

"Is that right?" Harrison replied slowly, considering. "What happened to the Negro soldiers who rioted?"

"Loaded 'em up and shipped 'em to Fort Sam. Threw 'em in the stockade. Rest of' em got shipped here…to hell. Our horses is livin' better un us," Charlie growled. "That's 'nough questions. Ya ask too many questions."

"Yup," Jonesy agreed.

"Where did ya say you's from?" Jonesy asked, the heavy smoke streaming from his mouth and nose.

"I'm from Kankakee, Illinois," Harrison answered. "Near Chicago."

"Don't know no one from there, I guess. You, Charlie?"

"Don't know no Yankees an' don't wanta."

"I'm from Harrisburg, further south," Jonesy stated. "I'll show ya to the camp if ya want. Since we both from Illinois. That ok, Charlie?"

"None a my bus'ness what ya do, kid," Charlie mumbled. But I don't want ya carryin' no bags fur the Yankee, now."

"I'd greatly appreciate the escort, private, but I've decided to go directly to the hotel and find a room. Any suggestions?"

"There's only one for a man like yurself, sir," Jonesy said, thoughtfully.

"Like myself, private?"

"Yeah, a white man."

"And what hotel is that?"

"The Hotel Hoover. It's the best place in town. An' on the other side of town. We'll take ya there. It ain't that far. Columbus ain't a big place, is it, Charlie?"

Charlie, still staring at the Yankee, only grunted. Somethin' 'bout him, he thought. Act like some rich dandy.

"Thank you," Harrison said, smiling at the young man.

"I like that fancy hat," Charlie said suddenly. "I bet you a banker, lawyer, something like that, eh? That suit must a cost a whole lot of money."

"No, just a businessman," Harrison replied. "What's your name?" he asked the other soldier.

"Jones, Abraham Lincoln Jones," he answered directly.

"Nice to meet you, Private Jones."

"How much a hat like that cost?" Charlie persisted. He reached to grab James' hat from his head.

"Careful with the hat." Harrison caught the shorter man's wrist in a viselike grip so quickly that Charlie jumped back, startled. "I'm superstitious about my hat, gentlemen."

"Leave the man alone, Charlie." Jones elbowed him. "A man's hat is personal, like his piece. Right? What ya say yur name is?"

"I suppose. Yes." James released his grip, but still held Charlie's gaze. "Harrison James."

Jones flipped the butt of his cigarette out the partly opened window.

"No hard feelings 'bout the hat, eh?" Charlie stuck out his other hand. Now he liked the Yankee even less.

Harrison shook Charlie's hand. "Of course not, Charlie," he said. "Of course not."

*

Two hours later, the soldiers escorted Harrison away from the train depot that consisted mainly of a long wooden, open-air platform. Most of the travelers he saw were soldiers, while most people standing or sitting around the station appeared to be Mexicans. The army camp began across the street from the depot. Harrison saw tents stretching off into the distance toward the southwest, disappearing in a cloud of dust. Other than street vendors selling fruit, vegetables, and hot tortillas, he saw no women anywhere.

"Don't buy nothin' from her," Charlie advised as they walked by a vendor. "It'll make ya sick."

Although still early, business appeared to be brisk along Broadway Street, several blocks from the depot. Broadway was obviously the town's main thoroughfare. Several motorcars mingled with horse-drawn wagons, riders on horseback, and pedestrians to clog the wide, dusty, unpaved streets at the main intersection that was also a crossroads. Harrison turned and looked south. "Mexico, eh?" He asked Jonesy, pointing in that direction.

"Yeah, Mexico," Jonesy replied.

"You don't get lost out there, now. The desert can git ya real confused," Charlie said.

"I'll remember that," Harrison responded, then turned. He casually considered the layout of the town, scanning the road running east and west. In both directions, the road disappeared into the flatness of the land. A dust devil swirled down the wide street toward the west, kicked up by several trucks pulling out of the army camp. He had a strange sense that he was being watched, then decided it was because in small towns like Columbus everyone seemed to know when a stranger was in town. He had learned that from living in rural pueblos in Bolivia. "Do those mountains have a name?" he asked, pointing to three nearby peaks rising out of the desert floor just to the northwest.

"The locals call 'em Tres Hermanas. That means 'Three Sisters,'" Jonesy answered, proud to demonstrate his knowledge of the area. "We use 'em to git ar bearin' out there."

"Shut up," Charlie growled for no special reason.

"Getoutaway!" someone yelled as the three navigated through traffic, attempting to reach the other side of the street. They sidestepped several autos, halted to allow a carriage to pass, and still the swirling red dust kept James from seeing two approaching motor trucks bearing down on them.

"Hey! Look out!" a driver growled at James. The rear fender of a Model T Ford covered in dust grazed his leg, missing his foot by inches as it passed.

"Hey, why didn't you boys say something?" he asked, dusting himself off. A young Mexican woman with three small children in tow walked by, all four staring at the well-dressed white man walking with the soldiers.

The two privates looked at each other and grinned. "Sorry, Harry. Ya gotta be careful 'round here," Jonesy said. "This differ'nt than Chicago?"

"No different from Market Street, I guess," James replied, throwing the grip over his shoulder again. "But Chicago is a large city."

The soldiers shrugged.

"May I buy you gentlemen a beer for helping me?"

"Yeah, that'd be right friendly, Harry," Jonesy said. "We in no hurry, are we, Charlie?"

"No, I guess not," Charlie said, indifferent to the offer. "We got a place right 'round the corner here." Leading the way, he directed them to a two-story, unpainted, clapboard and wood framed building. A double swinging door with large windows dominated the front. Turning to look out upon the wide dusty street, also congested with animal and motor vehicle traffic, Harrison judged that this could be the main thoroughfare of the small town. He saw soldiers everywhere.

"Last Chance Saloon," Harrison read as they walked by the dirty window. "I like that. Any reason for the name?"

"Don't reckon I know for sure," Jonesy said. "Maybe before a man crosses the border? Yeah, that's it. Mexico is only about five, six miles down the road. An' the next big town west a us in the U.S. of A. is Douglas. Yup, Douglas, Arizona. Mighty long ways if ya got a thirst." The three entered the saloon. Even this early, Harrison saw that the place was doing good business.

They headed through the tobacco smoke for the bar across the room. "Wait. Boys, I think we should find ourselves a table. No room up there, eh?" Harrison said, peering through the smoke.

The two soldiers followed his gaze, looking at the uniformed backs of men lining the mahogany. "You right, Harry. Ain't he, Charlie?"

"We sit over there, I think," Charlie said, pointing to three empty chairs in the corner. "I know them boys. They's in the regiment." Charlie and Jonesy walked over and sat down. Harrison followed, casually looking the crowd over.

"Hi boys," Charlie said. The two soldiers at the table looked up at James, not speaking. "He be a Yankee, but don't worry none."

"Harry, from Chicago," Jonesy added. "Sit down here, Harry."

James placed his grip behind the chair against the wall. He shook their hands, nodded, and sat down. A young woman immediately approached him. With thick splotches of rouge on her cheeks and blond hair piled on top of her head, she seemed like a grotesque caricature of his mother. She wore a brightly colored dress with a plunging neckline. Stooping to take his order, she presented him with small but firm breasts. Her perfume overpowered the table with its thick, heavy scent.

She could see money all over James. "What can I git fur ya, sir?" she asked with a wink. She ignored the soldiers.

"Three beers," he said. "And get yourself one, too."

"Well, thank ya, sir," she said with a Southern twang. "My name is Peaches. What yur name be?"

"Harrison," he answered with a smile. The young woman, James thought, couldn't be older than sixteen or seventeen.

She brought the beers quickly, set them on the table, then backed up provocatively to sit in Jonesy's lap, but facing Harrison. Jonesy was elated, and immediately placed his hands on her breasts. Charlie leered at her, but said nothing.

"I want to thank you gentlemen for showing me around town," Harrison said, appreciative. "And Jonesy, if there's anything you want me to take to your family back in Illinois, just let me know."

Jonesy smiled, but was preoccupied by the young woman. His hands covered her small breasts. "Yeah, sir," he said, fondling her.

Charlie sat staring at Harrison.

"So, Charlie," Harrison said, feeling his eyes. "When do you think you'll leave for France?"

"Don't know," he said. "Why ya wanna know?"

"Just asking," he replied, sipping the beer. "So this is the frontier, eh?"

"The frontier? Yeah, I guess. So what?"

"Seems like there could be plenty of opportunities here for a man who worked hard. Have you ever thought about settling down around here?"

"Hell no." He threw down the mug of beer. "I don't wanna talk my business with the likes of you," he growled. "What doya know 'bout it, anyway?"

"I didn't mean to offend you," Harrison said. "I'm just making small talk."

"We best be headin' back to camp. Git up, private, he ordered Jonesy. "We gotta git." He stood up.

Jonesy looked at Charlie, surprised. "I was jus' gittin' comfortable, Charlie." His hands were still on Peaches' breasts.

"Charlie, cain't ya see the private here is preoccupied?" Peaches said, appearing to enjoy the fondling, or recognizing potential business in the young man. But it was the civilian who caught her eye. "Where ya stayin' mister? Mister? She listened closely for Harrison's answer.

"The name is James, and I don't know for certain where I'm staying." He grabbed his grip and prepared to leave.

"Let's go," Charlie said.

"You come back later, Mr. James, and you see Peaches now, ya hear me? You too, slim," she said as an afterthought.

"I surely will," Jonesy said with a wide grin on his face.

*

After walking about two blocks east, the three arrived at the Hoover Hotel. In another three blocks they would have reached the eastern limits of town.

About one block before reaching the hotel, they passed a charred ruin. Only the stone foundation and an adobe wall remained. "That's where the Commercial used to be," Jonesy told him. "The Mex burned it out when they come in 1916. They say 'cause Villa don't like the owner. Said he cheated 'im on a gun deal."

"People take their business seriously down here, don't they?" Harrison said. Charred pieces of wood still lay about on the ground where they had fallen. They kept walking.

"Here ya go, Harry," Jonesy said, having walked another block. "The Hoover." They stopped on the wooden sidewalk.

James looked up at the two-story clapboard building dominating the entire block. It was the largest building in town, he observed. Originally painted red, it had since faded to a grayish pink in the hot desert sun. Entrance was through double wood doors inset with large windows. "THE HOOVER HOTEL WELCOMES YOU" was painted across the large plate glass window to the right of the double door. There was no front promenade. The doors were open wide. A young, neatly dressed Hispanic looking man leaned against them.

The two soldiers turned to walk back toward Camp Furlong. There were no further words spoken. Jonesy had pointed to the entrance, and Harrison demonstrated his appreciation with a nod. He entered the building, the grip still over his shoulder.

The young Hispanic man followed him into the lobby. "Ahh señor, you will stay at the Hoover Hotel?" he asked with a smile.

"Yes, I will," Harrison responded. "You have a room available? I want the best that you have, please." He looked around, impressed with the large, well-decorated lobby. Small groups of men stood about talking and smoking.

"Claro, señor. For you we have only the best," he said, taking hold of Harrison's one bag. "You will be staying long?" The young man immediately noticed the expensive cut of the white man's suit.

"I don't know yet," Harrison answered. "Perhaps."

CHAPTER SEVEN

Later that day, after a bath, a nap, and clean clothes, Harrison James stood on a rocky promontory looking down at Camp Furlong from the north. Standing there on the overlook, he observed three or four wooden buildings clustered around the road that ran south to Mexico. The railroad tracks, running east and west, were just behind him. South of the wooden buildings he saw row after row of tents arranged symmetrically in city blocks, stretching toward the west and southwest. They were organized around an empty expanse of field approximately 100 by 40 yards. The only complete wooden structures he saw among the tents sheltered horses. Small formations of men could be seen drilling on the open field, kicking up clouds of brown dust as they marched. The entire, sprawling camp stretched out on a flat desert plain, with mountains rising in the west and southwest.

He was stopped at the main gate by a Negro military policeman. The young man had stepped out of a small wooden guard shack. A Ford motor transport truck turned in at the same time as Harrison, sending up a screen of dust. He turned away and covered his face.

"Wait suh," the young MP said. "I gotta check the truck through. Quickly he looked into the back, poking under and around sacks of grain with his night stick. He then walked around to the driver. "Where ya goin', private?" He asked the soldier.

"Feed for the horses. Came in on the train," the soldier said. He was older than the MP and white.

"Pass," the MP ordered. He turned to walk back to James. The driver put the engine in gear and slowly moved forward.

"Yur bus'ness, suh?"

"I'm going to the Third Battalion, 24th Infantry," James replied. He quickly noticed how the MP was armed—a .45 caliber automatic was strapped to his waist.

"Follow me, suh." An aimless gust of wind suddenly blew up. It swirled down the roughly graded streets between the squares of tents, dusting everything with another layer of hard, red grit. Directly ahead, James watched the activity. Marching men on the parade field passed again and again through the curtain of dust without breaking formation. Very harsh, bleak conditions, he thought, as they made their way around the parade ground to a regimental headquarters area. He could tell by the banner waving in the breeze out in front of one of the larger tents that it was the 24th Infantry's headquarters.

He deliberately slowed the pace to observe the Army camp more closely. He recalled what Jonesy had told him about their duties at Camp Furlong: "to catch gun smugglers and Mexican rebels crossing the border…and to keep an eye on the Niggers."

They continued walking until they came to another large tent with the Third Battalion banner out front.

"Just like hell," Harrison mumbled, remembering what Charlie had said.

"We is here, suh," the MP said to James. "He'll help ya fine." He waved to another Negro soldier standing at parade rest with a Springfield rifle in front of the tent. The MP departed the same way he came.

"Yeah, suh," the young soldier stated firmly before James could climb the three steps into the tent. "Ya bus'ness, suh?"

"I'm looking for Major Kneeland Snow," Harrison said. "I'm expected." "Inside, suh," the soldier said, holding the tent flap open. Trucks rattled by, churning up more dust in the camp.

"Thank you," Harrison responded, entering. His young escort turned and returned to his duties.

The command tent was oppressively hot and stuffy. "I'm looking for the Battalion Commander," Harrison announced to the tired looking Negro soldier at the first desk he encountered.

"Sir, who ain't," the man replied slowly without looking up.

"I mean, I have an appointment with Major Snow."

The soldier finally looked up. "And yur name, sir, is?"

"James," he announced. "Harrison James." The other soldiers in the tent stopped what they were doing to stare at the civilian. "An appointment was made with the major four days ago."

"Yes, sir," the clerk said, flipping through the pages of paper on a clipboard. "Here it is, sir."

An officer entered through the front opening, swiftly marching up the two steps into the wood-floored tent.

"I've been expecting you, Mr. James," the tall, heavily built white soldier called out as he entered the tent a short time later, followed by the clerk. He was hatless, and Harrison noticed the thinning dark hair outlining a broad, fleshy face with small, brown eyes and a rather large, bulbous nose. "I received a telegram from Mrs. James. She said you would be arriving today."

Harrison faced the army officer.

"Welcome to the 24th Infantry. I'm Major Kneeland Snow." The major held out his large hand to the civilian."

"Thank you, major." He extended his hand. It was immediately engulfed in the larger man's hand. Weak grip, Harrison noticed, and the soldier seemed heavy on his feet for an infantryman. He wasn't what James had expected.

"May we talk…in private?" Harrison asked quietly.

"Yes. Of course," Major Snow said politely. "Let's go to my quarters. Please follow me." He led Harrison through the large tent. The Negro soldiers still watched as the two white men left by the rear entrance.

Crossing one of the dusty streets, they entered another, smaller tent. Harrison was careful to maneuver over the tent's anchoring lines as he stepped into the major's quarters.

"Please sit down." Major Snow motioned with his hand to one of the two chairs in the tent. "Forgive the lack of accommodations, but we are on a war footing here." He smiled. "You can understand."

"Yes, of course, major. I'll try not to take up much of your time." Harrison then pulled a yellowed envelope from his breast pocket and unfolded its contents. Inside was a letter written on simple white stationary, and a Western Union Telegram.

The officer recognized the contents. He had written them.

"Major, in this letter..." he held it up, "You state that my brother put a gun to his head and..." Harrison suddenly choked, feeling sickened and bereaved. "And shot himself."

"Yes, sir. That is correct," Snow nodded. "I'm very sorry." Sitting at the small writing desk, the major looked down.

"He took his own life because he was depressed. Is that right?" Harrison struggled with his sudden emotion.

"Please, sir. Let me explain. This unit recently had a very unfortunate experience while stationed in Houston, Texas. Many of the men mutinied. A horrible time, really. They mutinied and went on a rampage. People were killed. Civilians were killed. These boys are a difficult bunch. Coloreds, you know...."

"What does that have to do with the death of my brother, major?"

"I'm trying to explain," the major replied, standing. "Captain James was a good company commander. But, I'm afraid he over-sympathized with his Colored troops. Too long out here in company with them."

"One year, sir. Do you consider that too long?"

"He failed to provide the leadership that the army expected of him. Mr. James, his concern for his men clouded his judgment."

Agitated by the criticism of his brother, Harrison, too, jumped to his feet. He towered over the soldier. "You're saying his death was because he blamed himself for the Negro troopers rioting in Houston? Your letter indicated as much. However, sir, I'm afraid the family still does not quite understand."

"The cause of your brother's unfortunate death was the Houston riot." Snow was intimidated by the tall man now coldly staring at him. "Yes, your brother blamed himself for what happened. He was Officer of the Day during the riot. Captain James couldn't live with that dishonor. But, Mr. James, I'm not saying the Army blamed him. I'm not saying that at all, sir. He blamed himself. When we got here to Columbus, well, Bart just wasn't himself."

"He wasn't himself? What does that mean?"

"Your brother seemed sad, out of sorts. He was acting strange. He kept to himself, not talking to anyone, and always seemed busy. He traveled by train the day before he died, but he wouldn't tell anyone where he was going, or why. Lieutenant Floyd asked him, but Captain James told him only that he had to go to El Paso on personal business. He refused to discuss the troubles in Houston with me or the other officers."

Harrison filed that information. "Who discovered his body?" he asked quietly.

"I discovered him. I found his body late, around 11:00. He was lying across the floor of his tent, between two cots. He was alone. His .45 was beside him. It had been fired."

"His gun was fired," Harrison repeated. "How many times?"

"Just once. I checked it myself. No other bullet holes anywhere. Just the one. There were no signs of a struggle."

"No chance of an accident? Perhaps his gun accidentally discharged?"

"Accidents happen," the officer agreed. "But this was no accident. His weapon had to have been charged, cocked, and the safety released before it was fired. In any case, the coroner ruled out accidental discharge due to the wound."

"The wound?"

"Yes sir. An entry wound to the temple. At extremely close range." The major paused. "Mr. James, again I'm extremely sorry."

"What else did you find at the scene?"

"Nothing out of the ordinary. It was late, as I've already stated, sir. On a Saturday evening."

"Did you hear the gunshot?"

"No, I didn't. L Company is quite a distance from my quarters here. Only his orderly, Private Peck, heard a gun discharged. Most everyone else was gone. It was Saturday night, after all."

"Is that unusual?" Harrison asked. "That only one person would have heard the gunfire? We're in the middle of an Army camp, major."

"No, it is not, Mr. James. Out here, random gunfire is not unusual, in any case. Everyone carries a sidearm. After the Mexicans raided last year, people took to arming themselves." The major continued. "Gunfire is commonplace on a Saturday night, and it's something we've grown accustomed to hearing. The town is a lethal mix, guns and whisky."

"Had my brother been drinking...in your opinion?"

"No, sir, not in my opinion."

"I see." Harrison frowned, pausing to focus his thoughts. "You didn't hear his gun fire, yet you found him?"

"We were to meet in his tent. I entered and saw him. He was there on the floor."

"You were to meet that late, major?"

"Yes. I was the duty officer that Saturday...to give the other officers a night in town. I know that sounds strange, but it's true. We were the subject of an investigation by senior officers from Washington. The Adjutant General's office. Their visit proved to be a very trying time for all of us."

"There was a high level investigation?" Harrison asked.

"Yes, sir. The AG staff was preparing for the Colored's court-martial. They were conducting a review of the Houston troubles. They had questioned Captain James that day. They asked him if he had refused a direct order to fire on the mutineers before they left camp. That had re-opened wounds...between your brother and me." He stared at the ground. "We, all the officers under my command, had been interviewed that week regarding the events in Houston. The other officers left camp earlier in the evening, after the Washington people were taken to the train, to relax in Columbus. They had earned it. But your brother declined, stating that he had some business to take care of. We arranged to meet because I needed to talk with him. That's when I found him."

"Do you know what kind of business he had, major?"

"I don't know exactly. I assumed he was taking care of personal correspondence. We found his fountain pen on the floor, but no papers, notes or anything else on his desk."

"Curious," Harrison said, thinking about it. "Sir, may I review those investigation transcripts?" he asked. "It's important that I know how my brother answered those questions."

"Not at present, Mr. James. Not until after the court martial is concluded." The major was absolute. "All interviews are material evidence."

"Who gave the order to fire?"

"I beg your pardon, sir?"

"Who gave the order to fire on the Negro troops?"

"I gave the order, sir. They were mutineers…. They had to be stopped."

"What happened then, major?"

"It was mutiny. The damned Coloreds went marching through town to the police station." Major Snow's lower lip trembled. "We should have fired on them immediately…to disperse them. It would have saved trouble, saved lives, and a lot of grief. Mr. James, your brother's refusal to follow my order was a serious breach of his military responsibility. I believed it was a problem your brother and I needed to settle between ourselves. He refused my direct order to stop them, sir."

Harrison noted the anger.

"We needed to talk further about it," the battalion commander said, then paused. "Sir, I want you to know…this was a highly respected unit. They distinguished themselves in Mexico. However, like any other unit, it had its bad apples. Trouble makers, stirring up the others. With Coloreds, I've come to understand, more discipline is required rather than less. Race troubles being what they are in Houston…well, sir, I feared something bad was bound to happen."

Harrison listened without interrupting.

"Your brother refused to open fire. I told him it was a direct order from his commanding officer. Still he chose to disobey it."

Harrison watched the Major grow more agitated.

"He treated me with contempt, sir. He spoke of our disagreement openly with other officers. This has seriously affected morale. Captain James was my subordinate." The soldier turned to stare out the tent opening, making an effort to master himself.

"I wanted to settle the whole matter so that the unit could overcome this, this terrible event. As soldiers in the United States Army, Mr. James, we both understood what was expected of us," he said, turning back to the civilian. "And, sir, I want to tell you that I never charged Captain James with disobeying a lawful order, nor did I convey my own feelings to the Board of Inquiry."

Harrison studied the officer for a moment. "Did you tell anyone else you were meeting with my brother?" he asked calmly.

"No, I did not."

"Was the reason you went to his tent that night to discuss my brother's shortcomings?"

"To discuss how we could better work together to improve things, Mr. James, not to discipline him. I was not angry, only disappointed. I had hoped we could resolve our differences as two officers in the United States Army." The major gave James a straight look.

"I did not like your brother, Mr. James. That is well known. However, the captain was a gentleman and an honorable officer. I would be the first to admit that I respected him."

"What else can you tell me about my brother?" Harrison asked, noting the officer's anger whenever he spoke of Bart.

"That's all that I can tell you, sir."

"Thank you for your time, major. You've been most helpful. May I visit my brother's company? Talk to his men?" Harrison asked.

"Of course, Mr. James. I can arrange that. I'll get someone to escort you."

CHAPTER EIGHT

"This was my brother's tent?" James asked, following the shorter man up the two quick steps. The stuffy, oily canvas smell in the desert warmth made him slightly dizzy.

"Yes, sir," the sergeant responded crisply.

"Did you know my brother well, sergeant? Sergeant...?" he asked. The soldier was a slim, light skinned Mexican American of about 40 years of age. His dark hair was cut short and he wore a neatly trimmed mustache. The sergeant's eyes were a soft brown, but James detected the steely determination in them. In their handshake, the grip was firm and the hand was rough and horny. A lifetime of physical labor, James thought. He also noticed that the sergeant didn't walk, but marched, erect and military-like. His manner was polite and respectful.

"Parilla, sir. Juan G. Parilla." His back stiffened. "I knew your hermano for one year, sir. He was my commanding officer." In the tent's shadows, the sergeant looked directly at him without wavering.

"How did you get along with my brother, sergeant?"

"No problemas, sir. Su hermano was a fine man."

"No problems," Harrison repeated softly. He continued to scrutinize the shorter man. "You must be infantry?"

"Yes sir."

"Who was living in this tent with my brother?" Harrison asked as he walked around the narrow area, examining its layout of two cots and a few pieces of furniture on a rough wood floor.

"Lieutenant Floyd. He is en el campo with his men, sir."

"Does he still live here?"

"Sí, señor. Aquí."

"And where was my brother's body found?"

Sergeant Parilla slowly stepped to the open area between the bunks and squatted down on the floor. "Aproxima aquí, Señor James." With his hands, he outlined an area on the floor between the sparse furnishings. Harrison noticed two kerosene lanterns hanging at each entrance. There was just one writing desk and two chairs in the tent.

"Show me how you found him, please." Harrison knelt on the floor beside the soldier.

"Señor, I did not find him. The major find him, señor. I come mas tarde. Major Snow, he was here already. I come maybe one hour later from mi casa en Columbus. Private Goode tol' me to come," he said softly, then he looked down. "He was here on the floor, Señor James. Blood everywhere. His head…." He paused. "His head mostly gone…. Everywhere." He motioned at the canvas walls, at the spattered brown stains and small tear, while he spoke. "I wrap him up. My men take him away quickly. The major say, 'take him away now.' We do it as he order."

"I see." Harrison paused for a moment to examine the tear in the tent's side panel. It was about six feet up from the tent floor. He walked over to touch it. The edges were ragged. The bullet must have made that hole, he thought. "When you arrived, had he been moved from the spot where he fell."

"I don know, señor," Parilla said. "Señor, I am not a police."

"How was he lying on the ground, sergeant?"

"Señor?" he asked.

Seeing the hesitation on the soldier's face, Harrison paused and asked again, in a different manner. "Please sergeant, it is important to Captain James' mother and me that we understand exactly what happened."

Without a word, Sergeant Parilla sprawled out on the wooden plank floor, lying across the darkened areas where someone had attempted to scrub away the blood. He lay face up with his entire body situated in the space between the two cots. His feet pointed toward the open doorway of the front entrance. "Maybe like this, señor."

"Hmm." Harrison studied his position. "In your opinion, sergeant, is it reasonable to believe that was the final position of a man who shot himself?"

"Señor?"

Both men stood to face each other.

"It seems to me that a man would not take his own life sitting in a chair at his writing table or standing. That's what I mean." James continued to closely examine the premises. "According to a military police report we received only a week ago, the bullet entered here. An Army .45 caliber bullet." He touched his forehead. "The medical examiner described the wound as compatible with a self-inflicted gunshot. That is, powder burns indicated that the gun—Bart's own gun—was very close to his face. But I wonder, sergeant. Why in the forehead? And look where the hole is in the canvas." He pointed to the tear about ten feet away from where the body was found. "What do you think, Sergeant Parilla?"

The soldier stared at the civilian. "No se, Señor James. Es posible. I have seen many different ways that a man falls as he dies. And the bullet? Quien sabe?"

"You may be right." Harrison said. "The stains are over there closer to that entrance, near where he supposedly fell. But look, sergeant, at the hole in the canvas." Juan looked to where James pointed. "Bart was supposedly sitting at the desk or standing between the cots." He pointed to the blood stains on the floor behind him on the far side of the tent. Then he ran a forefinger around the edge of the tear. "That is what the medical examiner stated in his report. And way over here we have the bullet exiting the tent. Hmm." Harrison sat in the chair and contemplated bullet trajectory. "I don't think the hole is at the correct height or angle, and the blood stains don't seem right, either. The scene is confusing to me."

"I do not believe he here like they say," Parilla said slowly. "But I cannot know. I think he sit in his chair at his desk, facing this way." Juan's back was toward the rear entrance, away from James. "He was maybe sitting like this when he shoot. He fall back and the chair turn over." He turned the chair over for closer examination. "Look, Señor James. Blood, no?" The Sergeant pointed at the dried spots on the wood back. "Maybe he die falling, I think. And the bullet go in that direction." He pointed at the tear.

"Then you think he was sitting at his desk when he shot himself?"

"Sí, es posible, no?" the sergeant replied.

"Where was the chair when you arrived?" Harrison asked.

"It was at the desk like we see today, señor." Juan replied. "The major order me to clean everything in this tent. I discover the blood then, no?"

"Someone could have been here in the tent with Bart." Harrison thought out loud. "They disagreed, struggled perhaps. My brother was shot at close range and he fell backward. Maybe the killer moved his body after he was already dead. That's why the blood stains are over there by the front entrance. To make it look like suicide"

"Señor James, that is not the way they say it happened. The colonel and the major investigate, eh?" But the Sergeant was wondering also. The blood stains on the chair and the position the body was found seemed confusing.

"Yes, but it could have happened another way," Harrison said, still going over the scene. "You left the stain on the chair?"

"Sí, señor." Juan paused, and then said quickly, "Evidence, I think."

"Where did my brother keep his gun when he wasn't wearing it?" Harrison's mind was racing ahead.

"Captain James keep his pistola in his tent. When he did not wear it, he lock it up in his desk. Aquí." Juan tried to open a lower desk drawer. It was locked. "'Juan, too damn many accidents' he say to me."

"How many people knew Bart did this?"

"No se, señor. I know only because he show me."

"So others may have known as well?"

"Sí, señor. Es posible."

"Who else would have a key to the drawer?"

"No one. But the lock, it is simple. See?" Pushing a small strand of wire he produced from his pocket into the keyhole and shaking the front of the drawer lightly with his other hand, the drawer easily slid open. Juan smiled. "Many old desk around. I must open them sometimes."

"Where are all the weapons kept? Do the rest of the troops keep their own weapons?" Harrison asked.

"No, señor. They are all kept in the quartermaster's tent. There is a guard on them. Only officers keep their pistolas. Sometime they wear, or sometimes they lock up, like Capitan James."

"Is there a record or log of when Captain James checked his out of the quartermaster's tent?"

"Sí, the record is clear. He write down the date he took it. Every soldier must do it this way. The colonel ordered. We check the record carefully."

"What did it say, sergeant?"

"Your brother took his weapon from the tent three days before he died. The record does not say he bring it back."

"Sergeant, why do you think he checked his weapon out then?"

"I do not know, Señor James."

"Do the officers need a reason to take their weapons out of the armory?"

"No, señor. Out here along the border, is very dangerous. If they need them, they take them. Sometimes they keep them."

"I see. Who keeps track of all the company's weapons?"

"I do, señor."

"So an officer could take his weapon wherever he wanted? Could he sell it and no one would know?"

Juan eyed the civilian. "No, es no posible. I watch closely all weapons and records. But...." Parilla shrugged. "The records only say your brother didn't sign his pistola in again. There was no sign. That I know."

"Then he had it here with him, either locked in the desk or holstered?"

"Sí, I think so."

"Was he wearing a pistol belt when he was found?"

The sergeant thought a moment before answering. "No, no pistol belt. It was on his foot locker. Here." Parilla walked over to the locker and pointed.

Harrison considered, going over to stand beside Parilla. "Yet there's one more possibility, isn't there?" he said, looking back at the desk.

"Señor?"

"Someone could have opened that desk, just as you did, and stolen it without my brother's knowledge. Isn't that true, Sergeant Parilla?"

"The captain did not report a stolen pistola. He would have reported it, Señor James."

Harrison thought. "Do you believe Captain James took his own life?"

"It was a great surprise to me. He was not a man of fear." Juan shuffled his feet uncomfortably. "I must return to my duties now." Without speaking further, he grabbed the pencil from the desk and hurriedly scratched out an address on a slip of paper he tore from a notebook in his pocket. "Señor James, maybe we talk more." Handing it to Harrison, he abruptly turned to leave the tent. "Come. I will take you back to the gate."

"Wait!" Harrison called after him. "This Lieutenant Floyd. I would like to speak with him." He stuck the slip of paper into his coat pocket.

"Sí, señor. Follow me. The major orders that I escort you while you stay in camp. I think, Señor James, that he wants to watch you, eh?" Juan smiled slightly.

"Are you keeping notes of my activities here, Juan?" Harrison asked.

"Ah, no, señor. He say to report to him after you leave. Only this. Anyway, I do not write Ingles so well."

As they walked together toward the parade field, neither spoke. James wondered how much more the sergeant knew.

When they reached the field, Sergeant Parilla stopped. The soldier indicated a formation of 40 men marching toward them with their rifles at shoulder-arms. Parilla waved to the officer.

"Platoon, halt!" the man ordered the formation.

Parilla approached the lieutenant and quickly briefed him. He turned back to James. "Señor," he called. "I give you privacy with your talk. When you are ready, wave and I will come to take you."

The lieutenant waited with his soldiers standing at attention. The sergeant walked over to the formation and saluted. Lieutenant Floyd returned the salute. "Sergeant Parilla..." he called so the troopers would hear, "...take over." The tall man stepped away from the formation and walked toward James, taking long, measured strides.

"Lieutenant, I am Harrison James, the brother of Captain James," he said as the officer reached him.

"First Lieutenant Roger Floyd, United States Army, sir."

The two men shook hands.

"I have some questions, sir. Could we talk privately?" Harrison noticed that this officer seemed more relaxed. He hoped the man would feel more comfortable answering his questions than the major.

"Of course, Mr. James," the tall soldier said. "Let's stroll…if you don't mind, sir."

Sergeant Parilla watched out of the corner of his eye as the two Anglos walked away into the dust. "Señor James, I return for you, eh?" he yelled as he marched the formation of soldiers away across the field.

"Yes," Harrison said, distracted. "I'm trying to get an accurate picture of my brother's death," he explained to the tall lieutenant. "Lieutenant, were you nearby when my brother died?" They walked slowly across the dusty field, avoiding other groups of soldiers around them

"Sir, I want to tell you how sorry I am about your brother's death. He was a fine man."

"I appreciate that," Harrison said. "Again, when Bart died, were you near the tent?"

The soldier hesitated, and then blushed. "I'm afraid I was indisposed."

"Indisposed, lieutenant?" Harrison turned to see the suddenly red face beside him.

"Yes, I had had too much tequila. It's a major pastime in these parts," he added.

"You served with my brother in Houston, lieutenant?" Harrison continued, ignoring the confession.

"Yes, sir. And in Mexico. Chasing Pancho Villa."

"Did it strike you as strange that my brother would commit suicide?"

"No sir, it did not. Considering recent events, it was certainly possible, and even likely. Houston was a difficult time, Mr. James. The pressure on all of us has been extreme. The question of what went wrong there haunted the battalion officers, and most of all, your brother. We all tried to keep busy, to not think about the court martial. Yet, your brother.… I thought he kept more to himself after we returned. He was always busy with something, and never wanted to talk and relax with his brother officers."

"I see." Harrison paused. "Tell me, did my brother's Negro soldiers mutiny?"

"No sir, they didn't. No one from our company left the area."

"I don't understand," Harrison said. "If your company wasn't part of the mutiny…?

"Captain James was Officer of the Day, responsible for keeping order, ensuring the Battalion was secure. Our men were on police detail that day. Doing gate duty, patrols around the camp and keeping an eye on the civilians there."

"Civilians?"

"Yes sir. The Third Battalion was there to provide security while the camp was being built," Floyd explained. "It is to be a training camp, built to house thousands of recruits coming south for training for the war. Our company—L Company—had the guard detail that day."

"When the mutiny began?"

"Yes, sir. It started with trouble in town with the police. A misunderstanding, really. But one thing led to another, and soldiers from two companies broke formation, rushing the quartermaster's tent for rifles. First Sergeant Henry led them. They began to march into town. 'Free Corporal Baltimore,' they chanted. Crazy Niggers." Floyd shook his head.

"What action did my brother take when that happened?"

"When we saw what was going on, Captain James formed a skirmish line with all our L Company troopers, to reinforce the guard. I was with him when he ordered the men to block the gates."

"Did you stop the mutineers?"

"Hell no. It was too damn late by then. One hundred or more armed Niggers were marching through. They started shooting—in the air, mostly, but we lost one right there. Our boys were overwhelmed.

"How would you describe my brother's actions that night?"

"He did his job," Floyd said. "Then the major ordered him to stop them right there before they could march into town. Major Snow ordered him to stop them. A direct order. I heard it. The Major was yelling, 'shoot them!' But your brother refused to obey it. The Niggers marched right into town, shooting the place up. They killed civilians. Hell, even shot a couple of Houston policemen right off their horses. Fifteen people were killed. It took about three days to put out all the fires. It was a damn mess, Mr. James. And we could have prevented it right there at the gate. Our boys were armed, too."

"That is a tough decision to have to make, isn't it?" Harrison said, thinking out loud.

"I'm sorry, Mr. James. I don't want to second guess your brother, but I think it would have saved lives to have followed that order." Floyd stopped, turned painfully to face the civilian. "Our orders were clear, sir. We were ordered to stop them. Major Snow ordered Captain James to halt the mutineers. But...."

"But, lieutenant?"

"He was under orders to fire, yet he refused to obey that lawful order. Perhaps even a necessary order to protect lives and property."

"I see," was all Harrison said in response. Bart's refusal confused him. He knew that the French routinely shot mutineers, and the British hung them. They did it to preserve discipline. Had his brother failed in his duty? Had he then killed himself from shame?

"Our most basic duty, sir, is to follow orders. Please understand that. As officers in the United States Army, we are trained from the beginning to follow orders. Even the Nigger soldiers understand that."

"Would the men have obeyed such an order, to shoot their own?" Harrison asked.

"I don't know. But they, too, are soldiers in the United States Army. To quote the regulations: 'Obedience to orders is the vital principle of military life. The fundamental rule in peace and war, for all inferiors through all grades from General of the Army to the newest recruit.' Sir, not only West Point graduates, but all soldiers entering the Army are instructed on this point."

Harrison shrugged. "Do you think his actions that night had something to do with his suicide, Lieutenant Floyd?"

"Everything, sir. His life was the Regiment. When the color'ds mutinied, the Regiment was disgraced. The mutineers marched into Houston shooting at civilians. Your brother blamed himself for the resulting loss of so many lives." The young officer's hands were frozen at his sides as he spoke. He paused for several long seconds. "It was a dark stain on each of our careers," he finally said.

"You didn't take your life, lieutenant." *Our careers*, Harrison thought.

"We are all different, sir. We all see things differently. And the decision was—had to be—your brother's alone."

Harrison paused, thinking. "Do you think I might speak with some of his men?"

"That can be arranged through Major Snow, sir," Floyd told him.

"Can you add anything else, lieutenant? Anything at all?"

"Yes, sir. One more thing needs to be said. The men say your brother had…. I'm sorry to have to tell you this, but you may as well hear it from me, sir. Your brother was keeping a woman who is a Negress, sir. It was the talk of the company, I'm afraid."

"Does that relate to my brother's death?"

"I wonder if this liaison affected his decision not to follow that order," Floyd said, now speaking in a whisper. "He traveled to El Paso, I suspect, to visit her on many occasions. The last was only several days before he died."

"Could you tell me something about her?" Harrison asked.

"She is known as an outlaw—a smuggler of guns to the Mexicans," Floyd said, looking down. "She may have been using him. These people aren't like us, Mr. James. They will do anything to accomplish their purposes."

"I still don't understand, lieutenant," Harrison said.

"She preyed upon his love for her," Floyd said. "That's what I think."

James remained silent.

"One day, when the captain was gone," Floyd continued, "I was called to the front gate. A man was waiting there—a large, older Nigger. He had a letter he was ordered to deliver to Captain James. I took it. It was from the woman—probably a love letter."

"You read this personal correspondence?" Harrison was startled.

"No, of course not," Floyd said.

"Then why do you think it was a love letter?" Harrison asked.

"I could smell the perfume, sir," Floyd answered simply.

"His behavior became more erratic, less predictable after that. A few days later he was dead," Floyd said.

"A coincidence, perhaps, lieutenant?" Harrison asked.

"A captain in the United States Army cavorting with a Negress and known gun smuggler, a bandit whom we've been trying to arrest for months? I don't believe that, Mr. James."

"You have evidence of an affair?" Harrison asked.

"No, I don't."

"Then, lieutenant, your suspicions are just that." Harrison said. "Unless you can prove it, I suggest you be careful what you say."

Floyd said nothing. They began walking again.

"Did you speak with my brother the night he died?" Harrison asked.

"No, I did not. Sir, I'm usually in town when I'm not on duty. At the hotel."

"The Hoover Hotel, lieutenant?"

"Of course, sir. Where white people stay. The Negroes and Mexicans have their own. But the Hoover is the only decent lodging in town for us. I assume you are staying there, Mr. James?"

"Yes, lieutenant, I am." Harrison agreed. "I checked in this morning."

"Then we will probably be seeing each other," the officer stated. "I'm afraid I must go, but if I can be of further assistance, please call on me. I'm usually in Room 212."

"I will, lieutenant. I certainly will. And thank you." The two men shook hands, and the lieutenant turned to locate his men. Harrison watched him walk stiffly back across the parade field. He didn't know how to take Floyd's observations about his brother's relationship with the woman. But Harrison didn't believe it had anything to do with his death.

Harrison waited for the sergeant to escort him from the camp. He and Sergeant Parilla did not speak on their way to the gate. Harrison was thinking about the conversations, and the address the sergeant had given him.

CHAPTER NINE

Exhausted, Harrison returned to his room and collapsed into bed. He didn't awaken until the afternoon of the next day. Finally feeling refreshed, he stood in the lobby of the Hoover watching the crowds of people coming and going. It was after dinner, and the variety of evening activities and the mix of people surprised him. Soldiers, businessmen, local residents, and well-dressed prostitutes all flowed in and out of the hotel lobby. No one seemed to pay any attention to the hour. Harrison's business sense told him that contacts were being made everywhere around him. The lobby smelled of money.

He paused at the desk, considering. Did the lieutenant say Bart was in love with a smuggler? That she may have been using him in some way? Who would know more about this woman? Bart's first sergeant might know, he told himself. The man who had followed Bart's every step, perhaps sharing some of his thoughts and concerns. And I have his address, James thought, reaching into his right vest pocket.

He pulled the slip of paper from his pocket. "Señor," he called, turning to the desk clerk. "Where is this?" He handed it to a young man.

"Esta casa, señor?" The young clerk asked, staring at the hastily scrawled address. "I know this place, señor.The barrio has many bad hombres."

"What is your name, young man? Harrison asked. "I want to go there now."

"I am called Miguel. No, señor. Ahora, no. Pero mañana," the young Hispanic man stated excitedly.

"No, I must go now. It is very important." James handed the young man a five dollar bill.

"Pero señor, the barrio ees very dangerous. Very dangerous to go there at night. Too many people who don't like Anglos. Me comprende?" The clerk had been working two years at the Hoover, and this was the first time anyone had asked to be taken to the barrio. He knew it was a place filled with banditos and rebels. Maybe the rich man is crazy, he thought. And what can I do about that?

Harrison took another five-dollar bill out of his wallet. "If you won't help me, I'll find someone else." He was determined.

"Sí, señor." The clerk eyed the bills. He had a pregnant wife and needed the money. Besides, this gringo's health was not his concern. "I will go, señor," he said with a shrug. But you must stay behind me. It is much safer, I think."

"Agreed," Harrison told him.

The clerk summoned another man, similarly dressed, to stand at the counter.

Once out in the clear, almost cool night, Harrison followed the younger man down dark, dusty alleys, through narrow passageways, and across neatly scrubbed brick patios. After walking several blocks, he found himself in a neighborhood made up of single story, one and two room adobe houses. There was a stench of garbage and decay hanging in the air. Except for the occasional barking of a dog, this neighborhood was quiet, with an almost unnerving silence. Lacking street lamps, he carefully navigated this way through the dark maze behind the clerk. The smell of horses, gasoline, and burnt corn mixed with that of the garbage. Smoke from low stoves and fireplaces stung Harrison's eyes.

Eventually, the young man reached the address written on the slip of paper. Harrison stood in the shadows of a stable several feet away and watched as the young man paused in front of a small adobe house. He then turned and walked quickly back past where James was standing

"Aquí, señor," the young man whispered to Harrison as he went by quickly, disappearing into the deep shadows.

Harrison stepped forward and knocked at the door.

"Quien es?" a male voice asked through a crack in the door. In the stillness, Harrison thought he detected the sound of a slide action on an automatic pistol. He instinctively thrust his right hand under his coat.

"Harrison James," he announced quietly. "I've come to speak to you again, sergeant."

The door swung slightly open. Standing there ready to greet James was Sergeant Parilla. Even in his bleached white woolens, the Hispanic sergeant presented a military bearing. The Army .45 in his hand was pointed to the ground. "Welcome, Señor James," he said simply. "How did you come?"

"A young man. He showed me the way."

"Miguel?"

"Yes, Miguel."

"Miguel does not like to come to the barrio. He is like his father, I think. Afraid of his own people," Parilla said sadly, squinting beyond Harrison into the darkness.

"Hasta luego, Miguel," he called into the night.

The man's greeting reassured Harrison. Behind Parilla, in the shadows of the room lit by candles, he could make out a woman with an infant in her arms. The child was crying fitfully.

"Come in," the sergeant said, and turned to the woman. "Consuelo! Tequila, por favor." He smiled at the child. "Mi hijo, Juanito." Both men looked at the frightened child. Sergeant Parilla gently stroked the child's tear-streaked cheek. Almost immediately, the baby stopped crying.

The young woman obeyed her husband, but did not speak. She poured tequila into two small transparent glasses without looking at James, then placed the baby in a small crib in the corner of the brick adobe room. The filled glasses remained there together on the table.

"I hoped you would come, señor." The sergeant gestured slightly. "This is mi casa, where I am el jefe...the boss." He motioned for James to sit in a simple wood chair. His pride in his home and family was obvious.

Harrison sat down at the table and looked around the small, freshly plastered room. The walls were painted white. The floors were of a simple brown tile. "You have a very handsome family," he said, smiling at the woman. Woven tapestries, brightly colored with simple pastoral scenes, adorned the white walls. There was no stove, but a simple adobe fireplace was built into the far wall. He saw that cooking utensils and earthen pots surrounded the opening. Embers of an earlier fire still glowed under the grate. The sparsely furnished room was very clean, almost spotless. He turned back to Parilla. "I have questions which I think, sergeant, you can perhaps help me with."

"Por favor, señor, call me Juan. For, it is Juan to the hermano of Captain James." He handed a glass of tequila to his visitor and took one for himself. "My wife, Maria, and the little one is called Juanito," he said with great pride.

"Please call me Harry," James said, nodding at Consuelo. He smiled at the child.

The woman, who Harrison saw was much younger than her husband, was very pretty, with long dark hair and eyes that watched him cautiously. She did not speak, but smiled and curtsied when introduced to him.

The sergeant lifted his glass. "To su hermano. A fine officer and a very brave hombre."

"To my brother," Harrison replied softly, surprised by the sergeant's obvious sincerity. He emptied the glass with one, quick jerk of his wrist.

Both men sat silent for a moment.

"Now, amigo, your questions. Here, ahh, how do you say? There are no ears. More private for talk. You want to know about the captain?" Juan poured another drink for each of them.

Harrison felt the warmth of the tequila rising from the pit of his stomach. He stifled a belch.

Juan observed Harrison closely. "Es bueno, no?"

"It's very good," James said. But he sipped cautiously at his second glass. "Sergeant Parilla...."

"Juan."

"Juan, I'm trying to learn more about my brother's life here..." Harrison paused, "So that my family can understand how he died. So that I can understand. It has been very difficult for us."

For a few seconds, Juan did not answer him. "Señor Harry, I understand these things. It is difficult to comprende when men like su hermano die," he said, then stared into his own empty glass. "So much trouble in our regiment. It is bad, very bad."

"Tell me about those problems, Juan."

"Houston was no good for the Negro soldiers. It was no good to go to that place, at Camp Logan. Better for the soldiers to stay in the desert. I think that white people in Texas fear.... In their fear, they hate people of color. They want to keep the old ways." He sighed.

"Are the problems here also?" Harrison asked.

"Señor Harry," Juan paused to consider his words carefully. "Things here are no better. The men are angry and afraid. They think there will be more punishment. And the guns...."

"Yes?"

"The guns, señor. Machine guns disappear. The machine guns the Army take to Mexico are gone. The major watches everybody, but still he cannot find how this was done."

"Your Lieutenant Floyd suggested to me that my brother may have been involved with a gun smuggler. A woman, he said. Do you know anything about that?"

For a second, Juan was blank faced, his eyes hard. He frowned. "The lieutenant say that, eh? Be careful with that man, Harry."

"Why?"

"I cannot say nothing more. He is my lieutenant, comprende? But remember what I say." Juan cautioned. "There is a woman who sells guns in Mexico." He paused. "You brother knew her. He had respect for her."

"What kind of woman is she?"

"She loves her people," was Juan's only response. "They respect her too, Harry."

"Did she steal guns from the army?" Harrison asked.

"Others, I think, steal machine guns from us. Not la Señorita Washington. The captain would tell me this."

"How can you steal something as big as a machine gun and not have someone see it?"

"Claro. But the men, they see nothing. They know nothing. Private Peck say he lock all the guns up. But the thief, he take them anyway. Six machine guns gone."

"Who is Private Peck?" Harrison asked, recognizing the name.

"Your hermano's orderly. He keep the records for me. Guns are locked in the quartermaster's tent. This is on the major's orders."

Harrison nodded that he understood. "My brother wrote of him in his letters."

"Sí. Peck was in Mexico with us. Two years in the regiment, Señor Harry."

Harrison sipped at his tequila. "Tell me, Juan. How did my brother act the last few days before he died?"

"Señor Harry, the captain was all the time alone, in his tent or away in other places. He was in his thoughts, I think. He worry much about the trial in Texas. The officers from Washington ask him many questions."

"What about the other officers? They were also questioned about the riot, weren't they?"

"Sí, Harry. They ask everybody about the troubles in Houston. They want to know where all of us were, what we do. Those kind of thing."

"Major Snow and the officers from the other companies—where were they during the riots?"

"Ah, Harry, the other officers try to stop their men from mutiny. That is what I know. Some did and some did not. But Major Snow...." Juan ran a palm over his short hair, thinking.

"Yes?" Harrison asked.

"I do not know. He gives orders for them to stop, but the men, they get their Springfields and go to town. My friend Vida Henry lead them."

"I see. Did my brother try to stop them?" Harrison watched Juan refill his glass.

"Captain James say, he say to me, 'Sergeant, order the men to prepare to fire!' I order the guard to load and prepare to fire. The captain say 'Sergeant Parilla, fire only when I give the order. Not before!'" Juan took a sip from the glass, then a deep breath. "He never give that order, Harry. But I understand why."

"Tell me, Juan."

"Your hermano was a soldier, Harry. We fight together against Pancho Villa. All of us, together. He cannot kill his men. They are his family. I know, and I respect him for this."

Both men sat, thinking their own thoughts. James thought of his brother, of mutiny, of failure to follow lawful orders, of shame and of suicide. What Parilla had said confirmed his information.

"I've been thinking more about who found my brother's body," Harrison said. "If you could answer a couple of questions...?"

"Ask me. I will try to answer for you."

"Who was there when you arrived?"

"I see the major, Captain Blaine from M Company, Private Peck, two military police and the Provost from the Regiment. Two troopers come with me. We wrap the captain in a blanket and put him on a stretcher. That is what I see. I have two more privates come to clean up the tent. The three officers leave together before me. I tell Private Peck to stay and clean.

"Any sign of a struggle?"

"No."

Harrison thought for a moment. "Tell me more about this woman, Senorita Washington. I'm surprised that my brother would be involved with someone like her. Do you know her, Juan?"

"Señor, some things are better left alone." Juan threw down the tequila remaining in his glass. "This may be no good for you."

"I must speak to this woman." Harrison continued, still sipping at the cloudy white liquid in his glass. "Will you help me find her, Juan?"

He sniffed the empty glass, and then looked over at his wife and the child. "This is not so easy. This woman is, how you say? Wanted."

"Wanted?"

"Sí, Harry. The Army has a large reward for her."

"Then you can't help me. Is that what you're saying?"

The sergeant shrugged. "I must think about this, Harry."

"I'll find someone else, if you don't want to help me." Harrison still couldn't understand. Bart and a smuggler? "I must meet her, Juan. It is important."

"It's dangerous, Harry. The reward of five thousand dollars is for 'dead or alive.' Every bounty hunter look for her, eh?"

"I must know if my brother committed suicide. She may have information." James pressed the man as much as he dared. "I will pay you whatever you want."

"I will consider this," he said finally. "But I do not want your money." He turned to the corner, to where his wife and child were. He smiled. "Harry, I will think about helping you. Tonight, I think.

Tomorrow, in the morning, I tell you what I decide." Juan knew he was the only man who could help the gringo meet la Senorita.

"Fair enough," Harrison said. "I'm staying at the Hoover. Just leave a message with Miguel if I'm not there." He stood, nodding to Consuelo, who smiled quietly in response. "Good evening then." Harrison turned, put his hat back on and headed out the door.

*

He threaded back through the alleys until reaching a street with gaslights. Broadway—Harrison recognized the street from earlier in the day. He had observed yet another side of the New Mexico town. Nearer the well-lit street, the small adobe homes of Juan's neighborhood had given way to two story, wood frame, clapboard houses, once brightly painted and trimmed with ornate latticework. Walking slowly back to the center of town along Broadway, Harrison encountered increasing numbers of soldiers.

Harrison stopped in front of a well-lighted saloon that he recognized from the day before. Why not, he thought. It's still early. He entered the Last Chance Saloon.

Upstairs, he saw men leaning against wooden banisters, talking or watching the crowd below. A thick haze of dark blue tobacco smoke hung in the air. The smell of stale beer and cigars permeated everything. He saw saloon girls strolling through the room taking drink orders or making other arrangements with the soldiers, but he saw no Negroes anywhere.

Sipping their mugs of beer, several soldiers turned to watch as James walked to the bar. "A beer," he ordered. He leaned over the polished mahogany and placed one foot on the brass footrail.

The short, stout bartender nodded and drew a mug for the new arrival. Harrison slid a quarter across the bar toward him. The man picked it up and smiled. "Evenin'," he said, flashing his black and brown stained teeth. The man had a belly that pushed against the front of his grimy white apron, and an even larger bald head. But Harrison saw that he was quick on his feet as he watched him move around behind the bar, satisfying his customers.

Harrison stared up at a wooden framed lithograph of the battleship U.S.S. Maine hanging behind the long bar. To its right was a lithograph of John L. Sullivan in his glory days. Seeing it, he smiled, remembering how often and in how many places he had seen the same picture of the great fighter hanging in a saloon.

"Hey, Harry," someone behind James called.

He turned to see the two soldiers he had met on the train.

"Gentlemen," Harrison said. The two approached him, mugs of beer in hand.

"Ya know, Harry, for some reason I know'd I'd see you again. You're fast at findin' yur way 'round town. Ain't he, Jonesy?"

"Sure is. Howdy, Harry."

"You drinkin' alone, Harry?" Jonesy asked.

"Yes I am," James answered, smiling at the mismatched pair as they leaned against the wood railing on each side of him. "Isn't it a little late for you boys to be out of camp?"

They both grinned.

"Harry, we's off duty. We can come ta town if we wanta, eh?" Charlie said.

Both soldiers laughed out loud.

"You boys need another?" the bartender asked in a thick Irish brogue.

"Give us one. You buyin' Harry?" Charlie asked with a sneer.

"What about ye, sur?" The bartender asked Harrsion.

"Not for me, thanks," Harrison responded, still looking at Charlie. "But give my good friends here each a beer." Harrison then gave the short soldier a nasty smile.

"Ye be new lad 'round here, ain't ye?" the bartender asked.

"That's right. Harrison James."

They shook hands.

"Patrick Derry. Call me Paddy," the bartender replied. "This be me own place here. Now where ye be from, if ye don't mind me askin'?"

"I'm from Illinois."

"Illinois," Paddy repeated. "Be travelin' through, now?"

"No, Paddy," Harrison replied.

"Come on, Paddy. Where's ar beer, eh?" Charlie was irritated.

"Comin' up, boys. Jus' hold yer horses," Paddy said, tapping two draughts, then sliding one after the other across the mahogany.

"You boys come here often?" Harrison asked Jonesy.

"Sure do," Jonesy answered, then took a long swallow from the mug.

"Tell me more about what the army has you gentlemen doing out here. What with the real war on in Europe," Harrison said.

"We makin' sure the Mex don't come 'cross the border again," Jones continued. "Now, we's gettin' ready for the big 'un. Yessir. Give us our steel helmets today." He looked at Charlie.

"That's right," Charlie responded, taking a deep swallow of beer. He wiped the froth from his face with the back of his forearm. The bastard Yankee buys me a beer and expectin' me to sing fur it, he thought, kicking viciously at the sawdust that covered the dark wood floor.

To Harrison, Charlie had trouble written all over him. This encounter only confirmed his earlier opinions. He easily pictured Charlie as one of the big rats that lurked in all of Chicago's alleys.

Charlie leaned real close to Harrison so no one else could hear. "Ya got money on ya, Harry?" he whispered, his hand holding Harrison's upper arm.

Harrison reached across with his other hand. He grabbed Charlie's fingers and twisted hard to force the smaller man's arm behind his back. "Go to hell," Harrison whispered, putting pressure on Charlie's arm.

Charlie struggled to free himself.

Harrison gave him a slight push, then let him go.

"Let's go," Charlie suddenly ordered Jonesy. "We got bus'ness." He turned and left.

"I'm sure we'll see ya agin, Harry," Jonesy said, and followed Charlie to the door.

"Why we leavin' so soon, Charlie?" Jonesy asked when they were outside on the wood walkway.

"I don't like the Yankee none," Charlie answered. "Come on. We'll go across the street. Wait fer 'im ta leave."

Harrison finished his beer.

"Havin' 'nother?" Paddy asked.

"No Paddy. I think I'll be retiring for the evening."

*

From the mouth of an alley across the street, the two privates watched the civilian leave the bar and walk down Broadway. They then crossed the street and re-entered the saloon.

"I don't like that Yankee none, Paddy," Charlie told the bartender when the two got to the bar. "He needs to be taken down a peg."

"Ye think ye the man to do it, now?" Paddy asked, serving them two more beers.

"Ya sayin' I can't?" Charlie asked angry.

"I be sayin' to ye that the man be dangerous," Paddy said. "I can tell it when I looks at 'im. Ye best be leavin' 'im alone."

CHAPTER TEN

Harrison did not receive any message from the Sergeant the following day. He stopped by the front desk twice to speak with Miguel. With time on his hands, he asked around town about Bart's woman. But mostly, he stayed in his room thinking.

Early the morning of the second day, Harrison heard a knock at his door.

"Señor James?" the clerk said through the door. "Señor, I have message for you. From my uncle."

"Slide it under the door," Harrison responded from bed. He had spent much of the early morning planning his next move. He waited, listening for the clerk's departing footsteps on the waxed wood floors, then got out of bed. Seeing the single sheet of tablet paper on the floor, he reached down to retrieve the note.

The message was simple and direct. "La Señorita will meet with you. Tomorrow, at six of the clock we travel. Come to the livery off Broadway." It was not signed.

*

Sergeant Parilla and James departed as the sun's rays broke the horizon. Parilla had rented two horses and packed provisions for two days. "This is enough, amigo. No worry. I am a soldier in this country for many years."

Harrison listened, reserving judgment.

Juan saw the expression on the white man's face. "You have pistola, Harry?"

Harrison hesitated, finally smiled and answered, "Sí."

"Good. There are many animals in this country. Some dangerous. It is good to be armed." Juan looked him over carefully. The weapon was well concealed.

Still smiling, Harrison drew his coat back to reveal an ivory handled .32 caliber Colt automatic in a shoulder holster.

Juan nodded.

Harrison pulled his hat down tight over his brown hair. He wrapped a scarf around his mouth and neck, more to hide his identity than for protection against the early morning chill. Only his eyes were exposed.

"Muy bien," Juan laughed heartily. "We are ready. Now we go to meet La Señorita." He led them out of town, moving due south toward the border.

"Now where do ye think they be goin' in this wide land?" the bartender asked, standing at the door to the saloon as the two riders passed down Broadway. He had just unlocked the door to get ready for the early morning trade.

"I dunno, suh," the young Negro shrugged. "But, they ain't goin' to no picnic. I knows the first sergeant, an' he not a man to travel in a desert fur no good reason." Using a slow, choppy motion, he deliberately swept the dirt and dust from the night before into one large pile in front of the door.

"Do ye know that lad with 'im?" Paddy asked, stepping away from the pile of sawdust and dirt.

"No, suh. I surely don't. He wears those fancy clothes. He don't need to go picnicin' in the desert, no way."

"Ever seen 'im before?"

"Yeah, suh. I seen 'im a couple a day ago, I reckon. Seen 'im in the company area. He was askin' 'bout Capt'n James, Mista Derry. The one that kilt hisself."

"They goin' someplace import'nt, maybe, to meet somebody, to git somethin', maybe." Paddy narrowed his eyes.

"They say he's the capt'n's brother, but I never heard his name."

Paddy only said, "Ye hear something, Peck, ye be lettin' me know. There's a good lad."

"Yeah, suh, Mista Derry. I surely will." The young Negro resumed his sweeping, gradually moving the pile out the door onto the wood sidewalk. Peck had been working at the saloon on and off since his company returned to Camp Furlong. Like many soldiers from the camp, he needed the extra money. And Mistuh Derry rewarded him well sometimes for his information. Mistuh Derry always wanted to know what the army was doing.

*

When the two riders had gone several miles and were safely out of sight of Columbus, Juan abruptly changed direction and headed northwest. "Where are we going?" Harrison asked.

"Columbus has many eyes, amigo. We go toward Tres Hermanas." He pointed to the three peaks standing side by side in the distance.

They rode slowly all day through the arid, rocky plain. They stopped only once to eat, rest, and water the horses. Juan pointed out landmarks to Harrison, and explained ways to survive in the desert. "Always look for landmarks, and do not let the distances fool you, amigo," he told him. "The land is very flat here. You see?" He pointed to the mountains. "How far you think?"

"I'd say several miles—three miles, maybe," Harrison replied.

Juan smiled. "No, amigo. "A half day by horse."

When the desert turned suddenly to scrub forest, Juan knew they had reached the foothills, nearing the meeting place. The day was hot, and the dry air and dust had taken their toll on both men.

Making their way carefully through a narrow canyon, the two riders came out into an open area surrounded by sheer cliffs on all sides. Higher up, rocky promontories towered over them. Harrison knew that from those high points someone could observe any approaches into the widening canyon. He felt they were being watched as Juan led him through a stand of scrub pine. They reached the rendezvous just as the sun set behind the peaks. There, they finally dismounted.

"We make camp," Juan ordered, and began to unpack the horses. "I feed the horses. You build a fire. Build a big fire." Juan knew they were being watched. "Make us some coffee." It was autumn in the high country and the evening air was cooling quickly.

Harrison did as he was told. He filled the tin coffee pot with water from his canteen, then he scooped in ground coffee and closed the lid. When the coals were red and the fire was hot, he set the pot on a larger mesquite log at the edge of the fire. Within a few minutes it was boiling. The aroma of fresh coffee slowly filled the small clearing. He opened a large can of beans and dumped its contents into a large pan. Then he added a tin of meat to the beans. Ravished, they ate.

An hour passed.

"Make more coffee, Harry," Juan ordered softly. "For our guests."

By the time the coffee had begun to boil, they heard horses approaching in the darkness.

James was intensely curious about this woman, supposedly Bart's lover, who he had heard so much about. But he wasn't taking any chances. He positioned himself against a tree, from where he could cover most approaches to the fire.

There was the increasing sound of hoof beats and then, suddenly, two riders appeared out of the darkness. They had rifles. James saw the barrel of a Springfield pointed at his head.

"I will speak," Juan whispered. "Hola, amigos! Que pasa?" he called to them. "Por favor, join us by the fire," he said, his voice pleasant.

The two dismounted warily and lowered their rifles. They moved closer. Finally, they squatted down to warm their hands.

Where was the woman? Harrison wondered, watching the two men.

"Coffee? This gringo brought coffee all the way from New York to share with you, amigos," Juan lied. "Take some." He pointed to tin cups sitting near the pot. "Do you have hunger? Eat the frijoles. This is for you, amigos."

The men helped themselves.

Harrison saw that one of the men was Negro, and the other appeared to be Indian or mestizo. Both were dressed like Mexican compesinos—dark blue cotton shirts and faded brown pantaloons, but with high leather boots. They were well-armed. In addition to modern Springfield rifles, they carried Model 1911 .45 automatic pistols. Bandoleers of rifle bullets crisscrossed their chests. The younger looking Negro was short but angular, with knotted, muscular arms. His hands were huge. Harrison noticed a scar, pinkish in color, that contrasted with the dark skin. It began just below his right ear and ran down his neck, disappearing under the collar of his shirt. The man's slow, methodical manner of sitting and pouring coffee gave the impression that he was not naturally quick.

He seemed sullen and angry, Harrison thought, seeing the young man's dark eyes burning in the firelight. His hair was cropped close, like the soldiers at Camp Furlong. There was a huge bowie knife stuck in the man's wide leather belt—probably his weapon of choice.

The young man's companion, about the same height, was lighter skinned, and much thinner. His features were chiseled, as from polished walnut, but marred by deeply pocked scars. Small pox, Harrison knew. The young man, although he guessed he was several years older than the Negro, had black hair that had been cut—chopped—straight across the back. The dark eyes seemed vacant, with a chilling lack of expression. Neither wore a hat.

Without speaking, the Negro directed the other, pointing to where he wanted him to sit. The other man paused briefly, frowning at the younger man, but did as he was told.

Harrison noticed, and sensed little warmth between the two. They were not friends. The Indian concerned him more than the young Negro. Harrison wondered why they were here, and why he had yet to see the woman. Some sort of ambush? No. He was willing to trust the Mexican sergeant, a soldier in the United States Army.

The men continued to stare at James without expression.

"Hola Juan!" James heard a female voice say from the shadows. "Who have you brought me, eh?" Her voice was clear and melodious. Harrison turned to look. The figure, taller than her two companions, finally stepped from the darkness, moving nearer to the fire. Like the others, she wore no hat. The long curls of black hair radiated out like a midnight sun, falling to her shoulders. Her sculpted brown face was alive with emotion. He saw her dark eyes sparkle in the firelight. And, Harrison saw, they were intent upon him as she openly examined him. He was certain she was measuring him against his brother.

But Harrison also took measure of her. Standing in the shadowy light of the fire, she was without doubt the most beautiful woman he had ever seen. The men's clothing she wore did nothing to detract from her beauty or her natural grace. Tall, yet not thin, she easily filled out the tan cotton shirt and trousers. In the firelight he could see her breasts pressing against the thin fabric of her rough cotton shirt. Small hoops of silver swung from each ear.

Harrison continued to stare at her, unable to look away.

"Señorita Maria," Juan exclaimed, delighted to see her. They spoke in English, and Harrsion suspected that it was as a courtesy to him.

The young woman still stood there, looking at him. Her own curiosity was evident.

"This hombre is the brother of Capitan James," Juan stated, motioning for the young woman to sit.

"Of course he is," she said, smiling at Harrison. "And does he have a name?" she asked. Her English, with its melodious Mexican lilt, was excellent.

"Harrison," he answered. He watched as she knelt easily in front of the fire to pour a cup of coffee. The young woman, like her companions, had an Army .45 strapped to her narrow waist. He guessed her to be about 22 years of age. "And your name, I've been told, is Senorita Washington."

She laughed from deep in her throat. "I've been called many things, Señor James, but my amigos call me Maria. Maria Pasquel Washington."

"'Maria' sounds almost Mexican."

"Yes, my maternal grandparents were Mexican. But on my father's side…. He claimed to be related to George Washington." She laughed again. "I suppose all Negroes claim to be related to Mr. Washington, or Mr. Jefferson, or some other famous white slaver."

Bright and charming, Harrison thought. He tried to picture Bartlett with her.

"Harrison," she repeated. "Harrison and Bart." The young woman again studied his face. "Your brother and I were friends." She paused. "And lovers. Does that surprise you?" She asked the question directly.

He was surprised by her openness. "Yes." He smiled. "I had no idea my brother had such good taste." That's one question answered, he thought, captivated in spite of himself.

She turned her head slightly. "Juan, your amigo speaks graceful compliments, does he not? Like his brother."

Juan said nothing, simply smiling in reply.

Maria set down her coffee cup and abruptly turned back to James. She was no longer smiling. "Señor James, you have come a long way. You wish to talk to me about your brother."

"I want to talk about my brother, and about how he died," Harrison said immediately.

"Yes," she said simply. She crossed her legs to sit on the rocky ground, and then slowly extended her arms, palms out to feel the warmth of the fire. The young woman was in no hurry, feeling her way into the conversation.

She stared into the cup of coffee poised on her knee. "Juan told me about Bart's death. I could not believe it. When he brought me the news, I was devastated. But, I am afraid I can tell you very little about that, Señor James."

"You knew him well, señorita," Harrison said slowly. "Do you believe he would kill himself?"

The brush in the fire crackled and popped as he waited for an answer.

"I was surprised to hear of the manner of his death," Maria finally responded. "I have thought about it…about him." Her voice was soft, almost inaudible. "For him to take his own life? I am certain he did not, could never, do such a terrible thing."

He studied her face in the flickering light, still struck by her beauty and her easy, yet almost aristocratic manner. He sensed she was holding back. The other three talked quietly in Spanish among themselves.

"You have reasons to believe so, Señorita Washington?" Harrison spoke quietly, but he could feel something in her denial.

"Your brother had enemies, Señor James. He was…" She paused, considering her answer carefully. "…involved in many things. Some things I knew. Some I did not know."

"Things? What do you mean, señorita?" Harrison asked, controlling his impatience. Careful, he thought. Don't push too hard. Out of the corner of his eye, James noticed that the younger, darker-skinned man had turned to look at them.

"We were good friends, as well as lovers," Maria began. She raised her head to look at Harrison. "And we were necessary to each other. Bart wanted to know things about the Germans in Mexico. And things about the Mexican freedom fighters, too. I wanted to know where Army patrols go, and when they go. We are traders, Señor James. We sell arms to the highest bidder, on either side of the border." She paused, her eyes suddenly opaque. "Your brother and I also traded information," she finally continued.

Harrison had listened closely. "Is there more?" he asked.

She ignored the question. "We both had our enemies: the Germans, the Mexican Army and, for me, the American Army, too."

Harrison nodded. "Did he help you find weapons to sell? And you gave him information about the Germans?"

"Many on both sides of the border," she said after a short pause, "are getting rich selling arms to the Mexican rebels and to the Mexican Army. The United States Army was investigating this. But your brother…he was not getting weapons for me, Harry. He would never smuggle arms…even to help me in my business."

"Selling weapons is a very dangerous and unpredictable business, or so I've been told," James said. "What did he do for you?"

Maria smiled softly, but said nothing in response.

"I'm trying to understand how my brother died, señorita. To do that, I think I must understand what he was involved in out here," Harrison said. "Your name has been mentioned." he finally added.

"The war in Mexico makes good business for me; for us," Maria told him, responding to his question in her own way. "We sell the generals what they need. Pancho Villa wants Mausers, so we sell to him. If General Carranza wants Springfield rifles, we get them for him. In war, all things can be had for a price. I think you know this, eh?"

"Yes, I understand the business of war," he said, not looking at her, remembering Paris.

"Sí. The American embargo against the Mexicans has made our business even more difficult. Now, American gun makers are afraid to sell, especially to Villa because of his attack on Columbus."

"I hear what you are telling me, but I do not understand how my brother was involved."

She sighed. "Bart's business I cannot explain very well. He did not want others to know what he was doing. Many desperados operate around here. Spies, smugglers, and rebels. It is very difficult to tell them apart." She paused again to consider. "You must understand the hatred between the two generals, Villa and Obregón. Obregón's German friends are devils. Bart wanted to find their agents here along the border." She sighed. "It is very complicated, this war."

James took a sip from this tepid coffee and considered her words.

She smiled at him. "But your brother was also a kind and giving man. To me and to my people. He was beginning to learn our ways." She shook her head sadly. "And then he was dead."

Her lovely face, for a second, changed. In that brief instant she seemed to reveal the depth of her own vulnerability and personal sorrow.

"Sometimes, Señor James, things don't work out the way we want them to."

"What do you mean?"

"Your brother discovered secrets that his enemies tried to hide. Too many secrets, I think." She sighed again. "I think Bart was murdered because he learned too much."

"But you do not know who may have done it?" Harrison asked.

"No, that was his business," she answered simply.

"How did you help him, Maria? May I call you Maria?"

She grinned at him suddenly. "Yes, Harry. I introduced him to people along the border and in Mexico. Most of them were in my business. Some knew things about the Germans or the Mexican Government. That was how I helped him."

"I see," Harrison said, but wondered if he should believe her. There must be more, he thought.

"Your brother was a fine man. Bart would have become a great officer in Europe in the big war. I could see this. It was what he wanted. He told me."

"Did you love my brother, Maria?" Harrison was surprised at himself that he asked.

She looked straight into his blue eyes. Then tears suddenly formed and ran down her cheeks. She did not stop them. "Yes,

Harry, I think I loved him," She responded in her own time. "Since I was a young girl I've cared for myself—for my brother and myself—here in this land. What we do, we do to survive. Bart began to understand. I loved him for that."

"Maria, bastante," the black man blurted out. "No habla más! Nosotros no asesinamos el soldado!" He spat. "If this gringo wants to know about the dead soldier, he must pay for it, yes?" He said it in English to ensure that Harrison understood.

It was the way he said 'gringo.' Harrison raised his head slightly, resting his right hand close to the holster beneath his jacket. Juan, noting the movement, grew alarmed.

"Don't tell me to be quiet, hermano," the young woman scolded him angrily. "Harry, please forgive my brother. He is suspicious of all whites." Again she looked over at her brother, anger reflected in her eyes.

Then she turned back to Harrison. "We lost an amigo, Vida Henry, in Houston during the battle with the whites. He fought to gain our people freedom as Americans. Do you believe that, Harrison James? That he died for us?"

Harrison said nothing. He was fully alert and flushed with sudden anger.

"Maria! He is a white man…., a fucking gringo," her brother hissed in English. "You've told him enough. We go now!" His companion did not speak, but watched Harrison, his rifle pointed down, but in Harrison's direction.

"Mind your tongue," Harrison said coldly.

The young man suddenly jumped up to confront him from across the glowing embers of the fire. With his right hand, he grabbed hold of the hilt of his knife.

But Harrison was already moving. His hand slid easily into his jacket. His palm squeezed against the ivory grip. He lifted the safety with his thumb, but kept his finger off the trigger. He was ready to draw and shoot if either man made another move.

The others watched, frozen.

Harrison waited for the younger man. In the light of the fire, he noticed the boy's free hand tremble slightly.

The Indian rose to stand beside the black man, rifle in hand. But, very carefully, he had positioned the barrel so that it pointed at the ground.

James watched both men without expression, still waiting.

"Enough!" Maria yelled at her brother. "Sit down! Now!" She was certain that the white man would kill her brother if he had to. "Daniel!" Maria demanded.

Pausing briefly, Daniel did as she ordered. Both men sat down.

Harrison spoke to the Indian while his hand remained on his pistol. "Lay the rifle down crossways, pointed away from the fire. Or I'll kill you."

The Indian did as he was told, his whole being radiating hatred.

"Señor, please. They will not do this again. Please, don't draw your pistola," Maria said.

During the confrontation, Juan had not moved from his spot. Now he stood up slowly. "I get mesquite for the fire," he announced, and disappeared into the darkness.

"I am sorry, Señor James," Maria told him.

"I understand, señorita. But I will shoot them if I have to," Harrison replied, still keeping a close eye on both men.

Finally, he relaxed his guard, but kept his hand in his lap, close to the automatic.

"We are at war," Maria said slowly. She wanted the white man to understand her. "My brother and I are also of the people fighting for a place in our own country."

"Señorita Washington, you said you were a trader," Harrison began slowly. I have information of value to you. It is about one of your competitors. In El Paso. I am willing to cut a deal—information for information. Think about it."

She looked at the white man, holding his gaze. "We will be in touch, Harry." Then she rose quickly.

Her two companions also stood.

"We must go now. It is very dangerous. This close to the border, army patrols are everywhere."

Juan returned with a handful of wood. He began to feed the fire one branch at a time, appearing to pay little attention to the conversation.

"You are the enemy, white man!" Daniel growled before his sister could silence him again. "Everywhere in this world, you are the enemy!" He spit into the fire. Then he spun around to disappear into the darkness, the young Indian close at his heals.

"We will talk again. Maybe to trade, eh?" Maria said. She followed her brother into the night. "Juan….hasta luego, amigo," she called with a wave of her hand. A few minutes later, he heard the creak of leather, then hooves fading in the distance.

"Hey amigo, thanks for the help," James grumbled sarcastically. "There were two of them." He knew the Sergeant was watching from the darkness, but who did he have his eyes on? The two young men, or him?

Juan smiled, saying nothing.

"At least I've met Maria and her smugglers."

"What smugglers, señor? I am a sergeant in the Army of the United States. I know of no smugglers." He continued to build the fire. After a last cup of coffee, each lay down in his bedroll.

"Buenas noches, amigo." Juan said. Then turning on his side, he went to sleep.

Harrison lay there awake, listening to the other man's steady breathing, punctuated by an occasional snore. He considered the meeting with Maria and her brother.

*

Early the next morning, traveling in a northeasterly direction from the campsite, James and Parilla had left the mountains and were again down in the desert when they saw a cloud of dust. It was far to the east when they spotted it against the morning sunlight, but it was moving steadily toward them.

"A patrol," Juan said, pointing. "Be careful what you say to them," he cautioned. "Remember, we are having a camping trip to see this beautiful country of New Mexico."

Harrison nodded.

Within an hour, eight cavalrymen were upon them. The patrol deliberately intersected their route of travel. A young officer rode forward of the others. His troopers halted behind him in line, obediently waiting for orders.

"Good morning, gentlemen," the officer called out to the two men.

"Good morning," Harrison responded calmly.

"First Sergeant Parilla, sir. Can we help you, lieutenant?" Juan asked, recognizing the young officer from Camp Furlong. The troopers sat on creaking saddles, heavily armed with pistols and rifles.

"Looking for smugglers," the lieutenant responded, casually looking over the two. He wondered why they were out riding in the desert.

"I'm afraid we can't help you," Harrison interjected. At that moment, he saw his two acquaintances from the train. They grinned at him.

"Do you know you're close to the border, sir? And may I ask your business?"

"We're just out riding and enjoying the country, lieutenant." Harrison answered. "I've never seen it before."

"Did you cross the border?"

"No, we haven't." James pulled up the reins. He motioned around him with his hands. "A fine place...New Mexico."

"And the sergeant?"

"I hired him to be my guide, lieutenant."

The lieutenant looked Parilla over carefully. "You picked yourself a good guide, mister?"

"Harrison James, from Illinois. Yes, sir. Thank you. I always try to have the best, wherever I travel."

"Mr. James. We're looking for two known smugglers in particular. Two Negroes. They've been running guns over the border to the rebels down south of Juárez. Have you seen any riders at all during your sight-seeing trip?" The lieutenant knew this man was not a smuggler or a bandit.

"Selling guns is against the law here?" Harrison asked innocently.

"They're violating a United States embargo against selling weapons to the Mexicans. One of them, Pancho Villa, is an enemy of the United States, with a reward on his head for murder. But that doesn't stop some people from smuggling guns." The young officer seemed conscientious and sure of himself. He paused to look the two over one last time.

"We weren't really looking, but we didn't see anyone," Harrison told him.

"A tall woman and a man. There may be a third rider with them, but we don't know who he is. They were spotted crossing the border. We've been tracking them since yesterday evening."

"We didn't see anyone, lieutenant," Parilla agreed.

The soldier decided the two were telling the truth.

"Lieutenant, sir." Charlie had moved up alongside. "Request permission to speak with Mr. James, sir. I know'd him."

"Why speak to him, private?"

"We're friends. Jus' a question, lieutenant."

"Permission granted, private," the young officer said and turned his mount to prepare to depart. "Men, get ready to move out," he called to the others.

"There's a big reward for them smugglers, Harry. How 'bout helpin' yur buddies, eh?" Charlie asked, moving his horse closer and lowering his voice. Harrison could smell tobacco, bad teeth, and yesterday's cheap whisky.

"I have never heard of them, Charlie."

"Hey, Harry, you lyin' to us?" Charlie asked, certain Harrison was holding something back

"I beg your pardon, trooper?" Harrison answered coldly.

"Lieutenant, he know'd somethin' that he's not tellin'," Charlie shouted.

"Lieutenant, I could cut short my camping trip and we could return to the fort. Then you could explain to your commanding officer why you detained me." Harrison smiled, trying to appear calm.

"Lieutenant, stop him. He knows them smugglers, sure," Charlie insisted.

"That's enough, private. Let 'em go," the lieutenant snapped. The last thing he wanted was some damn civilian making trouble for him.

"The man's lyin', sir. I know'd it," Charlie said angrily.

"Lieutenant, I have met this man before," Harrison told the lieutenant, deciding it was time to act. "But he is not a personal acquaintance of mine. And I hope he's not a reflection of the U.S. Cavalry, which until now I've had only the greatest respect and admiration for."

"Sir, I apologize for this man's rude behavior. Private, return to the ranks now," he ordered Charlie. "Men, allow them passage." The troopers pulled aside so the two riders could pass. "Good day, Mr. James. Sergeant."

Before Charlie left James' side, he leaned over. "We be a watchin' ya, Harry," he murmured.

"Don't get in my way, Charlie."

James and Parilla rode south and east toward Columbus. Watching, they saw the cavalry patrol move in the opposite direction, toward Tres Hermanas.

An hour later, Harrison abruptly reined in tight, forcing his mount to stop. He dismounted and waited for Juan to pull up close. "Sergeant Parilla, where do you stand on all this?" James asked directly when Parilla was closer. "I need an answer before we get back to town."

Juan also dismounted. "Señor?" he asked, caught off-guard.

"You are a soldier in the U.S. Army, yet you are a friend of smugglers," Harrison said. The two men were standing a few inches apart. "I don't know what side you're on, and that makes me nervous."

Juan thought before answering him. "The señorita is my friend for many years. She does not disrespect me. I have respect for her. Your brother was my commanding officer, who I always respected. I do not know how he died. But I tell you this: I am a man of honor. If you do not like me or what I do, tell me to my face. We settle it now." He stood facing Harrison, casually ready, a compact man with no sign of fear about him.

"You've made your feelings clear," Harrison said, pulling on his reins to bring the horse closer. "Let's ride." He then remounted.

Juan remained standing. "Listen to me, Señor Gringo."

"What?" Harrison replied, surprised. He sat was on his horse, studying Juan's quiet intensity.

"This. Every hombre has a right to be respected. No man can take it away. It is for him only to lose it. Without respect there is no friendship and no justice," Juan said. "We could be friendly, gringo. But you must first respect me, and I must respect you. From this comes friendship, then trust. If you do not respect my life—the way

I live—I will give you time to get off your horse. Now choose your answer."

"I respect you, Juan," Harrison answered, not used to being spoken to in such a manner. This man has an honest way of seeing the world, he thought. "And I appreciate your helping me."

"Okay, Harry." Juan smiled. "Now we can go on."

CHAPTER ELEVEN

Harrison sighed, massaging a tense neck with his left hand. The Jack Daniels began to work its magic. He sat in an old wicker chair—the only chair in his hotel room—with his vest unbuttoned and his boots propped up on the windowsill. He had returned to Columbus with Sergeant Parilla several hours earlier, without incident. Finishing the drink, he poured himself two fingers more. He needed to think things over.

"To mater," he toasted aloud, holding the glass up to the window. "And to Bart." He sipped. "Hell, to me!" He held the glass up again before taking a final gulp, throwing it down his throat quickly. "No, mater, you do not have a fool, a worthless dandy for a son," Harrison told himself. The whisky lay in his belly, warming his thoughts.

He was interrupted by a knock on the door. "Señor James?" the voice asked. "Señor James, I have a message for you. Muy importante."

"One minute, please." He set the now empty glass on the windowsill, buttoned his vest, and threw his coat over the holstered automatic. He opened the door to see the young desk clerk. "Yes?"

"Buenos noches, Señor James," the young man said with a smile.

"Good evening," Harrison responded politely. "You have something for me?"

"A message, señor. The man who come, he left it and went away." He handed over the note

"Who is it from?" James asked.

"An old man, Señor James. I do not know him."

"What did he look like?" James held the note in his hand without opening it.

"A very old Negro, señor. The old man did not speak, and when he handed la carta to me, he was gone muy rapido." The young clerk gratefully accepted a piece of silver and quickly pocketed it.

"Thank you, amigo." Harrison led him to the door without opening the envelope.

"If you need more assistance, Mr. James, por favor, ask for Miguel."

"Yes, thank you, Miguel. I will." He closed the door, then opened the sealed note and read:

Dear Harrison James, It was a great pleasure to finally meet you. I am grieved it could not be under happier circumstances. Forgive my brother, but he is a very angry man and blames white people for his troubles. I have valuable information concerning your brother and his duties here. But it is now too dangerous for me to cross the border to the United States. Please come to Las Palomas as my guest. An old man will come to your door in one day to receive your reply. He will know what to do. Do not tell anyone. You must come alone. Your friend, Maria.

*

He read and reread the note, then carefully folded it and put it in his grip. He slid the bag under the bed. It'll keep, he thought. But he suddenly felt restless. He needed another drink and some conversation.

Harrison meticulously brushed off his hat. Using a corner of the bedspread, he buffed up his boots and, finally, he strapped on the pistol harness and put on his coat. He carefully locked the door on his way out. Walking up the street, James was guided by the raucous sounds of the late night saloons.

*

The Indian watched the tall, well-dressed white man walk past him as he sat slumped on a wood bench outside the hotel where the whites stayed. A large sombrero covered his face. He had learned from the previous evening out in the desert that the white man was un hombre muy peligroso. The gringo could interfere in business and could ruin everything. Carlos stood and followed the tall gringo down Broadway at a safe distance. In his mind he considered his options for dealing with Señor James. Without thought, he touched the .45 under his long shirt.

*

Harrison entered through the double wooden doors of the Last Chance Saloon, stopping at the long bar. "A beer. Pabst Blue Ribbon, please." He recognized the bartender from his earlier visit.

"Evenin' squire. I might have a bottle, at that," said the broad, red-faced Irishman. With a flourish, he produced one from under the counter. He smiled and uncapped the bottle, still cold and dripping from the ice water.

"And a clean glass, please," Harrison said without looking up. He laid a fifty-dollar bill on the bar.

Paddy produced a clean glass. "'Tis a poor man I be, squire. Only a widow's son. And that bein' so much fortune in a single bit of paper, so it is," he said, staring at the large bill.

"So it is," Harrison said. He left the money on the bar.

The bartender looked at him more closely.

"And what might be bringing yer lordship to Columbus, sir? Business? Columbus is a long way from the big city," he said, polishing the bar with a rag. "And you bein' such a fine gentleman an' all."

"Business," Harrison replied shortly.

"A kind of business that would bring a man such as yerself to my humble establishment, sor?"

"Harrison slowly surveyed the room. "Perhaps you could direct me to some entertainment. A game of chance, perhaps? Poker is my preference. An acquaintance, Lieutenant Floyd, comes here often, I'm told." He looked down at the large bill.

"Aye, well ye come to the right place, so you have. Now, Lieutenant Floyd, you say?" Paddy looked down at the greenback, then peered through the smoke at the room filled with soldiers. "I know the lad, sure."

"He seems to be both a Southern gentleman and a sportsman. Does he like a drink sometimes?" Now Harrison tapped the bill.

"He be known to take a wee drop and indulge himself in a game of cards now and again." The middle-aged Irishman squinted at the well-dressed customer. "The lieutenant be a man of good taste, sor. In his women and his whisky. But he be luckier with his women than with his cards. If ye follow me meanin', squire."

Harrison smiled and nodded that he understood. "He being a man of such good taste, I suppose he comes here often?"

"Aye, he's one of me best customers."

"Is he?" Harrison looked at Paddy. "I wouldn't mind a few hands of poker tonight."

The bartender looked down quickly at the bill. "The lieutenant is a grand an' generous soldier who don't cause me no trouble." He paused to tap a mug of beer and slide it to a soldier across the bar. Then he eyed James cautiously. "I think I be helpin' ye thar. Jus' leave it now to ol' Paddy."

"Thank you, Paddy," Harrison said.

Paddy squinted at him. "Ye be alookin' fur other entertainment? I be helpin' ye with that, too. Jus' look 'round ye, eh?"

"Oh yes? What else do you have, Paddy?"

Derry looked around before answering. "Depends on what a lad likes. Ye know me meanin'?" He winked at Harrison, and then nodded to one of the few women in the saloon. She responded with a calculating glance at the stranger.

The woman approached the mahogany bar. She was a big boned blond with dark roots and large breasts, her skin was very pale. Harrison noticed dark rings shadowing her gray eyes. She wore a bright red and green colored dress cut low to show off her endowments. He guessed her for late thirties, but trying to look ten years younger.

"So old Floyd likes the ladies," Harrison said, guessing.

The woman put her arm around his neck, pressing a breast into his arm. "Hi sugar," she whispered with a husky voice. "Buy me a drink?"

"Get the lady a drink, Paddy."

"I don't say nothin' 'bout his habits now, squire," Paddy said as he poured whisky. "But ye might ask the lieutenant yourself." "He might be willin' to share his 'speriences." Paddy quickly handed the woman a shot glass brimmed with house whisky.

Harrison did not respond.

"Me place is the place ta be. Money everywhere, an' it buys a lot of entertaining, squire. Women, all ye want." He looked at the woman. "Or a friendly game of chance? Well, ye come ta the right house. Yes sir, right here."

The woman finished her drink in one swallow, without expression.

"Another, Paddy, but some of the good stuff," Harrison said. "For the lady."

"Tell me yur name, handsome," she said, purring in his ear.

"Where's all the money coming from out here, Paddy? Harrison," he said to the woman.

"My name's Sal," she said, running her hand up and down his back.

"It be a rich lan' and no need to dig potatoes, squire. Opportunity fur ever'body, I think. Ye come here lookin' for a pot a gold, now, Mr. James?"

"More than that, Paddy.

Paddy gave him a hard look.

Sal listened attentively.

"Hey Sal!" a soldier yelled from behind, but close to the bar. "Sal, git over here!"

"Shut up now, Stewart. I'm talkin' to a gentleman. Cain't ya see?" Sal answered, turning to face the man.

"I don't care none 'bout yur gentleman," the soldier told her. "Hey boys," he called loudly to three soldiers sitting at the table. "Sal's found herself a gentleman."

They laughed and began to whistle and yell at her.

"Leave her be, boys. She be busy now," Paddy called over. "Drink up, lads."

"Mr. James, I hope ye enjoy this fair country, now."

"I appreciate that," Harrison told him. "You appear to have one of the better establishments that I've seen." He was looking around the room. "Business is good." He smiled at Sal.

The bartender laughed. "Oh, aye, lad, business is good. For now, anyways."

Sal smiled back at Harrison.

"Mostly soldiers who come in?"

"Aye, soldiers. But businessmen, too. Things are moving in Columbus these days, squire."

"What kind a business are you in?" Sal asked. "One a them travelin' salesmen come in on the train from the East? They's ma favorites."

"No, I'm not a salesman. Another for the lady," Harrison said, noticing that she had finished the second shot. "You ever meet a soldier in here by the name of James—Captain Bart James, from the camp?"

"No, I sure haven't met that one. He some relation of yurs, is he now?" she asked.

"He was my brother."

Another customer tapped his glass on the mahogany to catch Paddy's attention.

He poured a drink for the customer, then one for Sal.

"Well, thank ya, mister," Sal said.

Paddy just grunted, then walked down the line to wait on another customer.

Sal moved even closer to press her breast firmly into James' arm. With her left hand, she began softly to rub his thigh and crotch. "I could show you a real good time, handsome," she whispered in his ear.

Harrison smiled, but wouldn't allow himself to be distracted. He had other things on his mind.

Sal threw down the third shot like a pro.

Harrison felt her swerve slightly on his arm. "Lieutenant Floyd—do you know him, Sal?"

"I know that one real good, Harry," she said with a slight slur, looking at her empty glass.

"Does he talk with you much?"

"We talk, Harry," Sal answered. "He's here almost ever' night. Cain't avoid 'im."

"A good man, is he?" Harrison asked. "I mean, does he treat you right, Sal?"

"Jimmy is good to me, 'specially when he's got money to spend."

"Give the lady another," James called to Paddy.

"Bartender, I need a couple of beers," another customer called from the end of the bar. "Right now!" he demanded.

"I heard ye now, sergeant. I'm comin'," Paddy called back.

"How often is that, Sal? That he has money in his pocket, I mean?"

"He had a lot of money last spring, but not so much since he got back from Texas. Told me he does some kind of business."

"What kind of business?" Harrison saw that she loosened up when the bartender was gone.

"Don't know an' don't want to know. You understand?"

"Tell me, Sal. Do Paddy and the lieutenant know each other very well?"

"Those two know each other real well. I hear Jimmy does things for Paddy. An' Paddy pays 'im real good."

"What kind of things?"

"Like I tell ya already, I don't want to know. Paddy can be real mean sometimes 'bout askin' questions. But I'll say one thing: It pays money." Sal winked.

Derry returned. He gave Sal a hard look.

Harrison saw it. "Sal, I thank you for telling me about the beautiful views you have around here. I think you and me should take a buggy ride out to those mountains. Maybe on Sunday?" he said, then he leaned over to kiss the nape of her neck. Sal smiled. "She was describing what a nice place Columbus is, and that I should stay around for a while, Paddy."

"Yeah?" That gomerel be lyin' through his teeth, Paddy thought. He be the devil himself. "She don't have the time, gov. I keep her busy here," he growled.

"That's too bad. You and I were talking about Floyd's friends, Paddy?"

"Why don't ye ask 'im yurself. I take ye up and set ye in the game, gov. No problem."

"I'd appreciate that," James smiled. "Drink up, Sal." He threw down a twenty-dollar bill.

"You a real gentleman there, Harry. You different from the rest, I can tell," she said, grabbing the twenty from the bar and sticking it between her breasts. "Later maybe, eh?"

"Yeah Sal, maybe later. And I'm not really a gentleman," he said with a smile from watching her dispose of the greenback.

"Ye want change for this?" Derry asked.

"If you get me into Floyd's game, I'd call us even, Paddy."

"C'mon, gov. Follow me," Derry said. Then he walked around the end of the bar. "The game be upstairs."

Harrison caught up to the shorter man and followed him up the stairs. He took his beer with him.

"Sal, ya my woman, ya are," a soldier said, now standing behind her grinning. He ran his hands over her buttocks slowly then, in one hard thrust, he pushed himself against her.

Pushing him back, Sal turned quickly with knee raised. In one great effort she rammed it into his groin.

The private doubled over in pain. "Oh Sal," he moaned between clenched teeth. "I still love ya."

She remained there, legs wide apart and hands on her hips, prepared for anything. She watched him, a slight smile creasing the painted red lips. "Go 'way, Stewart, like I tell ya. Cain't ya hear? I'm busy workin'."

Stewart finally raised up, but very cautiously. Swaying slightly, he gave her a big smile. "Kiss me, Sal."

"Stewart, you go find yourself two bucks and I'll kiss ya."

Harrison, seeing Stewart assault Sal, had been prepared to intervene. But before he could take a step, Sal had made her move. "Take care of yourself, Sal," he said, and headed up the stairs, a couple of steps behind Paddy.

"An I ain't no lady neither, Harry," she said with a wink, looking up at him.

Stewart turned, staggering back to his table and into the laughter of his friends.

Before James reached the top of the stairs, a gun fired in the room below. Instinctively, his hand went for the shouldered Colt as he fell to the steps and turned. Looking down through the layer of tobacco smoke, he made out the figure of a man sprawled across the saw dust covered floor near the door. He looked for Sal and saw her still glowering at Stewart.

"Boys!" he heard one of Paddy's waiters yell. A huge man also in a stained white apron, wide at the girth with arms the size of tree trunks. "Boys, there be no shootin' in my 'stablishment now, ye hear me?" he called above the crowd noise. "Paddy don't allow it in here." He did not move from his spot behind the mahogany., but he reached down quickly to retrieve a sawed off shogun. "Stand back, boys, or I'll hurt ya," he yelled, brandishing the weapon for everyone to take notice of.

James spotted the shooter. He was one of the few civilians in the saloon, hatless, and dressed in a brown suit. He could make out the revolver still in his hand. Several soldiers now hovered over the wounded man lying on the floor. Everyone else was standing. Soldiers ringed the shooter in a half circle. Then slowly they moved in on him.

"Stay where you are or I'll shoot," he heard the civilian yell. "That man was cheatin'. He pulled a knife on me and tried to stab me. I got witnesses who seen it."

"Don't ye worry none, Mr. James," Paddy said, turning back to locate Harrison. "Charlie'll handle it."

The last words they heard Charlie call to a soldier standing nearby were: "Sergeant, git the constable right quick."

Soldiers hung over the banister watching the excited crowd below.

*

Harrison followed Paddy through the cigar smoke to a corner table. He quickly recognized Floyd towering over the other players. Up here, no one seemed to have noticed the ruckus below. Approaching, he stood directly across from Floyd, waiting for Derry's introduction.

"Boys, give me yur 'tention, now," Paddy said. "I got ye a new player. He calls hisself James, Mista Harr-i-son James. Ye got problems with him, don't hold back on me, now."

At first, the four soldiers at the table looked up at the two men, eyeing James especially hard.

"Mr. James," Lieutenant Floyd finally said, looking up from his cards. "To what do we owe your presence this evening?"

"Lieutenant Floyd. Delighted to see you, sir. I am searching for some amusement. I have a special interest in the game of poker, in fact. I thought perhaps you and your associates…." Harrison saw that Floyd was flushed. The pile of colored chips in front of him was a small one.

"Of course," Floyd interrupted. He had an air of forced gaiety. "Sit down, sir. Sit down. We can find room for another, can't we men?"

The other two lieutenants at the table nodded without saying a word.

"What did you say your name was?" the captain asked, putting his cards on the table, face down.

"James," Harrison responded with a smile.

"Any relation to Captain Bartlett James?" the captain asked.

"Bart was my brother."

The soldier said nothing in response.

"Sit down, please," the youngest looking man at the table said. "Right here in the empty chair. Bart James' brother. Older brother?"

"That's right. I'm older," Harrison replied, looking around the table at the four soldiers.

Paddy disappeared into the crowd without another word, fifty dollars richer.

"Gentlemen, I appreciate your gracious hospitality," Harrison replied, sitting. "I met a friend of yours downstairs, Lieutenant Floyd," he said with a wink at the others.

"Who would that be, Mr. James?"

"She said her name was Sal."

"Yes, I may have seen the whore," he answered, looking at the other players.

The other three military officers at the table smiled when they heard her name mentioned, but said nothing.

"I guess I'm ready," James responded, setting his half empty glass of beer down on the floor beside his chair. "Chips, please." He handed Floyd several hundred-dollar bills. "Stakes, gentlemen?" he asked formally.

"New money." Floyd smiled with satisfaction and took a quick swallow from his drink. "We play a very friendly game here, Mr. James. Don't we gentlemen?" He shuffled the deck.

The others nodded, their eyes on the hundred dollar bills.

"Five card draw. The ante is fifty dollars. The limit is five hundred. Is that agreeable to you, Mr. James?"

"Of course." With the next deal, Harrison threw in a fifty-dollar chip. "Do you come here often, lieutenant?" he asked Floyd casually.

"Too often, I'm afraid, sir," Floyd answered ruefully.

The others said nothing, anted, and looked at their cards.

"The lieutenant is working hard to get his money back before we ship out for France," the captain said, not looking up from his cards. But it was statement of fact, lacking any humor. He was older than the others, with a shaggy mustache that covered his upper lip. The sad brown eyes looked out from a well tanned face. There Harrison saw the slight facial twitch of the right cheek. The captain was not a handsome man, he decided, but his bearing was one of command.

Floyd took the time to formerly introduce James to each of the other three soldiers at the table. Each man stood, shook his hand and offered his condolences.

"I'm honored to be in such company." During the introductions, James casually observed who seemed to be winning and losing from the piles of chips in front of each. A captain and three lieutenants—all infantry, he noticed. He could easily tell the branch of service by their hard, almost gaunt, tanned faces, worn boots, and faded uniforms with crossed rifle badges sewn on the collars.

Lieutenant Jackson appeared to be the youngest. He was a small, handsome man with long, fashionable sideburns. A dandy, Harrison thought. Jackson spoke with an ease that set him apart from the others. The captain was more taciturn. Harrison found it interesting that he would participate in a money game of cards with his juniors.

"I do hope to discover more about my brother's death," Harrison agreed, looking his opponents over carefully while they played their cards. "Perhaps you gentlemen could assist me."

"Assist you, sir?" Jackson said. "What more can we do?"

"Anything that was overlooked in the investigation, perhaps?" Harrison asked.

"I conducted that investigation, sir," the captain said. "And I can assure you nothing was overlooked."

"I'll take three cards." Harrison handed Floyd his discards, face down. "If you could answer a couple of questions, I'd be most appreciative." His card play appeared casual, but Harrison was a very experienced, coldly calculating gambler. Blocking out the saloon's distractions, he listened intently to each man at the table.

"As I told you already, I was here the night of his death, and a little too indisposed to be of assistance, sir," Floyd responded before James asked. He then shuffled out the three cards. The captain asked for one card. The two lieutenants folded.

Harrison saw that Floyd was impatient to bet. "Fifty to you, sir," Floyd said. The captain matched him, but only after careful consideration. He noted that all four were reluctant to discuss his brother's death. "I fold, lieutenant," he said tucking his cards into the bottom of the deck. Harrison saw that he had to find another way to approach the topic.

Floyd matched the captain's bet and raised another hundred.

"My father can never understand why he must send me additional money each month," Jackson finally said with a laugh.

Following one more round of betting, the captain laid down his hand. "Two pair, aces high."

"Ha!" Floyd exulted, "Full house."

Over the next four hands, Floyd consistently bet heavily and lost. With each loss, he increased his bet. He continued drinking, while the others stayed relatively sober. Harrison saw that the other two lieutenants were easily distracted by the activities surrounding them. They were not experienced card players. But the captain was.

Two hours passed quickly. Harrison slowly shuffled the cards. He noticed that the captain seemed stiff and uncomfortable around the others. "Is gambling a preferred past time of yours, captain?"

"I'm here this evening, Mr. James, because I had nothing better to do," he responded. "And Lieutenant Anthony invited me to accompany him to the saloon for a drink. I usually go to the Officers Mess and don't normally come here. For obvious reasons," he said, looking around.

"I see," Harrison said. He assumed the officer was referring to all the enlisted soldiers he saw in the saloon.

"I'm the commander of M Company. Lieutenant Anthony is my executive officer, and Lieutenant Jackson is from I Company," the captain explained.

"The bid's to you, captain," Harrison said.

"I fold, Mr. James." He threw in his cards.

"We were here the night your brother died, playing cards just like we are now. That is, the three of us junior officers. Funny how things work out." Jackson stated. "Two cards, sir," he said.

"What was my brother like that night?" James said. "Did he play cards here?"

"I never saw him play cards. Ever," Floyd said. "He was a man who generally kept to himself. Since Mexico, I rarely saw him."

"Did any of you talk with him the day of his death?"

"I didn't know your brother well, sir," Anthony said.

"We spoke just before I left for town. About 5:00," Floyd said.

"Yes?" Harrison said. How did he act?"

"He was preoccupied, deep into his thoughts," Floyd replied. "As I told Captain Blaine, he said he was working on important business. He had stacks of battalion records and logs in the tent."

"Yes, I remember Lieutenant Floyd's comments," Blaine said quickly. "I later determined that the business he referred to was routine and had no bearing on your brother's death."

"I see."

"I can't get it out of my mind. They were preparing for their court martial in San Antonio, and I still believe that was what drove your brother to take his life," Jackson said with increasing emotion in his voice. "Too much pressure."

"The Judge Advocate's men were interviewing us to build their case against the Negro mutineers," the captain said, looking sternly at Jackson. "Mr. James, while conducting the investigation into your brother's death, I concluded that your brother had not handled the pressures of command all that well."

James remained quiet.

"Those boys from San Antonio interrogated us, is closer to the truth," Jackson blurted out, still worked up.

"Interrogation, sir?" Harrison asked, reacting to Jackson.

"The Army has its way," Jackson continued. "The question was whether it could have been avoided. That is, could we have prevented the mutiny? Pot's worth another hundred to me," he said, throwing in two chips. "The Southern politicians are demanding that the Negroes be severely punished. Will the Army just blame the affair on drunken Negroes, or will it blame us, too?" It was a rhetorical question.

The others concentrated on their card play.

"The Texans want to hang them...as an example to the rest," Jackson added.

"Lieutenant, shut your month," the captain snapped. "These decisions are made by senior officers, not by Texans. And they are never questioned by lieutenants."

"Those color'ds broke the law. They deserve to be hung," Lieutenant Anthony asserted. He was almost as tall as Floyd, dour, and sounded angry, Harrison observed. "They have no discipline. I'll raise you another fifty. How about it, Mr. James? Are we too rich for your blood, sir?"

"I'm afraid you're too much for me, lieutenant." Harrison threw in his hand. He had noticed that Anthony never bluffed.

"The Negroes proved to be excellent soldiers down in Mexico. Well disciplined," the captain said more calmly.

"The battalion also had better leadership then," Jackson suggested. "Before Major Snow took command."

"Are you criticizing your commanding officer in public, lieutenant?" the captain asked with a sudden cold fury.

Jackson flushed. "No sir, certainly not. Here's your fifty, Floyd. I call. Three of a kind—all jacks."

"Good, but not good enough, lieutenant," Floyd gloated drunkenly, rocking in his chair. "Three aces."

"The Negro troopers will be tried and then probably hanged?" Harrison asked quietly.

"And damn good riddance," Lieutenant Anthony said.

"Just what happened that night in Houston?" Harrison went on.

They all looked at the civilian.

"Your deal, Mr. James," Anthony said finally. The lieutenant still sipped at the same bottle of beer that he had when Harrison arrived.

"Sir," the captain responded directly. He played with the deck a moment before giving it to the civilian. "If anything good happened that night, it was that your brother's company held firm. His troopers didn't march down Washington Street shooting up the town like the others."

Harrison shuffled and dealt five cards to each man.

The captain picked his up slowly and deliberately, without looking at them.

Let's play!" Floyd cut in with growing impatience.

"I knew when the boys from I Company stormed the Quartermaster's tent that the situation was out of control. Yes, sir," Jackson stated. He folded and slid his cards across the table.

"One hundred fifty of 'em left camp, marched right down Washington Street like crazed monkeys," Lieutenant Anthony added.

Harrison noticed the captain still holding his cards, as if trying to decide something.

"Negroes are good soldiers," Jackson contradicted. "I believe that. But Houston was an impossible situation. They were treated poorly, beat up, spat upon. Not even tough discipline would have kept them in line forever. Fifty, sir." He threw out a single chip.

Harrison thought about what Juan had told him out in the desert. "Respect."

"The major took the mutiny personal. An insult to his pride," Jackson said. "I Company was under Major Snow's direct command, and all of I Company, to a man, rioted. Isn't that right, Anthony?"

"Gentlemen, that is enough," the captain ordered before Anthony could respond. "That is army business, and this is a public saloon."

"But captain," Harrison said. "It's certainly not my intent to interfere with army matters. But it is very important to me and to my family that we understand the circumstances leading to Bart's death. I ask you to help me. Tell me anything that may shed light on why my brother would take his own life."

The captain stared at his cards. "Mr. James, it is all in the report I submitted on your brother's death. There is nothing more to add," he said.

"I found your report incomplete, sir," Harrison said directly.

Lieutenant Jackson glanced at the cold-eyed captain, then quickly looked at his cards.

"We lost our best damn NCO that night—Vida Henry," Floyd moaned. "Sergeant Henry distinguished himself down in Mexico, chasing Pancho Villa. And hell, gentlemen, he led the mutineers!"

"I still can't believe it. Henry was so damned Army," Jackson said.

"Yeah, Army enough to lead a mutiny," Anthony said.

"He was a brave man and an excellent non-commissioned officer for the Negro troops," the captain told them. He looked at Harrison. "Henry served with the 10th Cavalry at Carrizal and Torreón, then transferred to the 24th to go to Houston. I'll see that fifty," he said, throwing in a chip. "Mr. James?"

Harrison looked at his cards. "Here's my fifty and another hundred."

"Henry refused to surrender during the mutiny, even when wounded," Floyd told them. "He shot himself that night in some shack in San Felipe. I'll bet twenty-five, gentlemen. A National Guard soldier found him with three bullet holes in him, the last one to the head."

"Much like your brother, sir," Anthony said, looking at Harrison.

"Play cards!" Floyd growled. "You going to bet or not?" He looked at Jackson.

"I'll see that, Mr. James," Jackson said, adding his chips. "And raise fifty. Hell, for the Negroes, Henry's now the hero of Houston."

"I'll see that and raise you another hundred, lieutenant," Harrison responded. "What did my brother tell the Adjutant General?"

"And I," the captain interrupted, "match that bet. Mr. James, that testimony is not public knowledge," he answered for his subordinates. "I'm afraid we don't know. You'd have to go to San Antonio, be at the court martial, to discover what he testified."

"To San Antonio…I see."

"Play cards," Floyd repeated thickly. "The bet is to you, Mr. James. I'll see that and raise you fifty."

"You're too rich for my blood, gentlemen," Harrison said. "I check." He didn't force the issue, and he didn't want to raise the stakes too high and risk taking anyone out of the game. He had been observing Floyd. Beads of perspiration glistened on the man's forehead.

"Fold," Anthony responded finally.

"I want to say, Mr. James, that your brother was a very brave man, who distinguished himself in Mexico," Jackson said. "I think General Pershing would support my opinion, sir. I fold, sir."

The captain also folded. "Gentlemen," Blaine announced, "if you will excuse me, I think I've had enough." He rose from the table.

"And I," Anthony said, standing to leave with the captain. "Good night, and it was an honor to meet the brother of Captain Bart James." He bowed from the shoulders, turned and headed for the stairs.

"Good night, gentlemen," Harrison said with a nod. He watched as both men walked down the stairs.

"I call," Jackson stated, watching Floyd.

"What have you got?" Floyd slurred.

"Two pair, aces and nines." Jackson said.

"You boys are too good for me," Harrison observed.

"Beat!" Floyd growled, throwing his cards into the middle of the table. Jackson shook his head, amused. Floyd struggled to maintain some measure of decorum before a fellow officer. He muttered, examining his very small pile of remaining chips.

CHAPTER TWELVE

An hour later, Lieutenant Jackson finally quit to return to camp. "Gentlemen, it's midnight. Time to go," he announced, throwing in his cards.

That left only James and Floyd at the table. The lieutenant was completely broke and dead drunk. Harrison knew the time was right. "Lieutenant, we seem to be abandoned here. Suppose I buy you a drink and we call it an evening?" he said.

"It seems, sir, that you have me at a disadvantage." Floyd was at the point where he had to carefully articulate each word. "I believe I owe a debt to you, sir?"

"Perhaps." Harrison turned in his chair. "Bring another tequila for the lieutenant and a Pabst for me," he called out to a waiter. He turned back to Floyd. "But in exchange, I could ask you a few more questions about Bart. I would greatly appreciate your insights, lieutenant. You're a man of experience."

"Of course, of course, Mr. James." Floyd's head drooped while he spoke. "Your glorious brother, the great Captain Bartlett James. I, too, am a West Point graduate. Did you know that?" He took the drink from the waiter, then held it up as if toasting what he had just said.

"No, I didn't," Harrison replied, paying the waiter. He slowly gathered up his winnings and collected the cards, folding them into the deck. His movements were precise, experienced. Harrison had played poker all over the world.

Floyd sat, half stupefied, as Harrison cleaned up the table. "I think I've gotten drunk, sir," he slurred. But he was still able to finish his last shot of tequila. "I was right beside him for more than a year. Mexico, Houston. We were together." Floyd stared at the table, his memory in his clouded eyes.

Harrison quietly waited for him to continue.

"Your brother often disagreed with the rest of us on how to discipline Negro troops." Floyd eyed his empty glass. "Sir, I'm from Alabama. We do things differently there." He paused. "You Yankees think you always know what's best for everybody. Mister James…," he slurred, unable to form his thought.

"Does Major Snow share your opinions on commanding Negro soldiers?" Harrison asked.

"Major Snow," Floyd ruminated. "Major Kneeland Snow…. Sir, his opinions are never strongly expressed." Floyd shook his head. "Or, maybe he has no opinions. Easier for him that way." He stared blankly down. "I am an officer in the United States Army and a graduate of West Point. I was trained to follow orders." He took a deep breath.

"His order that night seems clear enough," Harrison said, sipping his beer. "Would you say Major Snow is a good commander, lieutenant?"

"Why do you ask me?"

"You've served under him since he arrived."

"In *my* opinion—between you and me—he's not much of an infantry commander," Floyd said. "And he is very inexperienced at commanding troops in the field. Especially Negro soldiers. And let us say he handles criticism very poorly and, from his junior officers, not at all."

"I see," Harrison said. "Why do you think my brother was so preoccupied the night he died?"

"He was investigating something. By all his diligence, I'd say something important," Floyd replied.

"Or someone, perhaps?" Harrison suggested.

"That was possible, Mr. James."

"Do you agree with Captain Blaine's conclusions?"

For the first time the lieutenant, with bloodshot eyes, looked directly at Harrison. "Between us, James, I think he was in too much of a hurry. He's the major's man for everything these days, it seems," Floyd stated, wiping sudden perspiration from his brow with the back of his hand.

"Then his ruling of suicide may have been too hasty?" James said. "It could have been murder."

"Now, there you go, Mr. James." Floyd waved a drunken finger. "No one is talking murder except you." He ran his hands through his cropped, dark hair, attempting to pull himself together. "Captain Blaine is not an experienced investigator. Not like your brother, the great Captain James."

"I'm grateful for your help, sir," Harrison said. "Shall we retire?" He helped the soldier to his feet, and together they maneuvered down the stairs and left the saloon, walking clumsily through the double doors.

Paddy, standing behind the bar, silently watched them leave. Then he motioned over two men who had been standing at the far end of the long bar. "Ye see that civilian with the lieutenant, lads?" he asked.

"Sure do Mista' Derry," Charlie answered. "We knows 'im good. Somethin' not right 'bout 'im. That so, Jonesy?"

"Yup. Charlie and him don't see eye to eye on Niggers. Right, Charlie? He's gonna teach 'im a lesson."

"Charlie looked at his partner and nodded. "At the right time."

"What more would ye be knowin' 'bout him since the other night?" the bartender asked.

"His name is James from Illinois. He tol' us that," Jonesy said.

"Hell, I be knowin' that, now, private," Derry said.

"We caught 'im up out in the desert with a Mex sergeant from the Nigger battalion. Easy ride to the border out there where nobody would see ya," Charlie added. "He's up ta somethin'. Don't know what. Jus' don't smell right is all. Jonesy?"

"Yeah, that's right."

"Would it be the same Mexican who comes in regular then, lads?" Paddy asked, thinking.

"Yeah, the same. You know'd him. Name's Parilla, First Sergeant Parilla."

"Well now, that's surely int'resting how Mr. James gets 'round with the boys from the 24th so it is," the bartender said thoughtfully. His eyes narrowed.

"If ya want us to, we'll keep an eye on 'im fur ya, Mista Derry," Charlie offered.

"Ye'll not be needin' to, lads," Derry said suddenly. "Here," he added with a smile, drawing two beers. "On me own nickel. As for the squire…well, things have a way of takin' care o' themselves."

"Thank ya, Mista Derry," Jonesy said.

*

Two young women walking together, arm-in-arm, passed the two white men as they crossed the street. "Hi boys," one of them said. "Want to have some fun?" One of the women was darker skinned, while the other was a dark haired, dark eyed, white woman. Both were very slim and very young. The thick make-up and seductive dress could not hide their youth. Harrison guessed that neither was older than 17 or 18.

"Ladies," Harrison said, and nodded in passing.

"Like the whores, don't ya, James?" Floyd commented, patting the civilian on the back. "Don't blame you, don't blame you at all."

Harrison ignored him. "How does a young officer with, shall we say, excellent tastes, support himself comfortably out here on the frontier?" he asked casually as they resumed their staggering walk down Broadway toward the hotel. Their boots made soft, crunching sounds as they walked along one side of the street, James supporting Floyd. The buildings they passed were dark and silent, except for the occasional flickering of light from a window or lamps in a saloon down a side street. Broadway was now deserted. The gas lamps were spaced too far apart to provide much light. They walked mostly in shadows.

"What else do you do? To help meet expenses, I mean," Harrison asked.

Floyd laughed. "Sir, I believe you are prying." He stumbled and Harrison pulled him upright.

"I'm a businessman, lieutenant. I'm always interested in making money."

"There's money to be made out here, James. And it isn't in the army." Floyd smiled drunkenly. "But your brother wasn't interested in such things. He was an army man through and through."

"I'd like to know ways to make money out here," Harrison said. "Maybe I could take advantage."

"The embargo," Floyd mumbled. "It doubled the prices the Mexicans pay for guns and munitions. But they still need them: Mausers, Springfields, machine guns—it doesn't matter." Floyd began an exaggerated whisper. "A lot of smuggling goes on right around here, between El Paso and Columbus. Out there in the desert." He pointed to the southwest.

"Interesting," Harrison said. They had stopped in the middle of the street. "Would you know much about smuggling?"

"Everyone has their price." Floyd smiled. "Let me tell you a little secret," he said in his drunken whisper. He half swung from James' arms. "You're closer to the gold than you think. It's right up here," he said, tapping the side of his head. "But I'm not saying more. I'm drunk."

KRACK! KRACK! Two shots, and brilliant muzzle flashes lit up a darkened alley across from them. Harrison heard two bullets snap by his ear. He felt a tug on his arm as Floyd jerked, his body thrown to one side, falling in the dusty street. Harrison pulled his pistol and fired three quick rounds where his memory told him he had seen the muzzle flashes. Pieces of wood broke away from a corner building as his bullets walked upward from the recoil of the automatic.

The target was an alley immediately in front of them on the same side of the street. Harrison, crouching, rushed toward the opening, firing two more shots. When he reached the alley, he found nothing. Whoever had fired at them had disappeared back into the Mexican section of Columbus. Still crouched and alert, he scanned the area carefully. Something glistened on a wood barrel. Shell casings. He smelled them. Fresh. .45 caliber. The shots had been too close together to be anything but an automatic.

Harrison returned to the motionless form sprawled out on the street in the shadow of the sidewalk. He checked for a pulse, but Floyd was dead. His face and skull were partially exploded from the large caliber bullet.

"Police, police!" he yelled. "Over here. A man has been shot!" He bent down again to retrieve his hat. The second shot had ripped through it, piercing the corner of the brim directly above his left ear. The rounds were intended as killing shots to the head. Only an expert marksman would try for headshots in semidarkness.

A crowd gathered, seemingly out of nowhere. They all pressed around Harrison and the dead soldier. "Call the sheriff," he ordered, still kneeling beside the dead man. He scanned the faces of the civilians and soldiers. "Anyone see what happened? he called out.

No one answered.

Finally, the constable and a deputy arrived. "Stand back now," the constable said. "Who saw what happened here?" Again no one answered. The deputy pushed back the group of soldiers and townspeople. "See anything, boys?" he asked. "José, see if you can get a statement from anybody," he ordered. "Then clear the street." The constable bent over the prone figure of the lieutenant and mechanically checked the throat for a sign of life. He knew the man was dead.

"You with the lieutenant when he was shot?" he asked, looking at Harrison.

"That's right." Harrison was tense and shaky.

"Let me see your gun, please."

He handed over the weapon and the spent shell casings he had recovered.

The constable smelled them, then he handed his weapon back. "Nice pistola you have there, amigo. Colt automatic?"

"Thirty-two caliber."

"I'll keep these as evidence." The constable held the spent shell casings up to the dim light.

"From a .45." James said.

The constable dropped them in the pocket of his old dark woolen coat. "Had yourself a gunfight I'd say." They watched as two men covered the body. "José, get a call in to the MP's out at Furlong, pronto," he ordered. "Tell 'em to get their arses in here right away." Then he turned back to James. "What'd you say your name is? I already know who he was."

"Harrison James. And you, sir?" Harrison studied the police officer briefly. A shaggy mustache hung over the constable's thin lips. He had not shaved in several days, and wore his hair long and uncombed. Flecks of gray around the temples highlighted the dark mop of hair. The lawman wore his silver badge prominently on the lapel of the old jacket. An older .45 caliber Colt revolver hung from his hip in a brown, weathered leather holster.

Seems to know what he's doing, Harrison thought. An easy manner about him. But the man leaves no doubt that he's the law in Columbus.

"Constable Amos Arnold. You said James? From Chicago?"

"From Chicago," Harrison confirmed, surprised. "You know of me?"

"I knew your brother. He was a good man. I heard you were in town. Conducting your own investigation, I heard," the constable said.

"He was my brother," Harrison said.

The constable nodded. "Let's go back to my office. We can talk." It sounded like an order. The two walked several blocks back down Broadway, passing the "Last Chance." They entered a small adobe brick building, painted yellow with a red tile roof. A simple sign out front said "Police Station." A large window on each side with four vertical iron bars in front of the glass framed the thick wood door, which had a small peep hole cut in about a man's height.

Harrison followed the constable inside, then around a high counter stacked with papers in the first room. A case with four rifles and a shotgun was fixed to the wall. Arnold nodded to another deputy seated behind the counter. Then they passed through a doorway into an office right off the cellblock. "Sit down, Mr. James." He pointed to one of two chairs. "Tell me what happened." The constable folded his arms and sat on the edge of his desk.

Harrison described the ambush in detail, including the events occurring from the time Lieutenant Floyd and he left the saloon.

Arnold made notes on a yellowed piece of paper. Finally, he looked up. "Walking down a dark street. Kind of risky, ain't it?"

"Constable, I didn't expect to be shot at," Harrison said. "Are you saying you have a dangerous town here?"

"No, Mr. James, not saying that, exactly. Just have to be careful where you go that late at night." He looked again to his notes. "I figure I have what I need for now," Arnold said. "You'll be staying at the Hoover, of course."

"Yes, I am."

"Could have been an accident. Drunks shooting it up to make some noise. Happens too damn regular 'round here. Then again, it might have been deliberate. I'll look into it. And the Army will take a hand in the investigation." He stood and walked around to sit behind his desk.

The constable had a strong suspicion that this shooting was somehow linked to the death of Captain James. "That was a real shame about your brother dying the way he did," Arnold said directly, but with compassion. He wondered if this James brother was getting in over his head.

Arnold thought about the big smuggling outfit the Bureau was watching over in El Paso. He was part of that investigation. He had identified one man in particular—a Jackson Smith who maybe ran the operation. Smith was able to get his hands on good munitions from American armories. Arnold had learned about Smith thanks to the efforts of Captain James. He had told Arnold that he was going to meet with him. That was right before James died. Now he wondered whether he should tell this James about their meeting.

Arnold was preparing a report to President Wilson, but he needed witnesses and documents. More evidence, or the authorities could not act. Through persons unknown, Arnold had discovered that Smith had much influence in Washington. He'd just use that influence to get out of anything less than an airtight case. Arnold knew the game and what he had to do.

"I don't think he died that way," Harrison said.

The constable considered. "What do you think caused this shooting, Mr. James?"

"It was no accident, constable. And no drunk, either," Harrison said. "Lieutenant Floyd was murdered. They were trying for me as well." He held up his hat for the constable's inspection. "Whoever it was went for two head shots, and almost succeeded."

Arnold thought about Lieutenant Floyd's body, what he had observed. Examining the hole in James' hat, he added, "You're hat don't look so elegant now, either." The constable then gazed down at his boots, obviously thinking. "There's a lot of foolishness in town some nights," he said, finally looking up. "The boys like to let off steam by drilling some holes in the air. There's always that possibility. But like I said, you could be right."

"I am right, constable," Harrison said calmly, looking directly into the man's eyes. "You may see me lying there next time."

"Then best to be careful, Mr. James, damn careful," Arnold told him. "And stay away from alleys after dark."

CHAPTER THIRTEEN

Harrison had a fitful sleep that night. Lieutenant Floyd's murder, the attempt on his own life, and his brother's death seemed tied together. Yet in the back of his mind there was something very different about Bart's death.

Early the next morning, Harrison carefully cleaned and reloaded the Colt. When he had finished the familiar routine, he headed for the livery.

*

The weapon he now carried had belonged to his father, Randolph James. "You're going out to the frontier, Harrison. You will take your father's pistol, and use it if you have to," his mother had instructed him before he departed. Some mothers would have packed a box lunch, he thought wryly. Mine packed a .32 Colt. The weapon had a different feel than the pistol he normally carried—the .38 caliber Colt. That one had saved his life more than once in the mountain passes of Bolivia.

*

An hour later, Harrison rode to the main gate of the camp to speak again with Major Snow. He decided that the major had been holding back information from him during the last interview. He knew more about Bart's other mission than he let on. James was certain.

Harrison encountered great activity at the gate. Trucks loaded with white troops were queued up, waiting for orders to depart. Two Negro military policemen strolled slowly from truck to truck in the convoy, checking documents they held and counting heads.

"Yes, sir?" one MP asked while the other began waving trucks through the gate onto the dirt road leading to the rail station. The black Fords labored under the weight of their loads. The departing soldiers waved at James as they passed him. "To France!" one

133

young soldier yelled. They were singing a marching tune. "...and the caissons keep rolling along...." The muzzles of their Springfield rifles stuck out above the wooden sides of each vehicle.

"I would like to meet with Major Snow, Commander of Third Battalion, 24th Infantry," Harrison stated to the young military policeman. He tied his horse to a post near the guard shack.

"I'll telephone to Third Battalion Headquarters, sir. Yur name, sir?"

"Harrison James."

Harrison waited patiently while the young private cranked the telephone, hearing two longs and a short. Finally, the private spoke into the mouthpiece. "A Harrison James ta see the major, sergeant. Let 'em pass?"

"Come with me, suh," he said, turning to the civilian. "I must escort ya." He looked at the horse. "Please, leave the pony here. We'll watch 'im fur ya."

Harrison easily spotted the major out on the dusty parade field, watching several platoons of his troopers performing close order drill with rifles. Another man stood beside him. Approaching, he saw the two white officers were at parade rest with their arms folded behind their backs before the lines of marching Negro troops.

When Harrison arrived before them, Major Snow turned to face him. "Sir, please state your business quickly." The major was abrupt. "As you can see, we are very busy."

Harrison immediately recognized the captain from the previous evening. "Captain," he said pleasantly, ignoring the major.

The captain nodded. "Sir, we have heard of your near misfortune and the tragic death of Lieutenant Floyd. Shooting accidents seem to have become commonplace here, I'm afraid." The captain looked at his major, who stared impassively out over the field. "Perhaps we'd be safer in France." He laughed. Then, turning, he dismissed the MP with a quick salute.

Major Snow gave no indication of his own thoughts.

"It was no accident. Lieutenant Floyd was murdered last night. And I was almost killed myself," Harrison stated calmly, watching both men. "I'm asking you, major. Have you begun your investigation yet?"

"Mr. James, we have just been discussing it. Terrible. You must be distraught. First the death of your brother, and then Lieutenant Floyd shot while walking beside you," Major Snow answered without looking away from his troops. His brown campaign hat was set low over his eyes to offer some protection against the blowing dust and grit. "I can assure you, the incident will be investigated. I have asked Captain Blaine here to conduct an inquiry."

"I'm afraid, sir, that when we left the lieutenant he was quite intoxicated," the captain explained. "He and Mr. James, here, had evidently continued their activities in the saloon well into the early morning hours." The officer did not look at James. "When they did leave, sir, there were probably armed drunks all over town. Well, anything could have happened," Blaine said to his major. "But Mr. James, I will examine the case very carefully. We want to discover the truth as much as you." He turned to the civilian. "If we discover that the shooting was deliberate, you can be assured that the army will pursue it."

"I understand, gentlemen, that you are preparing for a war, so I won't take up much of your time." Harrison was tired, and still upset from the evening before. As an afterthought, he added, "The constable will also investigate Lieutenant Floyd's death. However, I have additional questions about my brother."

"Yes, Mr. James?" the major responded. "I believe I've answered all your questions. Nevertheless, again I will do my best to assist you."

His response lacked even the façade of sincerity, Harrison thought. "In private, if you don't mind, sir?"

"Very well, the major said, and sighed. "Captain, continue the review."

"Yes, sir." He saluted his senior officer, nodded to Harrison, and marched off across the field.

"Yes, Mr. James?" The major finally turned to stand squarely in front of the civilian.

"Thank you, major, for your time and consideration." Harrison recalled Maria's remarks about Bart's activities. "Major, I have some information which indicates that my brother may have been investigating illegal activities along the border. Is that true?"

Major Snow laughed harshly. It sounded forced, unnatural. "Forgive me, Mr. James. Gunrunning was and continues to be a serious problem here, and your brother was investigating it. It became apparent to us after the embargo was implemented that someone was stealing weapons from the Army and selling them across the border. To Villa's renegades. Through your brother's efforts, the stealing was greatly reduced."

"Why didn't you mention this when we spoke earlier?"

"Captain James' mission with regard to smuggling was highly secret," Snow said. "And I have had little involvement in it. Please keep in mind that I am only recently assigned to this unit. Much of this transpired before I assumed command. So, I cannot speak as a direct witness." He paused for Harrison's acknowledgement.

"Yes?" Harrison impatiently waited for the officer to continue. He realized his mood was too sour for this interview. But, after almost being killed himself, he was at last certain that his brother did not commit suicide. "Major, I think you're hoping that I will just go away."

"Mr. James, no one has given me approval to share army business with you, or any other member of your family," Snow answered. "I am a soldier, bound by army regulations, sir. Please try to remember that." Snow realized that this man would not go away until he was satisfied.

"I must insist that you tell me what Bart was involved in. I will not go away until you give me some answers," Harrison said, no longer able to control his temper. "I have evidence, sir, which suggests my brother was murdered."

The soldier stared at Harrison silently for seconds before responding. "Mr. James, I hear you are a very good poker player, but I must call your bluff," the major said. I know nothing about murder, and if you have new information I request that you share it immediately."

"To what purpose?"

"Good day to you, sir," Snow said, unable to mask his anger any longer.

"Forgive me, Major. I'm still recovering from events of last evening. What more can you add to my knowledge of what transpired just before Bart died?"

"Very little," Snow replied, pausing to collect his emotions. "Your brother had a liaison with a young woman, a Negress, who, as it turned out, had a great deal of information that she was willing to share with him. That information greatly assisted our efforts to reduce the weapons smuggling." The officer again paused. "She was an informant apparently more than willing to provide information to your brother, especially if it got rid of her competitors. And he compensated her very well."

"Yes," Harrison said. "I have heard that before."

"He met with her the day before he died, Mr. James. Your brother informed me that he was meeting with one of his contacts at the border, just south of here. He did not mention her by name, but I was able to discover their rendezvous. It was in the report that Captain Blaine was given by Constable Arnold during Blaine's investigation."

"I see," Harrison said, considering the new information. "Did the constable say what was discussed at this meeting?"

"He said he didn't know. Captain James told him of the meeting when he rode alone to the border. He evidently insisted that the constable not disturb them or attempt to arrest the woman."

"Did Lieutenant Floyd tell you his suspicions about the woman and my brother?" James asked.

Snow's face flushed. He made a noise to clear his throat. "I can't reveal my source. But we are a close group and his, ahh, liaison did not go unnoticed among the others."

"And, of course, the best interests of my brother and my family were paramount in your mind." Harrison was surprised at his own sudden anger.

"Mr. James, our conversation is at an end. If you wish to submit your allegations to the proper authorities, I cannot stop you. But I will not be subjected to your interrogation any longer. Good day to you."

"Yes," Harrison said, knowing he had lost control, but not caring.

"Mr. James," the major said before leaving. "Your brother had enemies. Some may have wanted him dead. But, I must remind you that circumstances all point to your brother's death as a suicide. Nothing has subsequently changed that finding. I—that is, the Army—does not believe that your brother was murdered."

"Enemies," James repeated. "What about those enemies? Could one of them as easily have killed him?"

"I can assure you, Mr. James," Snow replied, barely able to contain his own anger, "that Captain Blaine investigated that thoroughly. I think a greater understanding of the Houston troubles would help you to understand why your brother believed he had no choice but to take his own life. Good day, sir."

James watched as Major Snow walked away toward the drilling soldiers. He was left standing alone on the edge of the dusty field.

CHAPTER FOURTEEN

Harrison was still considering his conversation with the major when he heard his name being called.

"Señor James. Oiga, Señor James," Sergeant Parilla said, coming toward him. He had waited for the Battalion Commander to leave. "Please, Harry, come with me to my quarters. I have no duty now. We talk, yes?"

James raised his eyes to see the sergeant extend his hand. "Thank you, Juan. I'd like that," he said. They began walking across the parade field.

"I see that you carry your pistola today," Juan said softly, and smiled. "Be careful so the military police do not see it. They will take it. Go to the company area. I will meet you there, but I must take another way. It is better not to be seen. Comprendes? We talk in my tent. I have hot coffee. I think, amigo, you need coffee, no?"

Harrison smiled. "I could do with some, Juan."

The first sergeant departed, striding with authority across the field in another direction.

When Harrison reached L Company's area, Juan was already in the larger administration tent. They both sat down. Everything was covered with a thin layer of red dust. "Private!" the sergeant ordered. "Two coffees. Harry," he said, leaning close to the civilian "Que paso last night? The lieutenant es muerto."

"Yes," was all Harrison said, seeing two other men in the company tent. They seemed to be looking for things to do. The hurried activities so apparent at the gate among the white troops contrasted with the quiet here. A young Negro private brought over coffee in two tin cups.

"Gracias, private." Juan accepted the coffee. "Now, take Private Peck and inventory the new equipment in the quartermaster's tent." He handed the man a scrawled list.

The private nodded and departed with the other soldier.

Passing James a hot coffee, Juan said, "Now, señor, we are alone."

Harrison took the coffee, then froze. "Wait! Did you say Peck?"

"Sí. What is wrong?" Juan asked, surprised.

The two privates stopped in the doorway.

"Let me talk to this man Peck. In private," Harrison insisted. "About my brother."

"It is arranged, señor." Juan motioned to Peck. "Come," he said to the other private, and together they left the tent.

"Private Peck, please sit down," James said, offering the young man Juan's chair. "I'd like to ask you some questions about my brother, Captain James. If you don't mind?"

"Yeah, suh. I don't mind, suh," the young black man said, sitting down beside James.

"You were orderly to my brother, weren't you?" Harrison spoke calmly. He wanted to put the man at ease. "My brother mentioned you in his letters. He wrote that you were a good soldier."

"Yeah, suh, Mista James. I was orderly for Captain James. I al'ys done what the captain tol' me ta do, suh."

"Of course." Harrison sipped his coffee slowly. "Were you with my brother the night of the mutiny?"

"During the troubles, suh? Yeah, suh. All night."

"Did my brother talk with Major Snow that night? After 8:00, I mean?"

"That night ever'thin' was goin' on. But, suh, I was wit' the cap'n all night 'cept when he was called to the company, suh. By Sergeant Parilla. Yeah, suh, I seen the major come and talk wit da cap'n. It were out 'long the skirmish line. "

"Did you hear their conversation?

"No suh. They was speakin' private.

"Did the captain seem depressed or sad after you returned from Houston, private? Did he act like a man who might kill himself?" Harrison asked.

"Yeah, suh. I'd say so suh. He stay in the tent, suh, when he here. The capt'n don't speak ta nobody that I seen." Peck stared at the floor. "Jus' the men from Texas and the lieutenant maybe when they in the tent."

"How about on the night he died? Notice anything peculiar about him?"

Peck thought a moment, still not looking at James. "Yeah suh, I surely did. He stayed to hisself most a the night. He was sad, suh. He surely was. He had the blues. Jus' like they say, suh."

"Just like who said, private?"

"I hear the major say it, suh. After the cap'n die," Peck said.

"I see. Did he seem sad to you?"

"We's all sad after Houston, suh. And those officers from Washington ask ever' one questions 'bout the riot. Like we all done it."

"Do you think Captain James took his own life?"

"Yeah, suh, I do. I'm real sorry for ya an' all, but I think he done it to hisself. I'm truly sorry, suh."

"Yes, I see. Have you been in the Army long, private?"

"Five year, I reckon."

"And you're only a private?" James asked, curious. "Why is that?"

Peck hesitated at first. "I guess I don't see things ways I should."

"How's that?" James asked.

"When I first come in the Army, I go AWOL a lot, suh. Jus' ask the sergeant, suh. But the captain help me out 'cause I done good down in Mexico, suh."

"I see. Where were you the night my brother died?"

"In the quartermaster tent, suh. I was doin' my watch. Till the Sergeant of the Guard relieve me, suh."

"What were you doing there, private?"

"Al'ays, there be a guard on the guns, suh. 'Specially after what happen in Houston. Use ta be a lotta stealin' 'round here, suh," Peck said.

"Did you hear the shot?" Harrison asked.

"Yeah suh, I heard it. But I didn't pay no mind."

"Why not?" James wanted to know.

"Lots of shots fired, suh. It bein' Saturday night and all, and we's so close to town."

"Do the soldiers here in Camp Furlong do that on Saturday night, too?"

"No suh, not here. In town, suh," Peck told him.

"This shot was fired near here. Wouldn't that have caused you to investigate?"

"Yeah suh, one shot was loud. It surely was. I know'd it were close, but I have ma orders, sir." Peck fidgeted with his hands.

"And those orders are?" Harrison could see his discomfort.

"Ma orders are ta guard the guns, suh. We cain't have men raidin' the tent an' takin' their guns, like what happen in Houston. It's a important job. The cap'n say, 'Peck, never leave the tent,' so I stay put."

"You did nothing?"

"I couldn't, suh. I did look out ta see, 'cause like I say, it were close, but I couldn't leave ma post. So I jus' look 'round the area and I don't see nothing. So I go back inside." The young man was visibly disturbed.

"Yes, private?"

"When I looked 'round 'bout the area, suh. I thought, well Jeramiah, jus' some crazy Mex shootin' off out in da desert, maybe. The road south be real close and all. Yeah, suh."

"Were there Mexicans in the camp?" Harrison asked him.

"No suh, I know'd it weren't them rebels again. But maybe a Mex ridin' by the camp, bein' drunk, or a soldier comin' from Paddy's."

"Paddy Derry's saloon? Is that were you drink, private?'

"No suh, not me. Some a them white boys—I mean gennelmen—be drinkin there and comin' home."

"Did you see anyone at all in the company area around the time you heard the shot?"

"No suh," Peck answered.

"Did you see anyone later that evening here in the company area?" Harrison asked him.

"Yeah suh. I heard the major yellin', suh. So I goes out an' I sees 'im, an' I asks, 'what happened, major, suh,' and he say, 'In Captain James' tent.' I say, 'The Capt'n, suh?' An' the major say, 'private, come help me,' so I come. That's the truth, Mista James, suh."

"I see," Harrison nodded. "When you got to the tent, what did you find?"

"The capt'n was a layin' on the floor. Blood everywhere, suh."

"Where was the gun?" Harrison asked.

"I see the major wit' it. Yeah suh, I 'member," Peck replied. "The major had it in his hand. He ask me to take it an' lock it up."

"Do you remember anything else? Anything out of place? The furniture?"

"The furniture, suh? No, suh.. I seen the capt'n on the floor jus' starin' up. Blood ever' where. It were awful," Peck told him.

"Private, can you give me a better description of what you saw?"

"The capt'n was layin' on the floor wid his arm out like he be reachin' for somethin', on his back he was. Yeah suh, that's how I seen it. Blood was ever'where. An' his head…." Peck became nervous and agitated. He jumped up. "His head, suh. Oh, it were terrible. Terrible what I seen."

"Yes," Harrison answered sadly. "Anything else, Private? About the inside of the tent?"

"The inside of the tent, suh?" Peck said. "Don't know nothin', suh. Al ah could see was the capt'n and the blood."

"Thank you, private. Please ask Sergeant Parilla to come in."

"Yeah, suh." Peck turned and left the tent.

Juan returned shortly with coffee cup in hand. "Was the private helpful?" he asked.

"Nothing new, Juan," Harrison told him. Then he told Juan about his discussion with the bartender, and explained in great detail the death of Lieutenant Floyd.

Juan listened thoughtfully. When he was certain Harrison was finished, he asked, "Does La Señorita Washington know of the shooting last night?"

"I don't know," James shrugged. "Is it important?"

"I believe she has some interest in the hermano of Captain James." He smiled brightly.

"What about her brother?" Harrison asked. "He might take a shot at me, eh Juan?"

"Ah, señor, again you do not understand," Juan said, then paused, waiting for Harrison to speak again. When he didn't, he said, "What you do now, amigo?" He stared into his empty cup, but he was listening for Harrison's reply.

"Do you think I can find out anything new if I go to San Antonio? To the court martial?"

Juan shrugged. "No se. If you believe your brother's death is part of the Houston troubles." He looked around the tent. "Our troopers are punished because of Houston, amigo. Go to San Antonio, see for yourself," he said. And get out of Columbus to where it is safer for you, he thought.

"Did you know the leader of the mutineers personally? This man named Henry? I've heard things about him. Good and bad."

"Sí, señor. He was first sergeant, like me. He was with I Company. Henry was one very tough hombre with his soldiers, but they respect him."

"Was he a man who would lead rioters?" James asked.

"He did," Juan replied simply. "But that is an easy thing to say. And what does it mean? Go to San Antonio, Harry."

"He refused to follow orders in Houston, didn't he?"

"Is that important, Harry? Sergeant Henry and me, we fight in Cuba in '98. Against the Spanish bastards. I know he was a very brave man and a fine soldier. Now he is dead, too." Juan shook his head. "No comprendo."

"What drove him? Anger?" Harrison struggled to understand.

"He's angry with American laws. He speak to me mucho about African people. It make him angry, Harry, the way white people treat them. In Houston, he tell me, he say, 'Juan, I never get up for a white man on the trolley. I never do this. Negroes have rights, too.' He tell me this all the time."

"What do you think about that, Juan?"

"Harry, I am soldier in the United States Army. I do my duty. But I know this, eh? I know I am a man just like you. And Sergeant Henry also was a man."

"You're a wise man, Juan."

The sergeant smiled. "You are learning, mi amigo."

"What do you know about Lieutenant Floyd?"

Juan looked at James before he answered. "Harry," he said. Then he paused to collect his words. "I do not know what enemies would kill him. An hombre who owes money is better left alive, no?"

"He knew something, Juan. About gun smuggling. I think he was killed because of what he knew. I also think it involves this camp," Harrison told him.

"What do you know about this?" Juan asked.

"I think his information had to do with stealing and smuggling rifles to the Mexicans. This concerns money, lots of money," Harrison said. "I know that, Juan. Money is my business."

"Men will do many things, some not so good things, for money," Juan said.

"And it will buy a whole lot of honor. I've seen it."

"No, Harry, that is not true. A man makes his honor. He cannot buy it."

"I suspect that Lieutenant Floyd was not above breaking the law or forgetting his honor for money," Harrison said. "And his death was no accident, Juan. As I told you."

Harrison's comments didn't surprise Juan, but they saddened him. Harry is a good man, he thought. But Harry understands so little. He does not understand this place, or Mexicans, or Negroes, or even where his own honor lies. He wants a simple answer where there is none.

"I also think my brother was killed because of what he knew, like Lieutenant Floyd."

"You must understand more about things here in New Mexico, Harry," Juan said softly. "And you must watch what you say. And think before you say it."

The two privates returned to the tent.

Sergeant Parilla motioned for the men to get to work sweeping the tent's wooden floor. "Now, I am off duty," he announced with a smile after looking at his pocket watch, a gift from his father. "Vayámonos!"

*

James chose to walk beside the soldier back into Columbus, his horse following, reins held casually in his hand. Neither spoke again about murder. "What more do you know about Maria's business, Juan?" he asked, "that would have interested my brother?"

"Señor James, you must ask La Señorita," Juan answered firmly.

"Is Maria supporting Pancho Villa?" Harrison asked.

"Pancho Villa is a great hero to the Mexican people. Do not forget this," Juan insisted. "He fights to free the compesinos. Viva la revolución, no?" He smiled. "That is how Maria sees him. I know this, señor."

"He's not that popular these days on this side of the border, Juan," Harrison said dryly. "Many hate him because of his raid on Columbus."

"His attack on Camp Furlong was a military action, Harry. But General Villa did not plan on the American Army chasing him," Juan explained. "He want the Americans to make war, but, I think, not so quickly. He want all Mexican people to unite against the United States. In this, he make a mistake." Juan stated it without emotion. "Mexican still fights Mexican, and the people of the United States hate him more, I think."

"Yes," Harrison said. He was confused by the politics and the factions swirling about him. Who's right and who's wrong? He asked himself, trying to make sense of what Juan told him. The only reason I'm here is to find my brother's killer. *But there's only one reason I'm here—to find my brother's killer.*

"Harry, it is complicado, no?"

"That's a good word for it," Harrison replied, believing it did not affect him. "How does Maria fit in?" he asked again.

"Los compesinos fight against the rich landlords, and against the foreigners. The Mexican people demand tierra y Libertad. Everywhere we hear that, amigo. Everywhere! Your brother heard it, too. In Mexico. He tell me this." Juan saw Harrison looking at him. "It is her fight, señor." He flushed with embarrassment, realizing he had said too much. Calmase, he told himself. "I am sorry, amigo. Too much talk. But, I speak from here." Juan pounded his chest.

Harrison only nodded.

"Americans worry about their gold, Harry. Not about the Mexican people," the sergeant finished.

"The newspapers don't write about that. They write mostly about the fighting between the generals. And Zapata?" Harrison asked.

"Emiliano Zapata," Juan said. "He will take the land and give it back to the peasants."

"Like Robin Hood," Harrison smiled.

"Sí, like Robeen Hood. I heard this story. His plan for the Mexican people will give land to all the people. It is already written as the law, amigo. Zapata did that," Juan told him.

"It must have been difficult for you when you served with General Pershing against Villa."

"Not so difficult. Like I tell you, I am a soldier of the United States Army," Juan tried to explain. "And I know we never catch Pancho Villa. We chase him through northern Mexico, the land of my father, but we never catch him. Everyone, even General Pershing, knew this."

"Why did we do it then?" Harrison suddenly wanted to know.

"Ask your Presidente Wilson," Juan answered shortly.

"Do you support Villa?"

"Amigo, you are a rich white man from far way. You should not ask that question to me," Juan stated, and stopped abruptly in the middle of the road. "Escúcheme. As a Mexicano in this country, I must wear many hats and I must do many things. Some I do not want to do. But like you, Señor Harry, I am a cit-i-zen, too, eh? With opiniones."

"Yes, you're right." Harrison nodded and smiled at the shorter man. "I meant no offense."

They walked in silence, each thinking his own thoughts. The sun was now at their backs, casting long shadows in front of them. Overhead they spotted an airplane. It flew from the Army airfield north of town. "A Jenny," Harrison observed, pointing at it.

Still pondering their earlier conversation, Juan ignored the low flying plane. "The padre teaches us to forgive. But this is sometimes not possible."

"Juan, my brother is dead," Harrison stated flatly. "Today, that is all I care about. I forgive no one." He nodded once with cold determination.

The bi-plane flew off toward the north and the airstrip. The rays of the setting sun reflected off the brightly painted fuselage.

"Bueno, Harry," Juan responded after a long pause. "But remember, amigo: The truth remains the truth, but changes its color...like the desert. So, amigo, I say prepare yourself for what you find."

Harrison wondered what he meant.

The two men reached the outskirts of town, walking in silence. Then they separated.

CHAPTER FIFTEEN

There was a knock on the door several hours after dusk, waking Harrison from a sound sleep. Startled, he instantly reached for the automatic on the nightstand, rolled out of bed, then stepped lightly to the door. "Who's there?" he whispered. There was no response. Then, there was another knock. "Who's there?" he repeated. But this time, disengaging the safety, he moved up against the wall and prepared to open the door.

With his left hand James lightly grasped the knob. Then, throwing the door open, he turned into the doorway, prepared to fire. His first reaction upon seeing the giant figure, dressed in a dark suit and holding a top hat in his large hands, was that the Angel of Death had come. The man, expressionless, with kinky snow-white hair, filled the doorway. He reached slowly into the upturned hat. He pulled out a folded slip of paper and carefully handed it to Harrison.

Like the earlier message, he noticed it was written in a graceful long hand. In it, Maria introduced the older Negro as Mr. Jones and requested that Harrison go with him. He decided that he wanted to see Maria again, and that was worth the risk.

With the old man patiently waiting, he took what he thought he would need. Before holstering the automatic, Harrison released the magazine to check that it was full, then he reinserted it with a quick snap. The old man remained standing like a stone.

They left the hotel going down the back stairs, unobserved, and got into a shiny black Dodge with leather upholstery. The automobile seemed completely out-of-place here in the desert town.

They drove the three miles to the border under a brilliant star-studded sky. The road was empty after they passed Camp Furlong, except for a family in a horse drawn wagon heading north from the Mexican border. It was a high-sided grain wagon filled with blond-headed kids, stacked furniture, clothes, odds, and ends. Whatever they were able to throw together, Harrison thought. A team of two weary mules pulled the old wagon. A man and woman, both dressed in dark clothes, sat on the driver's bench. Harrison saw the old man cross himself as they passed.

"Mormans?" he asked.

The old man nodded.

Harrison had read that the Mormans had established settlements in the province of Chihuahua before the revolution. The Mexicans called them Colonia Dublan. They were now caught in the middle of the fighting. Bart had mentioned in his letters that Mormans had been useful allies during the Mexican campaign. Perhaps the Mexicans now thought of them as too useful.

When they reached the border crossing, a lone figure waved them through to the Mexican side. No papers or identification were requested, and no examination was made of their motor car. Just a simple wave of the hand by a younger, light skinned man dressed in civilian clothes. He had a Springfield rifle slung across his back. That was easy enough, Harrison thought. Mr. Jones waved back to the border guard as if he knew him.

Harrison saw two Mexican soldiers armed with older rifles standing in the middle of the dirt road as they crossed into Mexico. In front of them was a long pine pole positioned horizontally across the road.

One of the men motioned for the motorcar to stop, while the other walked over to the driver's side of the vehicle. Folding his arms, Harrison waited, looking to the old man for a sign.

The old man handed the soldier an envelope from his coat pocket and flashed a broad smile.

Of course, Harrison thought, as he watched the transaction.

"Gracias, señor," the soldier responded. "José, arriba!" he yelled to his companion. The other soldier immediately raised the pine pole and the shiny black Dodge passed through the gate.

Rounding a bend in the road a short time later, they saw a sprinkling of lights indicating a village in the distance. But the

Dodge did not enter Las Palomas. Before reaching the outskirts of the pueblo, the old man turned west onto a trail that wound upward into the hills.

The motorcar groaned as it labored up the steeper incline. The old man changed gears. Harrison could tell by the easy manner in which he shifted the transmission that Mr. Jones was a very experienced driver. The engine responded with an unbroken whine as it crept slowly up the hill. When they finally reached the top—a mesa concealed within a circling stand of scrub pine—Harrison guessed they were closing on their destination. The car rolled on a hard dirt track through the sparse pinion forest. A high adobe wall suddenly rose in front of them. The trees and a bluff had hidden it from his view.

The black Dodge, now streaked with brown dust, stopped at a closed, raw wood gate. Its headlights illuminated two solid doors held with immense iron hinges. Sitting forward in his seat, Harrison waited. His right hand rested in his lap, not far from the holstered pistol.

The driver sat patiently with the motor running and did not use the car's horn. Finally, the doors groaned as they slowly opened. Two figures carefully swung them away from the road to allow passage. No words were spoken. The two merely nodded at the driver to acknowledge him. They were very young, perhaps 13 or 14 years of age, and had no weapons, and no hats. They were barefooted. The boys looked at Harrison with simple but intense curiosity.

"This is a fortress," he said, admiring the thick adobe walls towering above the car.

The Dodge entered the compound to find a flurry of activity. Five large wagons were lined up in front of a two-story adobe building set against the eastern wall. Each wagon was stacked high with long wooden crates. He saw four men—all short with dark skin, dark eyes, and wearing sombreros—covering one loaded wagon with a large canvas tarp. Other men led a team of four mules out of the stables against the western wall to the front of the lead wagon. The men were either Mexican or Indian. Perhaps both, Harrison decided.

Mr. Jones stopped the car in front of the house, also a two-story wood and adobe structure with a red tiled roof. The windows were ablaze, with light streaming out into the night, even though the hour had grown late.

The old man parked the car, got out, and walked around to Harrison's side. He opened the door for the white man to step out. James emerged from the Dodge, thanking him. At that moment, he heard his name called.

"Señor James," a female voice called out. "You have come. Wonderful!"

Harrison turned to see Maria running lightly down the steps, illuminated by the brilliant light behind her. She was wearing a long, Mexican dress with a wide skirt of many bright colors and complicated designs. It was cut low in front, revealing the deep cleft between her breasts. Her shining, midnight hair was pulled back and held with a simple yet beautiful turquoise comb. Her dark eyes glowed. "Señorita?" he asked. "Is that you?"

Maria stopped in front of him, so close her dark eyes seemed to swallow him. Her breath smelled of honey and mint. Then, pressing her breasts against his chest, she kissed him impulsively on the cheek. Harrison noticed her perfume, dusky and promising.

The kiss surprised him.

"You brought your Colt, eh?" she whispered in his ear, smiling. Such a deep shade of blue, she mused, looking directly into his eyes. Like the feeling of steel on a winter day, they both chilled and gave her strength. She touched his face with her hands. "Come into my home, señor ," she said with a smile.

"Maria," he forced himself to say. "Your message...."

"Shhh...," she mocked him, "...Señor James."

"Come. We eat, drink, and then we talk." Maria took his hand and led him into the house. "I want to call you Harry. It is what your brother called you, yes?"

"Yes, my brother called me Harry. How did you know?"

"He spoke of his big brother often. I think he idolized you." Holding his hand, she led him into a foyer with a high vaulted ceiling, then she shut the heavy wood door behind them. The door itself was two inches thick, with iron hinges that growled as it was closed.

Entering the grand room, he was immediately struck by the rich colors. Painted in bright colors, the blend of reds, yellows and blues adorning the walls seemed to leap out at him. The adobe walls were framed with heavy beams of native timber. He saw brown ceramic tile floors with richly painted ceramic mosaics in the center of the room. Harrison stopped to admire it. He saw that it depicted a local scene—Indian women carrying baskets filled with fruit and vegetables on their heads. Only two paintings adorned the walls of this room. One was of an older man dressed in black, wearing a sombrero and mounted on a great white stallion. The other was of a family—the parents seated and surrounded by four small children. At first glance, Harrison couldn't tell boys from girls.

Watching him with a smile, Maria finally spoke: "That was my grandfather. A great man."

"Impressive," he said politely. "The family?"

"The smallest child was my mother. The woman was Dona Estrella, my grandmother."

Harrison nodded and continued walking through the large room. He felt a flow of cool air gently touching his face. He looked up and saw a fan with large wooden paddles slowing churning above them. Electricity out here? He was impressed.

Crossing the room, they passed through a wide archway to enter another room equally spacious, but well furnished. Tapestries depicting hunting scenes hung from the wall and blended naturally with the rich wood furnishings. Everything appeared thrown together, but Harrison felt a warmth and harmony here. A glass chandelier hung from a great beam in the center of the ceiling. In its light the variety of colors were reflected like so many rainbows. The room had the air of grandeur from an earlier age, brought to life through electric light.

Maria offered him a place on a dark satin couch done in an early French fashion. She sat beside him. "Your house is very beautiful," he stated simply. "There seems to be no order, yet everything is harmonious here."

"Thank you. But this is only the appearance of wealth, Harry," she replied, with a wave of her arm. "I inherited this house, these things, from my Mexican grandmother. La Señora Estrella was the wife of a very wealthy landowner and rancher. He loved her very much and built her this hacienda. Dona Estrella's only son—my uncle—was killed as a young man, fighting for Mexico's freedom. So, she bequeathed it to me." Maria paused to remember. She looked around the room and then back at Harrison. "But the land, the real wealth of our family, was taken long ago by the Dictator, Porfirio Diaz. Do you know of Diaz?" She didn't wait for him to answer. "My grandfather opposed that horrible man, and eventually paid for it. Diaz was a great killer of my people. What he wanted he took. He took our land, and then he took my grandfather's life." She shrugged.

"You still have this beautiful house," he said.

She did not answer directly. "Harry, things here are not so simple to explain. The land that he took was everything to us."

"Not so simple to explain," he repeated. "So everyone keeps telling me, Maria," he said. "But I'm not here to judge you and, for me, understanding who's right has been difficult. It's my brother's death that brought me here."

"Sí, I know this," she answered, caught by his striking blue eyes. They seem so sad, she thought. Do they hold the sins of the world, I wonder?

And Harrison was distracted and awed by her beauty.

"Someday the war will be over and we will have won. We will have defeated them."

"Defeated them? Who, Maria?"

"The revolution is against the rich landowners and the politicians and the Americans who make use of Mexico to enslave my people. It is to fight them that I must supply guns, but maybe tomorrow it will be corn and frijoles." Her dark eyes blazed with conviction.

Harrison suddenly wanted to believe in her passion and to share her conviction. For a moment, he felt a vast distance between them. "Those wagons outside? Are they loaded with smuggled rifles?"

We bought them legally from the Revel Brothers in Columbus. They are a respected American company. They buy guns the American Army does not want," she explained. "Since the Americans went to war in Europe, that is all we can get, and this shipment is the last even of those."

"Who smuggles them across the border?" Harrison asked.

"That is a stupid embargo. Two years ago, the border was open and guns did not matter to the Americans," Maria said. "Everyone on the border sold them to make money."

"I don't want to know how they come across," he said suddenly. "I shouldn't have asked."

"Harry, please...." Then Maria suddenly dismissed the subject by touching her thick, dark hair lightly with her fingers.

"I'm sorry if I insulted you," Harrison said, noticing her delicate fingers. He was distracted by them, by her presence. "You are a lady. Of that I'm certain," he told her, surprised to find he was sincere.

"And you are a gentleman with very good taste!" she said smiling. "Come, I want to show you a very special place." She took James by the arm and pulled him up. She held his arm while they slowly strolled through the large house. "Bart and I met at a fiesta in Juárez, hosted by the Alcalde and his wife. I noticed him immediately. He stood so proud and dignified in his uniform. And his Spanish was so, so like a Spanish gentleman's," she reflected fondly. "All the señoritas noticed him."

Finally, they stood in the doorway of a large study. Harrison could see from her expression that she was very proud of it. They were surrounded by dark mahogany bookshelves, each filled from floor to ceiling with bound volumes. He saw a different mosaic in the middle of the tile floor. This one had classical Greek figures—older men with boys. James thought the scenes illustrated learning. On the walls hung only one painting—of the same man, but sitting in a great chair. That chair, he decided, looking at the chair behind a large desk.

Maria waited patiently for his response.

The electric lighting from a single large ceiling lamp illuminated the desk set in the middle of the room, with the black leather chair from the painting neatly pushed in behind it. The only other lighting was from a double framed window directly across the room between bookshelves. Heavy cotton drapes dyed brown and green concealed the outside, making the room very private—perfect intimacy for a reader and his books. The desktop was bare of anything, even an ink well.

"I'm impressed," James told her.

"You like it?" she asked proudly. "My grandfather built this room. But, it was La Señora Estrella who collected the books," Maria told him. "Do you believe that she read them all?"

"She must have been a well-educated woman," he responded. But it was a map of Mexico that caught his eye. He noticed a line drawn from the New Mexico border almost to Mexico City with arrows in the Pacific Ocean pointing eastward, all marked in ink with dates and numbers. "And you, Maria? Do you read those books also?"

"Oh, Harry. When I was a child I came here often. Sometimes to read, other times just to sit in my grandfather's chair and think.

Now, it is different. I come only to visit the past, and to dream of a better future." She smiled at him, but her dark eyes betrayed her.

"Those moments are important," Harrison said, putting his arm around her. It felt natural.

"Come!" she said, pushing him away playfully. "You must have a thirst. Tequila? It is our custom," she said with a smile. She turned and left the room. Harrison followed her. They returned to the drawing room and the sofa.

A young woman entered with a tray of tequila. She appeared to be of Indian descent—short and squarely built, with dark eyes, dark skin, and black hair that she wore long. Her face held no expression. Maria took the decanter and two glasses, handing one to Harrison. "Harry, this is Luna. She is mama of the children you saw outside." The young woman smiled shyly. "Her husband was killed last year. He rode with General Villa."

"I'm pleased to meet you, señora," he said, standing and bowing.

The young woman smiled again and left the room.

"There are many widows in Mexico." Maria and Harrison watched the woman leave. "I do all that I can to help them," she added gently. "That is also part of our business."

"You have great responsibilities, Maria," he replied.

"To your brother," Maria toasted, holding the glass in the air. "A fine man."

Harrison responded by touching his glass gently against hers. He recalled Lieutenant Floyd making a similar toast. But Maria was sincere.

"And to the Revolution!" Maria exclaimed, continuing her toast. "Tierra Y Libertad!"

"Viva la revolución!" he responded.

She smiled. "Now we eat. Then I tell you more about your brother. And you will tell me of your life in Paris, yes?"

Harrison smiled back. "Yes, Maria, we eat. Then we talk."

"Come," Maria said simply. Holding his hand lightly, she led him into another room adjoining the second. It was a spacious dining room. Again, it was decorated much like the other two, but this room had a huge stone fireplace that covered an entire wall. A fire burned brightly in its hearth. He felt its warmth.

Harrison noticed two place settings on the long, deep grained oak table. Maria set the bottle of tequila between them. She motioned with her hand. "Please sit beside me."

He pulled out her chair.

"Ahh señor, you are a gallant caballero," Maria said. She brushed against Harrison's shoulder with her breast as she sat down. The gesture did not go unnoticed.

"Luna," Maria called, pouring each another tequila. The young woman returned carrying a tray. She served them while they quietly sipped their tequila, placing a bowl of soup and tortillas with chicken in front of them. Then Luna left them alone.

Harrison could not take his eyes from her. "How does one so beautiful survive in such a harsh world?" he finally asked.

"Do you like the food?" she teased, avoiding his question.

"Oh, yes," he said, rolling a tortilla and dipping it lightly into the soup. Harrison had seen that done at the hotel. "But I don't have much of an appetite. You've taken it away."

"Nor do I," Maria said, and smiled at him. "Are you so charming among the women of Paris?"

"What do you know of my life in Paris?" he asked, surprised that she knew anything about him.

"Harry, I know much about you, the worldly older brother," she said, touching his arm.

"I think Bart may have exaggerated," Harrison said. He did not want her to know too much about his wasted life.

"Perhaps you're too modest," she suggested.

"I don't think there's that much to talk about. I just run a business. Like you, Maria."

"Oh, Harry, Bart told such wonderful stories of your adventures. He told me about your battles with banditos in Bolivia. You are lucky to be alive."

Neither ate any more. Sipping at the tequila, Harrison quietly observed Maria. Her beauty continued to fascinate him. She, in turn, was content to glance at him, enjoying his attention. The time passed quickly.

Finally, Luna appeared. "Señorita?" she asked.

"We are finished, Luna. Gracias," she said softly.

Luna cleared the table. Harrison did not notice.

"Maria, why have you brought me here?" Harrison asked finally.

She looked at him smiling but, Harrison noticed, hesitating.

"Yes?" He asked.

"First we must make a deal and shake on it," Maria told him.

"We can do that," he said, curious.

"I will tell you something. In return you will tell me something. Agreed?"

She extended her hand with a smile and a sparkle in her eyes.

"It's a deal," Harrison responded, and gently grasped her hand.

"Harry, your brother was much more than an infantry officer. There were men, very dangerous men, he was working with. Mexicans and Americans. He paid them for information."

"On smuggling weapons?"

"Sí that, but also for information on what the Germans are doing in Mexico."

"German agents in Mexico?" Harrison felt almost a panic.

"Yes, the Germans were supporting General Villa then," Maria told him. "Your Army wanted—needed—to know what they were doing in Mexico. It was confusing. The Germans first helped General Villa. And when the Americans invaded to catch him, they worked with General Carranza—El Presidente."

"German spies," Harrison said softly, remembering what Butcher had said in Monte Carlo. "Do you think one of them killed Bart?"

"That is possible. I know this because I helped him. I introduced him to different people, people he wanted to know."

Harrison quietly considered her words. "Their names?" he asked finally.

"There were many people. I helped him contact a person in the home of the German Consul in Monterrey. A woman."

"A Mexican woman?" Harrison asked.

"Yes," she answered. "I told you. Things here are very complicated."

"Could I meet this woman?"

"No, you cannot," Maria said abruptly.

"Is it too dangerous?" he asked, watching for her reaction.

"She is dead. The Germans killed her."

"They killed her? Because of Bart?"

"Yes," Maria answered. "The Germans discovered what she was doing and they killed her. She gave Bart information, and they found out. Colonel Moltke, their military attaché, had her shot."

"Was it very valuable information that she gave my brother?"

"I don't know, Harry, but that would not matter. The colonel is a butcher."

Harrison sat, thinking. For a moment neither spoke.

"This woman…she was very brave to have done this," Harrison finally said.

"She believed in Bart. That was the reason she helped him."

"How did the Germans find out about her?"

"Oh, Harry, they were angry that the Americans stole this information. The colonel and General Carranza, they searched everywhere. Bart was in El Paso, out of their reach, but he could not save her."

"You didn't answer my question, Maria. How did they find out?"

"They received information that she was their spy. I don't know how."

"Was my brother operating some kind of spy ring in Mexico?" Harrison asked.

"No, Harry," Maria said slowly. "I think Bart was a spy catcher. Yes, he tried to catch German spies."

"Do you think the woman's spying for Bart might have something to do with his death? Revenge maybe?" Harrison asked.

"I think it is possible. Colonel Moltke is like ice. I know him. And the Germans punish everyone who will not help them," Maria told him.

"Help them to do what?"

"Colonel Moltke is working in Mexico to help Germany win the war in Europe."

"How do you know this colonel, Maria?" James asked.

She looked at him and felt his eyes on her. "I know him. We do business together. I also sell guns to the Mexican Army, as I told you."

"I see," Harrison said slowly.

She thought she could see accusations reflected in his blue eyes. "We sell arms. I do not concern myself with European politics. I have my own struggle here," she told him.

"Who were the Americans supporting when Pershing invaded?" Harrison asked, trying to understand.

"The Americans invaded to chase General Villa," Maria answered him. "At that time, General Carranza worked with your Army. But the Americans stayed too long in Mexico. General Carranza was afraid they would never leave. So, he asked the Germans to help him get the gringos out of the country. They talked of an alliance, I think." She took a breath. "This information was of great interest to your brother."

"What happened then?" Harrison asked.

"What then? Harry, the Americans chased Pancho Villa through northern Mexico for many months. They finally gave up and went home. Everyone knows that."

"My brother knew you were selling weapons to Villa?"

"I told him. That was not important to him."

"Then what was important, Maria?" Harrison sipped at the tequila slowly and looked at the young woman.

"As I told you—the Germans," Maria said, patiently. "He was concerned that a German alliance with the Mexican armies would threaten the United States. Maybe the American Army came to Mexico to keep the Germans from gaining too much influence? It is possible."

He looked at her skeptically. "What else can you tell me, Maria?"

"Harry, the generals always knew too much about where the American Army would go. Your brother began by investigating this."

"Their spies?" James wanted to know.

"Everyone has spies," Maria said. But with General Villa, the people are his eyes. The American Army invaded Mexico just like many years before. We did not support this. So many people, I think, helped General Villa. The Mexican people have long memories. Yesterday, today—it is all the same."

"From what I read, we entered Mexico only to catch Pancho Villa, and with permission from the Mexican Government. Maria, he invaded our country. His soldiers are considered bandits and murderers."

Maria bristled. "General Villa has the support of the people."

"It sounds like you know him well."

"Not well. We talk sometimes. He needed good weapons and I sold them to him. He wanted machine guns, so I found them.

Brownings from the U.S. Army, water-cooled. I helped him because he is like us. But now, I think it is too late for him."

"You still want Villa to win, don't you?" Harrison asked, wondering.

"Sí, claro. The American Army does not understand that General Villa is fighting for our rights," Maria stated matter-of-factly. "Like your own George Washington." She softly touched his hand.

Harrison scratched his head and suddenly grinned at her. "Politics can be very tiring." At that moment, he was very aware of her hand on his.

Their shoulders touched.

"It appears we won't have a war with Mexico, at least."

She shook her head. "Don't be so sure, Harry."

"What do you mean?" He asked.

"Today, the generals are only concerned with fighting each other." Maria took the decanter and poured each another glass, but kept talking. "But General Carranza, quien sabe? He has great ambitions, that one. And the Germans are still here, working for that war."

They both sipped from their glasses, considering.

"Forgive me, I become very emotional when I speak of the struggles of my people. I want so much for the country of my mother. It is very rich, too. But the people are very poor."

Again, Harrison envied her passion. But politics here seems so confusing, he thought. Loyalties pulled in one direction, then another—good and bad changing daily.

"One day things will be different," Maria said.

He could not help staring. She's so beautiful.

When Maria caught him staring at her, she suddenly looked down and blushed.

"The northern papers are not sympathetic to Pancho Villa since his attack on Columbus." Harrison forced himself to focus on the discussion, but he remained too aware of her. "Remember, Maria," he said, "General Villa was killing Americans and taking their property."

"And El Presidente Wilson—does he care about the suffering of the Mexican people?" she answered. "Like my amigos now imprisoned in San Antonio? They only fought against unjust laws, as Pancho Villa is doing."

Harrison tried to get the evening back on track. "Maria, I don't want to argue with you. I want answers to my brother's death. That's the reason I'm here." But now the words were empty, and he knew it.

Her dark eyes held his blue eyes.

"Maria, I'm not here to talk politics with you."

Maria was silent. Then she spoke, sadly. "I am sorry for my anger." She paused to think. "There is something else that I must tell you. I gave your brother information on where General Villa hid his weapons and ammunition. Bart passed the information to General Pershing. and the American Army traded the information to Murguia, Carranza's general. Murguia's men found the arms and made ready, so when Villa attacked La Ciudad Chihuahua in April, hundreds of his men were killed. It was a terrible defeat, Harry. I saw it.... Villa's soldiers ran out of ammunition. They were captured. Hundreds of his men were hanged on La Avenida Colon, left to rot in the sun."

"Why did you give him this information?"

"He wanted to know how the General armed his soldiers. I told him. Giving him information was part of our arrangement," Maria said. "But I did not think he would use it that way."

"My brother betrayed you?"

"He did not think it was so important."

"His action placed you in a dangerous position." James thought aloud.

"Sí," she whispered. "General Villa believes that I betrayed him, but I did not." There was a hint of fear in Maria's voice.

Harrison said nothing. He touched her shoulder lightly, and felt her warmth. He felt even more drawn to her.

"Harry, we live in a very dangerous world…all of us. In Mexico today, everyone must be watched, even our friends. Tomorrow, they may be our enemies."

"Maria, how can I help you? If there is a way, I will do it."

"Amigo, you are a man of honor." She took his arm, then she placed his hand between hers. "Somehow, I must prove to General Villa I did not willingly betray him, but you cannot help with that. Never mind," Maria said softly.

He reached out to touch her hair. "How does one so lovely survive in such a dangerous world?"

He sounds much like his brother, she thought, yet very different. She continued to hold his hand tightly. "I was raised in this world. It is all that I know. But I am surrounded by good men. Men who protect me."

"Yes," James said. "It's important to have them around."

"Make no mistake," she said, the tone of her voice firm, "I am the equal of any man."

"I believe that, Maria." He lifted her hand and gently kissed it. "But you will always be a lady."

This hombre has all the right words, she thought, and brightened. "Now, Mr. James, your information," she said with a smile. "You have heard enough about my problems."

"Last year," James replied, "my company employed a man who is now doing business with the Mexican Government. I don't know much about him except that he is selling munitions across the border. I will give you his name. That, I'm afraid, is all I have for you, but maybe you can use it to your advantage."

Maria studied him momentarily. "What is his name, Harry?"

"He's going by the name of Jackson Smith. I have his address," he said. "And when you find him, you will also find a warehouse full of munitions—if he hasn't already smuggled them across the border."

Maria repeated the name slowly. She seemed to recognize it. "The Mexican Government does not yet have money to make large purchases. I have been told this by amigos close to General Carranza. But they are raising it, Harry. I will look into this. Thank you. The information could be very helpful to us."

"I know Smith, but nothing else about his company," James said.

"A warehouse full of munitions, Harry," she said, raising her eyebrows. "It would do much damage to General Villa, if they can get it across the border. And it would make this man very rich," Maria added.

"That sounds like Smith," James said. He could tell the brain behind those beautiful dark eyes was working. "What would all those explosives and guns do to Villa's army?"

"Villa is in trouble. His men are tired and have few weapons left, and he has no money. I think the new supplies are all that it would take to finally defeat him," Maria answered slowly.

"Those supplies would buy Señor Smith and his company a lot of influence in Mexico, Harry," she said, still rolling the information over in her mind. "Mineral and oil rights; even land." She looked at him with a contemplative smile. "Thank you. Yes, I will see that your information is put to good use."

"Please Maria, with this information, I trust you will not make things here worse," James said, concerned that he could be adding to the suffering of the Mexican people. He was well aware that he could be repeating the mistakes of his brother.

Maria immediately noticed the concern on his face. Don't worry, amigo," she said to reassure him. "Come." She took him by the hand.

CHAPTER SIXTEEN

They arrived in the courtyard in time to watch the last team of mules hitched. A group of twelve riders prepared to leave. The leader, dressed like the others in homespun cotton with high leather boots, and wearing a sombrero, waved to Maria, then mounted his horse, a U.S. Army .45 strapped to his side. He was also dark skinned, with cropped black hair. Bandoliers of ammunition crisscrossed the other riders' chests, and Springfield rifles were slung across their backs.

Harrison noted the old Negro standing near the wagons. He appeared to be reviewing the details. "Who is that man?" he asked Maria, pointing.

"Mr. Jones?" Maria responded. "He was the dear friend of my father. Mr. Jones raised me. As you have already seen, he cannot speak. Drunken Anglos cut out his tongue many years ago."

"What happened to him?" Harrison asked.

"Mr. Jones was born a slave. As a boy, he was caught trying to run away. They were drunk. He was only a slave runaway." Maria tried to keep the bitterness out of her voice.

Harrison said nothing.

"This is what we do," she said, changing the subject by pointing to the departing train.

Harrison watched as the train of wagons and riders prepared to depart the ranch. "Where are you shipping the guns? Do you expect to be ambushed along the way?" he asked.

"Your brother always encouraged us to support General Carranza and the Mexican government against the Villaistas. Bart said that he is the government of Mexico," Maria said as she watched the wagon train move out the gate. "This shipment goes to General Carranza's men. We will meet them south of here at a place called Las Varas. It will be a dangerous journey for them."

"But you still support General Villa, Maria," Harrison said. "You believe that somehow he'll win."

"Yes, Harry," she said simply.

"It looks like business is good,, even with the embargo."

"Since the Americans began enforcing their embargo, it has been difficult to buy weapons of good quality. This shipment came through the Arizona desert. The border is dangerous everywhere. Harry, I'm worried." She crossed her arms and turned away from him. Tears welled up.

"But I think you've done the right thing to do business with General Carranza. You are protecting yourself and your people. You'll be okay." James spontaneously reached out to her and drew her close.

Maria did not resist, turning to bury her face in his chest. "No, Harry, if Villa is beaten, things will return to the old ways. They will arrest me, take my home and the people here.... I don't know. It is too horrible to speak of. I did not make this war," Maria said suddenly, her voice barely a whisper.

"We don't make them, and we have no control over them once they begin," Harrison said, trying to comfort her. "The strong survive, Maria, and you are strong." Nothing will happen to her, he thought, with a sudden, hard resolve.

She wiped away her tears and took him by the arm again to lead him into the stables. "Come, I have a beautiful thing to show you," she said, now holding his hand tightly. Inside, Maria pointed out a black stallion. "This is my horse," she said proudly, running her hand affectionately over the broad back.

Harrison patted the flank of the stallion. "A marvelous animal," he said. But he was more aware of the young beauty standing beside him.

Through the open stable doorway, he looked out upon the now deserted courtyard.

They walked hand in hand back toward the house. Harrison saw no sign of Maria's brother or his friend. "Where is your brother?" he asked carefully.

"He is in El Paso. He spends much time there."

"Who was the man with you and your brother that night?"

"You mean Carlos," she said, sitting again on the couch.

"Carlos," Harrison repeated. He thought again about that first encounter, and those dark, empty eyes burning into him from across the fire.

"He's a hired gun," she said, her lips near his ear. "Daniel must have a bodyguard if he goes to those places in El Paso. I insisted, Harry. It is so dangerous along the border. And now there is the reward." She sighed, her breasts rising. "So he hired Carlos."

"Because he's good with a gun?" he asked.

"Yes. Carlos comes highly recommended."

"By who, Maria? Who would recommend this man to you?" Harrison asked.

"A man I know in Columbus," Maria said.

"Was Carlos from Columbus?" Harrison asked.

"I don't know. He is Yaqui Indian. He came to us from Columbus." She smiled up at him, removed the barrette, and threw her head back to shake her hair loose in an unselfconscious, natural gesture. "Are you concerned about him?"

"I've seen that type before, Maria. Very quick on the trigger. Very cold in the head."

She smiled. "Harry, I think perhaps you see too much. Like a mirage in the desert."

Entering through the wide wooden door, Maria pulled him along through the wide arches to the room where he had seen the great glass chandelier.

"Sit, Harry." She sat on the old French settee, still holding his hand so he would sit beside her. "Another drink?" she asked. She moved closer until their bodies touched. The movement did not go unnoticed by James.

"Yes, please," he answered, and poured it himself. He felt her breath against his face.

She moved closer. "Tell me about yourself." She leaned forward deliberately to ensure he noticed her breasts.

Harrison and Maria spent the next hour on the settee, laughing and talking. He told her amusing stories from his many travels. He told her of the Champs Elysees with its wild mix of people; the smells of Rome in the spring; London's winter fog; and Christmas in Santiago's summer, delighting her with embellished anecdotes. Always he was aware of her.

Maria listened with fascination, laughing whole-heartedly at his stories. She imagined out loud strolling down the boulevards of Paris, or making love on a great ocean liner with a gallant man. "I will live in Paris someday. I have always dreamed of it," she announced. "I will be a lady, like my grandmother, educated, with a gentleman to escort me. Yes, and I will be respected, not looked down upon simply because of the color of my skin."

"Yes, I believe that," Harrison said.

"You've had a very exciting life," she said finally, touching his hand gently with a finger.

"Yes, Maria," he smiled sadly. "But you will not be a useless wanderer."

She sensed his inner pain. He was different from his brother. He was wounded in spirit. She bent and kissed his hand.

They embraced. Their lips met in a long and passionate kiss. Harrison held her trembling body tightly.

"Harry," Maria gasped, pushing him away. "Come!" She stood and took him by the hand.

She led him upstairs. "You will stay here tonight." It sounded more like a question than an order.

They entered her bedroom, a place he had not seen before.

"Yes." Harrison's throat felt constricted.

In the semi-darkness, Maria helped him with his coat. "I will take this." She kissed his neck as she took off his holster, then unbuttoned his shirt and trousers. In a moment, he stood naked and erect before her. He kissed her mouth, then the tops of her breasts. He was intoxicated by the scent of her. Slipping her dress down slowly, he gently touched her nipples. She stood swaying as he pulled the dress down over her thighs. It dropped to the wood floor soundlessly.

Harrison wondered at the soft, smooth curves of her brown body, her breasts firm, nipples erect. He reached out to touch, to feel her warmth and her passion. He moved his hands slowly over her soft skin, exploring the smooth contours that flowed into each other. Maria moaned as his fingers massaged her back. He kissed her ear, her neck, and then his lips touched the nipple of her left breast.

"I want you," he whispered hoarsely.

She kissed him on the forehead, caressing his chest. They embraced again. She felt the hard muscles of his back as her hands moved lower across his naked body. She felt the strength of his rigid organ pressing against her abdomen. She reached down with both hands to caress him. He touched her nipple again with the tip of his tongue.

"Come," she whispered in his ear, squeezing him gently.

Before she could move, Harrison swept her up in his arms as though she were lighter than air, kissed her, then laid her gently in the bed.

She refused to let go, pressing his head down hard against her breasts. Maria touched his earlobe softly with her tongue and, gently, she blew in his ear. "Come to me, gringo mio," she whispered.

They made love in the silent darkness.

Much later, Maria quietly left the bed. She searched for something in the moonlight. His jacket. She put it on and left the room, only to return a few minutes later. Watching, James saw her body framed in the large, unshuttered window, illuminated by the moonlight.

She knew he was watching her, was excited again by his obvious desire. Maria slowly removed the jacket and lingered for a moment in the light. She felt truly free to be herself. And exhilarated to be making love with this man.

Maria returned to bed. "Hold me, Harry," she whispered as she touched his hair.

In the darkness, he ran his palms over her hips and down her thighs. Wrapping his arms around her, Harrison held her close against him. "You are so beautiful," he whispered softly.

In response, she rolled on top to straddle him. "Oh, you are a man," she whispered."

They made love again, finding their own rhythm.

*

A ray of early morning sun streamed through the window. They lay together under a soft linen sheet drinking coffee served by the Indian maid. Maria played with Harrison's chest, her head against his neck. He smelled her hair.

She felt him stiffen slightly.

"Maria, if I could stay longer," Harrison said, and touched her breast with his hand. "You are a miracle for me. You're so real."

"What do you mean?" she asked, still stroking his chest.

He smiled sadly. "You seem so alive. I don't want to leave you."

"You are my good man," she answered.

"Did he love you, Maria?"

"He told me he did." She knew he meant Bart. "We made love, but we were not lovers. Not like you and I."

And Harrison believed her.

"Then he thought he had to protect me," Maria told him. "I helped Bart and, because of that, he protected me. But your brother was always a soldier on duty," she said. "Always, Harry. He could not give everything in love."

"Bart's life must have been complicated."

"He had many duties," Maria answered.

"Many duties," Harrison mused, stroking her soft, copper-colored skin.

"I was one duty for him," she said. "A kind of love and a duty."

"I am not my brother, Maria."

"Claro que si´. You are very different from Bart." Maria placed her thigh across his legs, kissing him on the shoulder. Her eyes sparkled. She ran her hand down his chest and across his thighs. "A man who knows American laws. This, your brother told me."

"What do you mean?" Harrison asked.

His fingers rubbed her breast gently.

Maria felt him growing hard against her. She coiled her body around his legs, squeezing him tightly. "Talk will come later. This is for now."

She's using me, Harrison thought, but in the moment he didn't really care. They made love again.

*

Finally, later that morning, they lay together in her bed, both exhausted from a night of love-making. Harrison knew he had to go, still he did not move. Maria rested her head on his arm. It seemed so natural for both of them.

"I feel safe with you, Harry," she said. "Now, I do not even worry that General Villa will come and kill me."

"Didn't Bart make you feel safe?"

"At first, yes. But everything changed, especially at the end. I asked him to protect me, but...."

"But?"

"Harry, the day before Bart was killed we met on the border. I asked him if he could protect me from your federales if I crossed the border to live," she explained. "I told him that General Villa was after me, that he would kill me. I begged him for protection in the U.S."

"What did he tell you?" Harrison remembered that Floyd had talked about a letter delivered to Bart, and Snow mentioned a meeting a day before Bart died.

"He said he could not protect me because I was a bandit wanted by both the Army and the federal police. Harry, he said we could not meet ever again. That was it."

"You think that my brother betrayed your trust?"

"We had an agreement. He broke it," she said. "That's what I believe, Harry."

Harrison sighed, saddened by her story. "I'm afraid, Maria, that my brother was a soldier in the United States Army before all else," he said. "And I know that's no excuse." Still, what Bart had told her surprised him.

"We each must do what we must," she said, still trying to understand.

"What must I do, my love, to demonstrate that I'm an honorable man who will not betray you?" He asked.

"There is one thing. I want you to rescue a man from the gallows for me. Harry, I know you can do it. You are a lawyer and a man." Maria raised up and turned to look Harrison in the eyes.

Harrison understood she was serious. "And how, my lovely bandita, will I accomplish this thing?"

CHAPTER SEVENTEEN

Mr. Jones drove him back to Columbus in the black Dodge motorcar. Well after dark, he left Harrison in the alley beside the Hoover Hotel. Walking in the front door, Harrison was still thinking about Maria's request to rescue one of the mutineers—a Grover Burns who Maria claimed was Mr. Jones' nephew. Maria believes the young man is innocent.—that he was in the wrong place at the wrong time. Do I have what it takes to defend someone charged with mutiny and murder? he wondered. But if not me who then? For him, that was even more disturbing. In the hotel lobby he saw the same nighttime activity he had seen on his arrival.

Harrison crossed the lobby quickly and hurriedly went up the two flights of stairs to his hotel room. When he reached the door to his room, he saw that it was slightly ajar. Stepping quickly to one side, he drew his automatic and thumbed off the safety. In one motion, he slammed the door back against the wall. Crouching low, he swept into the room with the .32 straight out in front of him.

Even in the dim light from the hall lamp he could easily see that the room had been ransacked. The thin mattress was overturned. The three dresser drawers had been torn from the piece of furniture and hurdled to the floor. They lay on top of each other. His grip sat on top of the mattress, open and emptied of its contents. Harrison's few pieces of clothing were scattered about the room. Both pairs of trousers had been completely shredded. He stood, momentarily stunned by the destruction. Then he reached for the bag. The letter and telegrams from the Army to his mother were there, but Maria's letter was gone. On the floor Harrison saw the photograph of Bart and him together. Whoever it was had only taken the letter. He dropped the grip, turned, and stalked out of the room and down the stairs, fighting to contain his rage. His eyes were blue ice.

An older desk clerk, seeing the tall man marching toward him, felt a sudden chill. "Where's Miguel?" Harrison demanded.

"No se, señor." The clerk trembled. He was used to handling angry guests from thirty years of service in hotels. But this tall man's hard stare and contained power made him shake with fear.

"Get him!" Harrison ordered. "Now!"

"Sí, señor." The clerk hurried away. A few minutes later he returned with Miguel at his side.

"Señor James. Una problema?" Seeing the gringo's expression, Miguel was very apprehensive.

"You don't know?" Harrison pressured him. "Someone tore up my room. Things were stolen. You knew I was out, Miguel."

"No, no, señor. Not me." He looked anxiously at the tall, angry gringo.

"You see who comes and goes. Maybe, Miguel, you saw someone come who doesn't belong here. The man who could tell me about this would be rewarded. The man who keeps silent may become silent forever," Harrison said grimly.

The young man was now frightened. "Come, Señor James." Miguel led him to a private alcove.

"Two soldiers," the young clerk whispered. "But they have no, aahh...." He pointed to his shoulder.

"They were enlisted? They had nothing on their shoulders?"

"Sí, Señor James," he answered eagerly. "One man, a shorter man, ask about you. He say he has informacion, muy importante, for you from the colonel. Only for you. Muy importante sobre el tenente. El otro was tall like you, señor. Lo siento. Lo siento muchisimo. I take them to your room so the short man can put a message." Miguel motioned with his hand.

"Under the door," Harrison finished.

"Sí, under the door. Then they leave. I see them leave, señor. They put it under the door," he repeated, still shaken. "We all leave together."

"When did this happen, Miguel?"

"Muy temprano. Maybe at 5:00 esta tarde. Before I go to mi casa para la comida."

"Gracias, Miguel." Harrison gave him a dollar bill, then turned to stalk out of the hotel.

"The bastards," he muttered. Short and tall. Charlie and Jonesy, of course. *Looking for money?* he wondered. Then why take only the letter? James was walking directly up Broadway, and could smell gas from the street lamps in the cool, crisp air.

Harrison entered the police station. "Where's the constable?" he asked the deputy sitting at the front desk.

"Un momento, señor," the young Hispanic said. He immediately turned from the counter and went to the rear office.

"Mr. James." The constable greeted James from his open doorway. Motioning for James to follow, Arnold let him into the sparsely furnished adobe room. Harrison noticed wanted posters nailed to one wall and the dried, aging whitewash pealing from walls and ceiling. "Sit down," Arnold said, pointing to a chair in front of his desk. "Now how can I help you?" He sat down behind his desk.

"I'm reporting a robbery," Harrison said, sitting down. Arnold, who James judged to be about his age, was heavier and deeply tanned, but appeared to be in fairly good condition. Just like at their earlier meeting, he was dressed in loose fitting cotton trousers, but with a rumpled dark jacket covering a white cotton shirt open to the middle of his chest

"A robbery? Where?" Arnold asked calmly.

"Someone broke into my hotel room, goddamnit. Completely tore up the place."

"You know who did it? You saw them?"

James was still angry and impatient, in spite of his attempt to remain calm. "I have suspects."

"Who are they?"

"Two cavalry soldiers from the army camp. I've met them before and know they're trouble. Charlie, and the taller one is Abraham Lincoln Jones."

"They take valuables, money?" Arnold asked.

"Valuable correspondence."

"Deputy," the constable called. "Take Mr. James' complaint."

"Yes, sir."

"José will do the paperwork, Mr. James. I can assure you this matter will be investigated."

"Thank you," Harrison said, frustrated. "One more thing."

"Yes?" The constable asked patiently.

"Have you found out anything about Lieutenant Floyd's death?"

The constable went to close the door. He came back and sat down again. Then he pulled a brown file from a desk drawer and quickly skimmed through the papers. He closed the file and returned it to the drawer.

Harrison waited, holding onto his appearance of calm.

"The Regimental Commander, Colonel Sizemore, I think…. Yes, Colonel Sizemore has, based on the recommendation of Captain Blaine, investigating officer, determined that the deceased died from an accidental shooting. Looks like the Army is satisfied, and their investigation is concluded." He sat watching Harrison

"Do you believe it was?" Harrison asked, very softly. Blaine, he thought. Snow's right-hand man.

The policeman sighed. He turned to slowly gaze up at the dirty, smoke stained ceiling before his eyes finally came back to rest on the man in front of him. "If the Army thinks it was accidental, why should I think otherwise?"

"You know why. Only two shots were fired at us. One aimed at me. The shots were deliberate. It's all in my statement," Harrison said.

"Yes, it was. And that information was given to the military police."

"And the army concluded their investigation without even interviewing me?"

"Seems to be the case," Arnold said, still watching James closely. *Can this James help me?* he wondered.

"They can't decide that way based on the facts," Harrison protested angrily.

"Are you are suggesting that they made a mistake?" The constable leaned forward across the desk, hoping for more information.

"More than that," Harrison answered. "They're concealing something."

"The whole regiment?"

Harrison considered his answer for a moment. "There was no love lost between my brother and his commanding officer—Major Snow. That stemmed from the Negro soldiers' riot over in Houston."

"Speculation," Arnold replied. "It takes a lot of hate to commit a murder, don't you think?"

"When careers and pride are involved?"

"Even then. But I'm interested. What else do you think, Mr. James?" the constable asked.

"There's the matter of smuggling army weapons to Mexican rebels. I'm told a lot of those guns are crossing the border from Camp Furlong and armories in this area. Suppose there were Army officers and men involved—there would be pay offs, bribery, and my brother or the lieutenant could have discovered who they are. Then they were killed because of it."

"And if horses had humps they'd be camels, Mr. James," Arnold said flatly. "Right now the United States Army says the lieutenant's death was an unfortunate accident. You say it was murder. Bring me something I can use. Get me proof."

"I don't have any proof," Harrison replied, frustrated. "But I'll get it."

Arnold listened closely. He had decided that Harrison James was no fool.

"I can assure you, constable, that I will not give up until I do," James said softly.

"I'll be waiting," Arnold replied.

They shook hands, and Harrison left.

"The deputy will write out your burglary complaint before you leave," the constable said.

Harrison walked back down Broadway to his room. He decided to trust the constable. A good man, he thought. He walked past the saloon, distracted, when two soldiers came charging out the double doors. The shorter man crashed into James. All three stumbled out into the dusty congested street.

"Get outa the way," Charlie snarled in Harrison's face.

"Well, if it isn't my two new friends," Harrison answered. "Did you gentlemen find what you were looking for?"

"Looky here, Jonesy. If it ain't our old buddy." Horses and motor cars swerved to avoid them. "Don't know what you're talkin' 'bout, Harry."

"Charlie," Harrison said quietly, "you boys are a couple of common, thieving bastards."

"Watch yur mouth, ya rich Yankee sumbitch. Or I'll have ta teach ya a good lesson. Real good, eh, Jonesy?" Charlie reached into his half unbuttoned tunic, but before his hand could pull the object from inside his belt, Harrison snapped a left jab square into his face. He followed it with a right hook to the shorter man's belly. Blood gushed from Charlie's nose as he bent, gasping for breath.

Before Jonesy could respond, Harrison had his automatic stuck in Charlie's neck.

Jonesy froze, his eyes wide.

Charlie tried to pull free, but before he took a step, Harrison slapped his pistol barrel down on the broken and bloodied nose. "That's for pure satisfaction, Charlie," he said.

Charlie squealed in pain. Jonesy's face turned pale, but he did not move.

A crowd began to gather along the wood sidewalk, but everyone carefully kept his distance.

Scanning the soldiers and whores collecting at the saloon door, Harrison saw no one who looked dangerous.

Paddy had been watching the action with interest through the grimy front windows of his saloon.

When Charlie finally staggered upright, James quickly pulled a small caliber Smith and Wesson revolver from inside his woolen tunic. It was an older weapon, worn from use.

"I wonder what your commanding officer would say about his troopers carrying concealed, non-Army issued weapons?" Grabbing Charlie's ear, James twisted. "Maybe I should tell him about it. Or maybe keep it. What do you think, Charlie?" Harrison twisted the ear again.

Charlie squealed louder.

Harrison then searched the shaking Jonesy, while covering Charlie. He did not find a pistol, but discovered an eight-inch hunting knife tucked in Jones' trouser belt. He inspected it carefully, and then dropped both weapons in his coat pockets. "Let's go," he told them.

Charlie spit blood into the dusty street. "Where ya takin' us?" he gasped. He could not quite cover his fear.

"Should I be mindin' 'em fur ye, squire?" Paddy said from the doorway of the saloon. "Take the lads out of yer road?"

"No," Harrison responded, without taking his eyes off the two."We'll take a walk to the police station, you bastards." He spun Charlie around and stuck his pistol into the middle of the man's back to nudge him along. Jonesy walked beside Charlie, careful to keep quiet.

"We don't care 'bout no civilian cop." Charlie's voice quavered. His nose was spewing blood as he spoke. "Do we, Jonesy?"

Jonesy did not answer.

Charlie suddenly stopped in his tracks. "You think you got what it takes ta shoot a man in the back?"

Jones said, "Christ, Charlie, don't."

Harrison raised the muzzle of the automatic to the back of Charlie's neck, releasing the safety with a loud click. "Goodbye, Charlie," he said quietly. "Say hello to the Devil."

"Jus' let us go, then," Charlie whimpered, his voice barely audible. "Be smart now. We didn't do nothin'." Charlie tried to stop the flow of blood from his nose with the back of one hand.

"You have something that belongs to me, Charlie," James whispered. "I want it back. Now."

"What's that?"

"Bang," Harrison said.

"We don't have it no more. I swear on my mother's grave," Charlie pleaded. "I swear. Tell him, Jonesy."

"That's right," Jones said woodenly.

"Where is it then?" Harrison twisted the barrel a little so Charlie could feel it.

"I sold it to a captain," Charlie said eagerly

"Which captain?"

"A capt'n of one of them nigger companies. I swear," Charlie told him.

"Now why would you break into my room just to steal a letter, Charlie?" James twisted harder.

The capt'n tole us. Said he needed ta know what ya was up ta. Ev-i-dence," he said. "Right, Jonesy?"

"Yeah, that's right. An' he paid us good money. He tol' us to keep quiet," Jones added, now also eager to please.

"Let us go," Charlie pleaded. "We didn't hurt ya none."

"What's the captain's name?"

"I don't know. Cain't 'member it." James twisted the barrel harder. "We only know'd him from ridin' the train," Charlie croaked.

"Last chance," Harrison said coldly.

"Tell 'im, Charlie," Jones begged.

"His name is Blaine, Captain Blaine. We know'd him 'cause we see'd him on the El Paso train all da time. Ya can find 'im. He's in the nigger battalion."

They were followed by several men from the group at the saloon, with others joining in as they slowly made their way down Broadway.

"The Army has a big reward posted for them outlaws, Harry. You know where they at," Charlie said. "We'll split with ya. What ya say to dat?"

"Shut up and keep walking."

The constable met the three on the street in front of the jail. "Trouble just naturally seems to follow you around, Mr. James."

"These two low lifes assaulted me, constable. I want to press charges." He reached into his pocket for their weapons and handed them to the policeman.

Constable Arnold raised his voice. "Now, you folks get back to whatever you're doing, you hear me? You've all seen this before."

Arnold took the weapons from James and examined Charlie. "Looks to me like they got the worst of it." He smiled. "I'll charge 'em if you want, but the military police will come down right smart and take 'em outa my custody." He escorted the two to the back of the jail and locked them into a cell. "José, take Mr. James' newest complaint."

Then the constable reconsidered. "Mr. James, come into my office and have a seat," he said. He waited patiently for James to sit. Then he continued. "I want to tell you something."

"Yes?" Harrison said.

Arnold smiled thinly. "There was something else I haven't told you. About those last days before your brother died."

Harrison leaned forward in his chair.

"Your brother stopped by my office. As usual, he was in a great hurry. But he wanted me to know where he was going," Arnold said. "He told me he was traveling to El Paso to meet a Jackson Smith. The Captain said this man had important information that he was willing to give him. For a price, of course"

"What was the information?"

"I don't know. We never met again, and your brother never mentioned the kind of information he was expecting from this man. Captain James said he would brief me later, but he never did."

"I see," Harrison said, considering. Smith again, he thought. "Thank you for sharing that with me, Constable."

"I thought you had a right to all the information concerning your brother's death. I hope that helps in some way," Arnold said. "We know Smith is a smuggler with powerful friends up north. What do you know about him? Anything that might help in my investigation? Anything at all?"

"I'm sorry, Constable," Harrison replied. "I'm afraid I don't know him. But if I find something, I'll certainly share it with you."

"Was Smith a business associate?" Arnold pressed.

"I never worked with the man," Harrison replied. "But I'll check with our home office. They may know something." I need to meet with Smith first before I tell Arnold what I know, he decided quickly.

"James, be very careful how you poke around here," Arnold said with genuine concern. "There's some things going on around here that could get you killed."

"Like what, constable?" Harrison asked.

"The problems across the border. The fighting going on there can spill over to our side easy enough. And I suspect there are people right here in town who have a hand in it. One way or another."

"Are you talking about smuggling?"

"Mr. James, I'll look into your concerns," Arnold said without answering his question. "I promise. Now, José will help you with your second complaint this evening."

"Thank you, constable," James said, knowing he would get nothing more from Arnold.

"José!"

"Sí, jefe." He motioned for James to sit. "Venga, señor. Sit here."

Harrison tiredly began dictating his complaint.

CHAPTER EIGHTEEN

January 16, 1918

The ride back to the ranch was a long one for Daniel. He had lost heavily gambling in El Paso, and knew Maria would be angry when she discovered how much money was gone. He looked over at the Indian riding beside him. In many ways, Daniel envied Carlos. He was his own man, free to come and go as he pleased, with no demanding sister. Daniel looked at the Springfield strapped across the Indian's back.

"Don't tell my sister, amigo," Daniel said. "About the gambling, I mean. She wouldn't understand."

"Sí," was all Carlos answered. His black hair whipped across his face in a late night breeze. He didn't listen to the silly Negrito, and did not care about his problems. The boy was already dead in Carlos' mind. He was busy working out the details of his next job. That was the big one they had paid him so well to do. It must be clean, he thought. No loose ends like the job he did for the local boys back in October. The rich gringo had escaped. Everything must go perfectly or it would fail.

He wondered why it had to involve the young Washington, and why it had to be done now. It would have been so easy to take care of both hombres, one at a time. If he killed the Negrito now, he could have his way with the woman when he returned to the hacienda. The thought of touching her made him hard. He would enjoy her in many ways before he killed her. Carlos looked across at Maria's brother and smiled.

The two men galloped on through the darkness, determined to make the Washington hacienda by dawn. Carlos enjoyed the solitude of the desert. The emptiness of the vast land matched the emptiness of his soul.

CHAPTER NINETEEN

The train ride from San Antonio back to Camp Furlong seemed to last forever. The car they were riding in was unheated, and the weather unusually cold and damp for west Texas. The weather had been the main topic of conversation among the passengers for the last four hours. Harrison, bored, peered out the window at the gray, sunless day. Dreary and dull, he thought, like the conversations around him. He squirmed on the worn seat, feeling the springs poking at his backside. His muscles ached, and he felt the beginnings of a headache, in the back of his neck. But at least the Grover's trial was over.

He thought about the quadrangle shaped building in the middle of Fort Sam Houston where the court martial for 64 of the 150 Negro soldiers who had mutinied back in late August in Houston had been held. Less than a week after kissing Maria good-bye he was there in San Antonio defending Grover Burns of M Company, one of the 64 men.

Flanked by huge portraits of Steven Austin and Sam Houston, the men were tried by a panel of 12 white army officers for mutiny and murder. They each faced a hanging if convicted. The opening day of trial—November 1st—was cool, but sunny for central Texas, he recalled. The trial dragged on for almost 30 days, with the Army's prosecutors presenting their case against each of the 64 men. Harrison had been one of only two defense attorneys for the defendants. He had represented only Grover. The others had shared one young army officer.

Feeling the chill of the coach car, Harrison longed for the warm Mediterranean breezes of southern France.

*

James looked over at the Negro soldier in the brown uniform sitting beside him. His chin rested on his chest while he slept. Occasionally, he gave out a loud snore. The young man's head, with a day's whiskers beginning to sprout in uneven patches, moved from side to side with the sway of the train, but the motion didn't wake him. Harrison envied him.

He remembered what Grover, frightened out of his wits, had told him when they first met in the stockade just before the proceedings had begun. "They tol' me they put a rope 'round ma neck. 'If ya don't talk, we gonna see dat you have a rope 'round ya neck.' Some boys already say they saw you downtown in Houston."

Grover had been suspicious of Harrison's motives for offering to defend him. "Mista Harry, ya believe ya can save me?" he had asked. "Ya ain't saved no Negro before. They gonna hang me, sure enough. I knows it."

Harrison told Grover he was sent by Maria and Grover's uncle, Mr. Jones, to get him out of a hanging. He assured Grover he knew what he was doing. But deep down, Harrison was not that confident. The last time he had litigated was five years earlier—and he had lost.

"Not guilty," the President of the Court had read, acquitting Grover of all three charges. "In the main," the general read, "these explanations given by the defendant are neither completely convincing nor entirely satisfactory. However, the Court, upon consideration of all evidence, entertained a reasonable doubt as to his actual participation in any of the offenses charged. Measured against this standard, acquittal is justified." Grover was the only one found not guilty.

Harrison realized from reading the witness statements and the other evidence presented by the prosecution that the case against Grover was weak. The Army, determined to make an example of the accused, presented witnesses that were easily rebutted. He also knew that it was his presence in the court room, more than anything else, that had saved Grover. He wondered how the other 63 defendants would have fared if they had been properly represented.

*

Carlos had sold the information for one thousand dollars. The white man from El Paso had bought it immediately when he told him where he got it. Not more than several hours later, he received payment in American dollars and orders to accompany Maria Washington on her journey south. That meant his decision to take her would have to wait. Carlos had already implemented his plan for getting rid of her brother and the important white man in Columbus. It was more complex than usual, but another man there would assist him. For a price, of course.

"Señor Daniel," he yelled from the gate. "Un mensajero de Los Estados. Muy importante."

"Digale a venir," Daniel called back. "I will meet him now. Maybe a love letter from her gringo, eh?" He laughed, but Carlos only smiled.

*

At the San Antonio train depot, Harrison had requested that the soldier be allowed to ride with him instead of in the car reserved for Negroes. The conductor absolutely refused, so Harrison sat in the Negroes' car with Burns. He looked up at the sign in the front of the car. **For Coloreds**, it announced in large black letters.

Harrison's hand trembled slightly. I could use a drink, he thought, still seeing the executions in his mind. He couldn't forget the image of 13 condemned men dropping into space to twist at the end of a rope. Several bodies jumped involuntarily, then all thirteen hung lifeless in the air. The Army had planned the hanging as an example, and they had wasted no time in carrying out the sentences. The prisoners stood in a line, blindfolded, with arms and legs tightly bound. They stood on a high wooden platform specially built for their executions in the courtyard of the Quadrangle at Fort Sam Houston.

James had witnessed the hanging only because he had assisted Captain Grier, the single defense attorney for the other 63 accused men, with last minute appeals for reprieve. President Wilson had refused to grant clemency, or even a delay. Harrison was sickened,

193

but not surprised. The whole spectacle was meant to appease the white Texans, and to discourage any other attempts by Negro soldiers to resist the Jim Crow Laws.

Harrison finally had an opportunity to read the witness transcripts, and he read them thoroughly. They were very informative. He gained a very clear picture of Bart's commanding officer. Harrison reviewed Major Snow's account of his own disappearance during the riot. "The men stampeded toward the center of town. My first thought was to get help. I had to notify the city of Houston then get to Camp Logan to act against these men," the major had testified. "I went down Washington Avenue, then ran down Washington Street to get help."

Harrison thought about Bart's refusal to fire on the mutineers. He had read his brother's testimony. And it was true, just like the soldiers at Camp Furlong had told him. Bart had refused to order his men to open fire. He admitted it. Reading the words again and again, Harrison sensed his brother's stubborn defiance, but not shame. "To shoot our own soldiers down in the street is against everything I believe in," he stated in his deposition. Harrison thought he would remember Bart's words always. Then the whistle shrieked in his ear as the train braked for El Paso station.

Burns began to stir. "Where are we now, Mista James?" he asked, first opening one eye, then the other. He raised both arms into the air to stretch, mouth gaping.

"El Paso, Grover."

Quickly realizing his campaign hat was missing, he stood up in a panic, looking about the floor. "Ma Hat? Where's ma hat?"

Harrison pointed above them. "I stowed it. It fell off while you were sleeping."

"Thank ya, suh," Grover smiled and stood to retrieve it. "Is thar food here, suh?"

They looked at the station platform coming into view. "Can we git somethin' to eat here, suh?" Grover sat back down quickly as the train jerked to a stop.

"I believe so." Harrison smiled. "But we stay together until we get to Camp Furlong."

"Yeah, suh."

Through the dirty window they both stared at the station platform and what lay beyond, then at the people still packed into their car. The passengers here were waiting patiently for all the whites in the forward carriages to exit first. Burns nodded slowly.

"Texas, Mr. James. Not a good place for color'd folk," he said.

CHAPTER TWENTY

Mr. Jones moved easily through the crowd to greet them as soon as they stepped off the train. He had been standing silently by the ticket window, watching passengers disembark. Grover noticed him immediately. "Uncle James!" he cried, the emotion clear in his voice.

Seeing Grover and then Harrison, Jones winked at his nephew and motioned to them with a turn of the head toward the black Dodge parked nearby. They passed him to approach the automobile.

"Harry! Harry, quick!" a female voice from inside the Dodge called out softly as they drew near.

Harrison smiled, took the private by the arm, and stepped to the window of the Dodge.

A hand reached out for him. "Harry, thank you," Maria said, squeezing his hand. "I knew you would not fail."

He bent down, looking into the car. Maria was in black, wearing a long full dress with high button collar. No gun belt was visible. Her fine features and hair were veiled. He saw the black cavalry boots sticking out from beneath her skirts and smiled.

"Get in, please," Maria ordered softly. Mr. Jones opened the door for the two and they slid into the back seat. She reached over and embraced Grover Burns, pressing him to her veiled face. "Now you are safe, Grover," she whispered in his ear, and lifted her veil to kiss his cheek. She held James' face in her gloved hands, looking into his eyes. "Harrison, you are my man of honor," she told him, her beautiful dark eyes shining with tears. She kissed him on his lips.

"Maria, this is dangerous," Harrison whispered intently. "You must go back over the border quickly. And I must get Grover back to Camp Furlong."

"I had to see for myself. When I heard the news, I could not believe it. Ah, Harry, my dearest. Mi amor."

She squeezed his hand. "We will meet later. Mr. Jones will bring you as before."

Harrison was worried. "Is that wise?" he asked, concerned.

"Don't worry, Harry." She smiled. "But you must be careful. Things have changed in Columbus. Now it is more dangerous than ever."

"Why?"

"The soldiers watch the border more closely." She touched him on his cheek, smiled, then kissed him on the forehead. "Mr. Jones, we must go," she ordered firmly. "Good-bye Harry, my love. For now."

Harrison and Private Burns slid out of the back seat as the big chauffeur started up the Dodge. Standing in the car's dust, they watched it pull away.

Harrison bought a copy of the *El Paso Sun* before they returned to the train. He opened it and began reading. In the lower left corner of the front page was a headline: "Fireball from warehouse explosion lights up night sky." Harrison opened the newspaper to the second page and read: "It was seen as far away as Columbus, New Mexico. Mr. Jackson Smith, a spokesman for Rio Grande Feed and Grain, stated that he had no idea why someone would blow up the building. Besides wheat, only several cases of dynamite for clearing tree stumps had been stored there. The cause of the fire was unknown, but arson was suspected, according to the El Paso Police."

Smith. Just like I figured, James thought with a smile, pleased with himself for getting the information on Smith's whereabouts from Jonathan before leaving Chicago.

*

The two men arrived in Columbus mid-afternoon of the same day. Harrison, with baggage in hand, went to his hotel with Private Burns. "I'll find us rooms for the night. We'll go out to Camp Furlong in the morning," he told Burns as they entered the lobby.

Harrison had already decided to escort the private back to camp. A good time to talk with the major, he thought. And with Juan.

"Yeah, suh," Grover responded. He was uncomfortable in the whites-only hotel.

One of the changes Maria had spoken of was obvious in the Hoover. The lobby was quieter, with fewer people milling about. Harrison saw only one Army officer. He looked for Miguel.

"Señor. Señor James," a voice called out from behind them. They both turned to see the hotel clerk approaching them from the dining room. "You have returned. Bueno!" He sounded pleased.

"Miguel." Harrison smiled. "I need the best room you have. And a hot bath. I'll be staying several days. Can you arrange everything?"

"Sí, Señor James. For you, no problema."

"The best," James said.

"Only the best, señor." Grabbing James' single piece of luggage, he led them both to the front desk. Miguel eyed the young Negro soldier. "Heem, too, Señor James?" he asked pointing at Burns doubtfully.

"Yes, amigo. Him, too. And he needs a hot bath." James produced a ten dollar bill.

Miguel looked resigned. "Muy bien. I will find something, but not in the Hoover Hotel, señor. I have another hotel for this man."

"No, Miguel," Harrison said directly.

"It's okay, suh," Grover intervened. "I'll take it."

"Make sure it's the best you can find, Miguel," James insisted.

"Sí, señor," Miguel answered.

"And a bath too, Miguel. For both of us."

*

Early the next morning, after a breakfast of steak and eggs, Harrison and Burns strolled to the livery and hired a buggy and driver to take them out to the military camp. Harrison was surprised that the ride was only a dollar. Prices had dropped. He gave the old man five dollars for his trouble.

"Gracias," the old man said with a dignified bow.

With Burns in uniform, an MP waved them through. The two men walked the short distance from the main gate to headquarters for the Negro battalion. Strolling down the dusty street, they passed empty rows of tents. The desert quiet had returned to Camp Furlong. It was slipping back into the sleepy frontier outpost of pre-Villa days. The empty tents, flapping in the desert breeze, held discarded pieces of broken furniture and equipment. He saw an overturned washstand with a cracked, dust-covered mirror nearby. Inside one tent, he glimpsed an abandoned pack with a broken shoulder strap. They came upon four Negro soldiers breaking down the tents. Probably to ship them to France, Harrison thought.

When he and Private Burns arrived at the headquarters tent for 3rd Battalion, 24th Infantry, they discovered that Major Snow had not yet returned from Texas, where he had testified for the prosecution in the court martial. The news frustrated James. "When can I speak with the major?" he asked. The young clerk did not answer. He was staring at Private Burns as though he were seeing a ghost. "Private?" Harrison asked again.

"Sir?"

"I want to speak with Major Snow. When will he be coming back?"

"Sir, he's expected tomorrow. I will inform 'im that you've asked, sir." He turned to Burns. "Burns, we weren't.... That is, you're back. We heard you was hung."

Burns shrugged. "So did I."

"Where's Sergeant Parilla," interrupted James.

"Sir, he ain't here, either. I'll tell the first sergeant that you asked for him, too, sir." The clerk continued staring at Private Burns. "He's off duty, sir."

"Good bye, Private Burns, and good luck to you," Harrison said, shaking his hand. "You know where you can find me if you need me."

"Good-bye, Mista James. I surely thank ya fur what ya done fur me. Yes, suh, I do," the private said with simple dignity. He left the tent escorted by another Negro soldier.

Harrison turned to leave, then he stopped. "By the way, is the cavalry still here?"

"Yes, sir. Still patrolling the border, sir."

"Thank you."

*

Harrison returned to Columbus and the hotel. At the door to his room, he reached for the Colt as he checked the door. He inserted the brass key, and entered cautiously. The room was undisturbed.

Shortly after dusk, he heard a knock.

"Señor...Señor James, venga! You have message. Muy importante, I think. Venga!" Miguel whispered through the door.

"Harrison opened the door. "Who's it from?" he asked.

"La policía, señor. Muy importante. The constable bring it. He give me to give you, señor."

"How long ago?"

"Ahora, treinta minutos, no mas." Miguel looked over his shoulder down the shadowy hallway. Lowering his voice, he repeated, "Muy importante, Señor James. He say to tell no one."

"Why didn't the constable deliver it directly to me?"

"You were not here, señor. He was in hurry and leave muy rapido." Miguel motioned with both hands.

James unfolded the yellowed slip of notebook paper. "Come to my office tonight. I have information for you." The message was signed "Amos Arnold, Constable." He reread it slowly. "You say the constable himself?" Harrison repeated to the clerk.

"Sí, the constable."

"I'll take care of it." Harrison refolded the note and slid it into his trouser pocket, already considering. He turned and went back down the stairway. The clerk followed.

"Señor James, I see you mas tarde," Miguel said at the hotel doors.

"Yes, later," Harrison replied absently.

CHAPTER TWENTY-ONE

The two riders tied their mounts behind the Columbus Jail in a dimly lighted area used to store harness and wagon wheels. The old adobe building, with its three small rooms, had been built during quieter times to handle the occasional small town drunk. The night was overcast and dark. They entered through the back door. It was unlocked. In the dimness, they walked past the two empty cells before they saw light through the barred window of the door leading to the front offices. The light was above Constable Arnold's desk. The door was ajar. The two men quietly opened it and stepped lightly into the small room.

Arnold looked up and smiled. He had been waiting. "Well now, I was about ready to give up on you, Washington," he said, watching them come through the door. "Who's your buddy?"

"Carlos. He works for us," Daniel said quickly. "You wanta talk about a deal?"

"Maybe. It depends," the constable told him.

"Depends?" Daniel responded. "Depends on what? That's not what you said in the message." The younger man leaned over the constable's desk in a threatening manner.

"Depends on what you have that I can use. That's what." Arnold said, looking the two over carefully. He saw that the Negro was unarmed, but he couldn't tell about the other man. "Your message said you was coming in to give yourself up. You got something to say, say it." His right hand dropped to the butt of his pistol.

"I never sent you a message."

Carlos stepped away from the young Washington.

"What's this? Some trick?" Daniel asked. He turned to look at his companion.

"Constable," Carlos said, stepping behind the large desk to stand beside the lawman. He reached behind his back.

"What the hell...?" Arnold looked up at the Indian, surprised. Then he pulled his gun and slid the chair back to stand. "Hold it, amigo," he said to Carlos as he started to rise from the chair.

A hand reached over to hit the light switch. The jail went dark.

*

James arrived at the old jail, surprised to find it silent and dark this early in the evening. Someone had to be on duty. He peered through the dirty front window but couldn't see anything.

He then stepped back to survey the building. The front door was slightly ajar. Harrison reached for his Colt as he stepped into the darkened building. The floorboards creaked beneath him.

*

"Daniel," Carlos was whispering in the dark, holding the constable's pistol. 'Venga!" Then they heard a noise. Someone comes, Carlos thought. Both men froze in the darkness.

"Constable," Harrison called softly. He felt for a light switch, but couldn't find one on the wall near him. His fingers gripped firmly around the Colt. "Anyone here? Constable? Deputy?" he called again.

He thought he heard a noise in the back of the building near the cells. Holding the automatic out in front of him, Harrison moved forward slowly and carefully into the deeper darkness beyond. He found the door to the constable's office open. He took a breath, then slid quickly through in a crouch. He felt as if all the air had been sucked out of the room. A bit of starlight shone through the narrow cell window, highlighting a corner of the constable's large desk.

Harrison moved toward that spot. Before he could reach it, the toe of his boot caught against something. He bent down to touch it with his fingertips. Soft. A man's leg. Kneeling, he lightly moved his free hand over the prone figure. A large man. No pulse. Still warm, but he wasn't breathing. Harrison touched the man's head. There was blood on top, in his hair. The man's skull had been shattered. It felt soft. Blood still trickled down to form a pool on the floor

204

Harrison remained in a crouching position, his pistol pointed ahead with the safety off. He began inching back to the office doorway, but saw something move in the shadows across the room. He raised the Colt. In the far corner, behind the desk—he was sure it was a man.

"Don't move!" Harrison yelled. Light from the window reflected off a gun barrel.

There was a clicking sound. In the stifling quiet of the room, it was the unmistakable cocking of a revolver.

James instinctively fired off two rapid shots. His target fell backward, firing his weapon into the ceiling as he disappeared.

I've got to get the hell out of here, James thought. Still holding his pistol out in front, he continued to move back toward the door to the front office. A board creaked. He turned to shoot, but he was struck from behind before he could fire. The hard blow across his wrist jarred the Colt free. Another caught him across the back of the neck. His knees buckled and he collapsed to the floor. Harrison fought to stay conscious. Flashes of pain shot up his neck and burst in his head. Stay awake, he ordered himself. He moaned at the pain.

He heard his assailant run across the wooden floor and out the back.

With his other hand, Harrison swept the area around him for the Colt. He found it and struggled to his feet. With his left arm he wiped the blood from the gash. In the outside light coming through the open backdoor, Harrison saw his assailant mount a horse. He struggled to reach the door, but too late. The man was already riding west down the almost deserted street.

"Stop him!" Harrison yelled. "Murderer!"

One horse was still tied to the post. He reached for the reins and mounted. Unsteady from the blow to his head, Harrison nudged the animal with sharp kicks in the flanks. The horse responded immediately, and Harrison pointed him west.

A deeper darkness began to overtake him after leaving Columbus, but he recognized a faint smudge that was a horse and rider ahead as a sliver of moon broke through. They were riding across an area south of Tres Hermanas. With a pounding head and arm, Harrison continued the pursuit. Turning south off the road, the rider ahead led him into a dry riverbed with large rocks strewn about. To avoid being ambushed, Harrison was forced to dismount and leave his horse. He walked carefully forward, his weapon in his one good hand.

James heard a boot scrape on a rock above. He turned, looking up, then raised the Colt with safety off. He saw no movement.

A figure leaped onto him out of the darkness, like a panther. Harrison fell, struggling to throw the man off. Overpowered, he was struck hard again on the side of his head. A deeper darkness rushed in on him.

CHAPTER TWENTY-TWO

Harrison first heard the wind as a humming in his ears. His head pounded. The space behind his eyes throbbed steadily, sending waves of pain down through his body. His right arm would not move, so with his left he reached up to touch his face, then the back of his head.

He felt dried blood. Moving his hand across his scalp, he felt another lump over his ear covering a large, jagged gash, again caked in blood. Slowly, his right eyelid opened, then his left. The first thing he saw was the hazy, deep blue sky. "Alive," he muttered. He struggled to sit up, but couldn't.

What day? The question formed in his mind as he tried to focus. Slowly, the pain subsided a little. His vision sharpened. He tried again to get up, and finally, with great concentration, got to his knees. But after a moment, he went down on all fours to regain his balance.

Get to the rock. With a fierce will, he forced his body to move. On all fours, he swayed toward a large boulder.

Bracing himself with his back, Harrison pushed upward against the boulder until he stood. He was shaky, but standing. Looking around, he saw the three peaks that were Tres Hermanas. Must be north, he thought. I'm close to the border, west of Columbus. Head still throbbing, he looked southeast, to face the morning sun. Nothing, as far as he could see. Not even a dust cloud. To the south and west the terrain appeared more rugged—gullies, canyons, more mountains. He knew that already. Best to walk east, Harrison thought. He sat again in the shadow of the boulder to gather his strength. "You'll walk," he told himself finally. "You'll rest 'till nightfall, then follow the stars."

Harrison's mouth was dry. He sat, feeling the dull, constant ache in his head and right wrist. Swallowing hard, he remembered

Juan's warnings about the dangers of being on foot in the desert. Look for land marks, and don't let the distances fool you.

When the day finally dissolved into desert starlight, Harrison, feeling better, began to walk. His gait improved as he established a shuffling rhythm. The stars guided him.

After an hour, he found himself on the weathered rim of a dry gulch. He stopped to rest and check his course. The stars seemed to be in the correct position. A distant light he'd seen ahead seemed to be larger.

Harrison looked down into the ravine. In the moonlight he thought he saw horse tracks in the pale sand. He slid down the embankment and felt them in the sandy soil. "They're still soft," he whispered hopefully. He couldn't tell how many, but they led down the ravine in two directions—east and west. Harrison started walking toward the east. His strength was fading, and a raging thirst began to overpower him. Long before the sun broke the desert darkness, Harrison had collapsed. He lay in the ravine, fighting to stay awake. His mouth was parched, and he could swallow only with difficulty. "Get up," he ordered in a raspy whisper through cracked lips. Standing slowly, he managed only two reeling steps before collapsing again, body sprawled full length in the sand. He thought of cool water, the ice of Lake Michigan, and of his brother.

*

Harrison awoke slowly, surrounded by darkness. The desert ravine was gone, and there were no stars above him. He struggled with his body and was able to move first his arms, then his legs. I'm in a bed…with linen sheets, he thought, touching the covers. They were soft against his sunburned skin.

He carefully raised his right arm to his eyes. The bandaged wrist was sore and swollen from the blow he had received in the jailhouse. Then he touched the cotton swathed around his whole head, above his eyes. His eyes had adjusted to the darkness. He looked around the room.

Harrison recognized that large, unshuttered, open window. He was in Maria's bedroom.

Stretching out one leg, then the other, he felt the floor of polished hardwood. It was real. He tried to stand. Wobbly at first, with the aid of a bedpost Harrison managed to balance on both feet. He reached out for the wardrobe against the wall. "That wasn't so difficult," he told himself. "Now see if you can navigate to the door."

Finding the knob was easy. Standing naked in the darkness of the room, he hesitated, then opened the door.

The first thing he saw in the lighted hallway was Maria walking toward him, carrying a tray of bandages and ointments. She stopped and looked him over from head to foot. Then she smiled that lovely smile. But Harrison saw the tears in her eyes.

"Harry, you have come back to me," she said, still standing in front of him. "For a while, we did not know. You have spent many hours between the living and the dead." She set her tray down on the floor to assist him.

He felt her strength under his arm as she helped him back into bed. They both looked down. She smiled and kissed his lips. "We have plenty of time for that, my love. But first, we get you well again."

"What happened? Maria, how did I get here?"

"Harry, there is much to tell, but first…."

"No. Now, Maria," he demanded. The exertion made his whole head throb.

"Harry, I will tell you when you are better. So lie down," Maria commanded. She removed the old dressings, then began to clean and re-bandage his wounds.

He fell asleep with the taste of salt on his lips from swallowing small teaspoons of warm broth. He dreamt of the desert and of Maria's beauty.

*

With several more days of bed rest and constant attention by Maria, Harrison's strength returned. At night, they made love in the warm darkness. At first, their lovemaking was slow and careful. Maria would rest astride him, moving over him in a slow rhythm. As his strength returned, their joining became more physical and passionate.

She would not answer any of his questions. She would only say that the time was not yet right. "Get stronger, Harry," she would say.

When Harrison awoke before dawn one morning a week later, he was surprised to find she was not beside him. He hastily threw on his shirt, trousers, and boots.

Opening the door, he peered down the staircase. He saw light and heard voices coming from her study, the command center for her smuggling operations.

Quietly, he walked down the stairs and made his way toward the room. He thought he overheard the voice of Maria's brother above the rest. "Vayámonos, Maria," he said.

"Tranquilo, hermano!" she responded in her strong voice. "Yo soy el jefe ahora."

"Pienso que el gringo, James, ese una problema—una problema grande. Es la verdad?" Daniel responded coldly, still in Spanish. "You put him above everything. We can all see this," he reverted back to English.

"Es su problema, hermano. Por que hombre?" she snapped back. "Are we murderers now?"

Harrison was unable to understand all the words, but he heard his name and that was enough.

"I would like to hear the answer to that question myself," he said, swinging the door open to stand in front of them.

"Ahh, the gringo," Daniel responded with open contempt. "The last time I saw you, gringo, you were stalking the shadows. Who did you think you were hunting, eh?"

Harrison went for the younger man in one swift, flowing motion. His eyes were blue flame. He saw only Daniel.

"Wait!" Maria stepped in front of him, but she could not stop him. Harrison picked her up and swung her aside as if she were a doll. "Mr. Jones, José," she commanded. There wasn't the slightest hint of fear in her voice. "Ayude me!"

Harrison lashed out, his fists a blur. Daniel's head snapped back. Blood poured from his nose. The younger man had no time to react to the barrage of fists. Then the other two men were on James. José caught his right arm in mid air while Mr. Jones, from behind, reached for the other. With some effort they were able to subdue him. At first, Harrison struggled, raging at them. But he gave in as he slowly regained his sense.

"Let me go!" he ordered finally. Neither man responded.

The old man's eyes were wary.

"You want to get even, eh, gringo?" Daniel said, smiling. He wiped blood from his nose and mouth.

Mr. Jones knew that Daniel was too young and inexperienced to be afraid of this man, even now.

"Harry, will you listen to me?" Maria asked, now standing directly in front of him. "No more fighting?"

"No more fighting," he replied. "Tell them to let me go."

She nodded and they released him.

"Now, I will tell you what you want to know, but first…." She turned to her brother. "Daniel, clean yourself and get ready to travel. Mr. Jones, take the men and make the preparations."

The three men departed. José was the last to leave the room, reluctant to leave Maria with the angry white man. He kept his hand on the small caliber revolver in his pocket as he spied on the two who remained in the study. Only when he was certain the threat was past did he leave the house.

Harrison sat down in the great chair. Maria sat on the desk, waiting.

"Maria, why did your brother almost kill me out in that damn desert," he asked.

"It was a mistake," she told him. "You were in the wrong place at the wrong time."

"Accident?" Harrison was still very tense. "Did your brother kill the constable?" James asked.

"Daniel said it was an accident but, before he realized what had happened, you came. They hid when they heard you."

"Your brother and somebody else just happened to come to the jail and accidentally kill the constable? Who was the other person?"

"It was Carlos," Maria answered. "Daniel did not kill the constable. He went to talk with him. Daniel swore it to me," she said, visibly upset. "My brother is not capable of murder."

"He was capable of hitting me, Maria." Harrison rubbed his scalp.

"He thought you were going to kill him."

"Why did he think that?"

"Daniel said he was hiding when you came and started firing." She sighed sadly. "He says he did not want to hurt you. But when he saw you shoot Carlos he knew he had to stop you or be killed himself."

"That man clearly tried to kill me, Maria," he said softly. "I shot Carlos, then?"

A single tear rolled down her brown cheek. "Daniel was very angry, but he did not want to harm you. He left quickly after he struck you. You chased him into the desert."

"So Daniel hit me twice?" he asked. "How did I get rescued?"

"Juan Parilla came to the hacienda the next morning. He told me he saw you ride into the desert. We waited for darkness to come again, but you did not come. We went to find you, Harry. We searched over many miles. I was almost crazy with you and Daniel missing, and the constable murdered."

"And Daniel? Where was he?"

"He did not return to the hacienda until two days later. After we found you, Daniel rode in and told us what happened."

"I see," he said, thinking about Daniel that night. "How did Juan know that I was out in the desert?"

"Juan, he followed you when you rode west out of town," Maria said. "He saw you were riding for the mountains. He tried to catch you, but he lost your trail in the rocks. When he could cross the border, he came here."

"Daniel did not know it was you," she repeated tearfully.

"What difference does that make, Maria? If not me, who then? The deputy? He left me out in the desert," Harrison said. "You can't always protect him." His temper flashed. "You know what could have happened to me out there."

She smiled sadly, hopefully. "It was not your destiny to die in the desert."

At that moment, Harrison realized completely that he loved her. He could not hurt her. "What happened in the jail?"

"It was a trap." Maria looked at him sadly. "My brother told me."

"A trap for who?"

"For Daniel. To arrest him for smuggling, I think."

"Why was I told to be there?" James asked. "The constable sent me a message to come to his office."

"I don't know," she went on. "I don't understand why the constable wanted you to come at the same time that they were there."

"Daniel didn't know I was coming?"

"No, Harry. My brother did not know. You were there when my brother was to meet with Constable Arnold." Maria walked over to sit on the arm of the big chair. She touched his hair with her fingers. "My brother went to Columbus to speak with him about a deal he offered us. Then there was a fight, and the constable was killed. Daniel said Carlos fought with the constable."

"But why was I supposed to be there," Harrison wondered. He paused. "A deal? What kind of deal?"

"The constable sent us a letter. He offered to give Daniel and me pardons if we came to Columbus. He wanted information about who smuggles rifles out of the armories and across the border." She pulled a letter from the desk drawer. "We received this note from Columbus. It was delivered to Las Palomas by messenger. See for yourself." Maria handed the envelope to James.

"So why take that risk by crossing the border? You knew it could have been a trap."

"It is time to stop this work. It is too dangerous. And now profits will be small," she said. "I was going, but the letter states that Daniel should represent me. The constable wanted to speak with my brother only. Carlos and Mr. Jones insisted that I stay here. So I consented. Daniel is a man now and can handle these things."

"And was Carlos invited to Columbus by the constable?" Harrison asked.

"No. But he was always with Daniel, for safety. He said he would go to protect my brother."

"Did Arnold know Carlos would be with Daniel?"

"No," Maria answered.

"I received a note also," Harrison said, examining the envelope. He read her note slowly, to compare the handwriting with that from his note.

"This writing is not the same as in my message. Here the penmanship is very poor and there is no signature, only the initials, A.A." He looked at her. "I think you've been tricked."

"The cowards. Assassinos!" she said with a scowl.

"Who?"

"Those hombres in Columbus and El Paso. Those who also sell weapons across the border. They want to get rid of us. Maybe they wanted revenge for when we burned down their warehouse," Maria told him.

"Did Juan know anything about this?" he asked, still examining the note.

"I told him to watch the jail. In case of problems, he could send a message back to me.

"Did he know I went to the jail?"

"Juan's nephew, Miguel, saw him in the saloon where Juan usually goes to play poker after work, and told him about your message. Juan said he went after you. To warn you to stay away."

"To warn me of what?"

"Juan knew that Daniel was coming to Columbus to speak with the constable," Maria explained. "I sent him a message. I wanted him to watch out for my brother. When Miguel told him in the saloon that you were going there, he wanted to stop you."

"Did he say what he saw at the jail?" Harrison asked.

"Juan told me he heard gunshots and saw Daniel, and then you, ride west from town."

"Who in town knew that your brother was coming to the jail?"

"We told only Juan. I think maybe he told his nephew," Maria said thoughtfully.

"Do you know what happened in the constable's office before I got there?"

"Daniel said there was a bad fight and the lights went out. Carlos beat the constable with his gun. Daniel said he tried to stop him, but it was too late."

"Do you believe him?"

"Yes. Daniel is my hermano," she answered.

"I don't think the killing was a mistake," Harrison stated. "I think Carlos planned to kill him. But I don't know why."

"Daniel did not know that. He could not have. And Carlos was not hired by me or my brother to kill a lawman. It had to be an accident," she insisted.

"Maria, it looks to me like a trap. But for what, I don't know," he shrugged. "Who found the bodies?"

"Juan said he saw a group of men come out of the saloon where the soldiers drink. They heard the shots and headed straight for the jail. They found Carlos and Constable Arnold."

"Who would have wanted the constable killed?" Harrison asked, thinking.

"I don't know," Maria said. "Someone worried much about him and they killed him to keep him quiet. Maybe they wanted to kill my brother with the constable. But you came too early. That's why I believe you are good luck for us, Harry. And fate was kind, yes?"

"Fate?" He smiled. "It's all about gun smuggling."

"Sí," Maria said.

"You have dangerous competitors."

"Sí, Harry. Where there is much money, there is always danger."

"Now a dead lawman. That's very serious."

James smiled. "I am in debt to you for saving my life, Maria." He looked into her dark brown eyes. "I love you."

She touched his cheek softly with the back of her hand.

"It was Juan who saved you," she said finally. "He followed you into the desert, but he lost you in the darkness. Then he came to me for help. As soon as we could, we left to search the area where Juan said you might be. For hours, my men and I looked for you, and my heart was breaking. We even used lanterns and risked being caught. But we found you, Harry. You were in the secret wash that we use to cross the border, and we found you just in time." She bent down to hug him, holding him tightly in her arms.

"This is a different world," Harrison said. "But it's where I want to be right now. We'll find out who is behind this," he told her, sounding determined.

Maria looked at him, alarmed. "More than just a few are smuggling guns across the border. It involves many. Some are very powerful Americans. They want more than dollars. They want power. Important people from Chicago, New York, Washington. Because of them the war in Mexico goes on forever and for them it is not about the people or liberty. They seek power to control minerals and oil. And the people of Mexico. They are very dangerous."

"Washington?" Harrison asked.

"Sí. Políticos. The war here is good for them. And I think some want the Germans to win the great war in Europe, so they keep the fighting along the border from ending. To keep the American Army here."

"And my brother was involved in all this intrigue," James said, amazed at all the subterfuge.

"Bart was investigating for your Presidente, as I told you before. He did not care much about a few missing rifles. He was looking for more important people."

"Not gunrunners, but spies." Harrison said slowly. "Who are they, Maria? Give me their names."

"I do not know their names. But if I did, I could not tell you," Maria answered.

"Traitors who spy for the Germans?"

"Dangerous men," she repeated. "That is why we must be very careful. They can kill us easily if they think you are after them. I will not allow you to die like your brother," she added fiercely.

"But the danger for you is really other smugglers—your competitors. Do I have that right?"

"Yes, Harry."

"I must return to Columbus," Harrison said.

"No, Harry. Not yet," Maria said concerned. "Mr. Jones tells me there is a warrant out on Daniel. And for you, my love."

"For me? I was only defending myself. And who besides Juan knew I was even there?"

"Only two shots were fired. One from your pistol killed Carlos," Maria said, concerned. "They say there were witnesses who saw you and Daniel run out of the constable's office and ride away. And your pistola? We do not know what happened to it, Harry."

"I think I can clear all this up. I just need to get back to town," Harrison said.

"Oh no, you cannot go back there. Not yet. Wait and we will find a way," Maria said, pleading. "Too many people want you now, I think. They've set a trap with no escape."

"What kind of trap?"

"They wait for you. When you arrive, you will be arrested. Then, who knows what they will do," Maria said, trying to frighten him. "The white man who rides with the Negro Washingtons?"

"Gun runners, rebels, and spies," James said, smiling tightly.

"Yes!" She looked at him. "When he does not expect us, then we will take care of this bad hombre," Maria said. "We must be patient."

James stared at her, not used to being put off. But before he could protest, Daniel entered the room.

He ignored James and spoke to his sister. "Maria, we are ready," he stated, and waited impatiently for her to respond.

"Yes, Daniel," she answered. "We will be there shortly."

"We're waiting," Daniel said, and turned to leave the house.

"Waiting?" James asked. "For what?"

She kissed him on the cheek. "Today, there is a big deal worth many thousands of dollars that requires everyone. When that is done, we will find your brother's killer."

"Thousands of dollars?"

"El Presidente Carranza offers a great reward to anyone who can break the American blockade and deliver weapons to General Obregón. The others have no weapons now, but I have worked out a plan to have guns for the general. I made a deal for the most modern rifles. So we have a good chance to make money."

"Maria, I have money. You don't need to take any dangerous risks."

"Harry," she told him with love, "I owe a debt. And I have a plan. It is a good plan." Maria looked out the window at the rush of activity in the courtyard.

"A plan?" Harrison asked. "Where will you get the weapons?"

"The Japanese have guns to sell, my love," she said with a smile. "We are going to ship arms across the Pacific Ocean, through the blockade, and up the Mexican coast."

Harrison was almost awed

"I see. Then you are going to deliver those rifles to the pro-German government of Mexico?"

"Not exactly," she said.

"What do you mean?"

"General Obregon believes he will get the guns, but he will not." She winked at him.

"No?" Harrison asked, confused.

"He will not get the guns because Villa will see to that." She smiled. "But, we will get the money. I cannot tell you how I will do all this, querido. I am not yet certain."

"Villa will just take the guns and hand over the money to you?"

"Of course," she said. "He will have his guns, and I will redeem my honor and my life. That is my plan."

Harrison stared at her. He could not think of anything to say.

"Harry, if he doesn't get them then he will surely lose."

"Then we will all be dead. Is that it?"

"Look out there," she said. "This is the beginning."

Harrison watched her men assemble the train of wagons.

"How do you plan to get Japanese weapons to Villa through the American blockade?"

"We, Harry." She kissed him on the forehead. "You and I are going to do it."

"Now I'm a gunrunner," he mumbled.

"You are a good businessman," she answered seriously.

He looked at her and smiled.

"We must move quickly," Maria told him.

"Move where?" Harrison asked.

"We go to the ocean. We ride with our wagons empty. "My plan must work. Come, Harry. The men are waiting for us."

"Who else knows of this other part of the plan?"

"Only Mr. Jones. You must tell no one," she insisted. "And now we will do a little play acting."

Harrison nodded.

"But later, when we have our shipment, you will meet with that German officer who killed Bart's spy. He advises the Mexican Army," Maria told him as they walked to the door. "He will meet us at the ships, and take the weapons," Maria said, as the two walked into the courtyard to join the others. "We will receive our payment at our meeting with him."

"What about the rebels?" Harrison asked.

"Don't worry, Harry, they are hiding in the mountains," she answered, now standing with the men. "They run from General Obregon."

James stopped to consider. He was still not convinced enlisting in her new adventure was a good idea. His business was across the border, in Columbus. Yet this German may just be the person he needed to speak with. He may hold the clues to Bart's investigation and his death. And I cannot allow Maria to go on this adventure without me, James thought. If something happened to her…. I have a duty to her, as well as to my brother. He had made his decision.

"Well then. I guess I'm now a smuggler, as well as a murderer and horse thief," he said with a weary smile.

CHAPTER TWENTY-THREE

An hour later, in the early morning darkness, six riders surrounded a train of seven heavy wagons, each driven by two well-armed teamsters. They had departed the walled hacienda and were following the well-worn road to Ascension, then through the Sierra Madres. The big grain wagons were each pulled by a team of six mules. The train moved faster than Harrison had expected.

The wagons were partially loaded with sacks of grain. When he asked why, Maria said, "The Indian people are starving. Six years of war have destroyed almost everything but the oil fields. This grain will guarantee our safe passage through Yaqui lands."

Harrison felt good being out in the country. He was a bit saddle sore, but his injuries had healed. The cool, dry air refreshed his skin. Maria had given him a brightly colored, woolen serape to hang over his thin cotton shirt. She had managed to rescue his felt hat, although by now it was severely worn, with the bullet hole and stains from his own blood. He had mended the hole, creased it, and reworked the brim. Fashionable enough for a gunrunner, he smiled. His .32 Colt was lost, but Maria had provided him with a new model Colt .38, much heavier than his own weapon. Harrison had carried one before and knew what it could do.

Riding next to Maria at the head of the train, Harrison looked over at his companion. Like him, she was draped in a serape. Hers was green and yellow. She wore no hat, and her pistol was riding high on her narrow waist. Boots covered her denim trousers to the knees. She rode her mount gracefully, something only a very experienced horseman could do in the rough terrain of northern Mexico. Seeing Maria poised on the stallion, he thought her a figure of exquisite beauty.

The column moved as quickly as the wagons allowed, until finally reaching the edge of the Sierra Madre Mountains. Around midday they entered a small, isolated settlement of adobe huts situated in the foothills. It was the first village they had encountered. Here they stopped to water and rest the horses and mules. Harrison looked around the Indian settlement, a dozen small adobe huts spread out around a central area. He saw garden plots with broken stalks of corn, brown and withered, just beyond. Dogs barked everywhere, announcing their arrival. He saw no horses.

At first, the adults stayed away from the village center. Only the children gathered around the riders as they dismounted. Finally, recognizing Maria, both men and women left their thick-walled adobe houses to greet her. The Indians had chopped, shoulder length black hair, and were dressed in brightly colored homespun cotton. They stood around the wagons. Harrison felt uneasy and stepped closer to Maria to protect her.

"Don't worry, Harry." She touched his arm. "They are friends." She motioned to her brother, who walked to the back of the lead wagon.

"Venga!" he yelled, waving to the men from the village. He threw back a canvas cover to reveal sacks of grain stacked three deep.

The men gathered around the wagon, but waited. Finally, an older man approached from behind the group. He stood directly in front of Daniel. Holding something in his hand, he began to speak.

"Who is he?" Harrison asked Maria softly.

"He is the Elder," she whispered. "He is thanking us for the grain."

When the chief finished speaking, he handed Daniel an object wrapped in sheep skin. Daniel unwrapped it. He held it up. It was a wool blanket woven of many bright colors.

"Gracious," Daniel said. He had taken off his sombrero and held it at his side.

The chief bowed, and then waved for the others to come forward.

*

They rode across the rough lands and mountains of Sonora, then down into the desert again. After three more days of hard travel, they met and followed a road near the sea. Late the fourth day, they arrived in Guaymas, on the Gulf of the California coast.

The night before arriving at their destination, Maria unexpectedly rode off toward the east. The hour was late. She had told Harrison nothing. He spent the time she was gone raging and walking around the camp. Shortly after dawn, as the sun inched above the mountains, she returned.

"God damn it," he said to her.

"Yes, my love?" she answered, smiling.

"I worried about you. Anything could have happened. They could have kidnapped you." Harrison did not bother to mask his anger.

"You are right," she said, pulling him into the shadows, kissing him. "But they did not." She wrapped her serape around both of them, then she fumbled with Harrison's belt. "Now," she whispered. I must have you now, my love." She threw off his belt and reached into his trousers.

Harrison's anger quickly dissipated. He unbuckled her gun belt and let it drop to the ground. Then he reached up under her blouse, feeling for her breasts.

Both giggled while they removed their boots and jeans. "Shhh," Maria whispered. "Or Mr. Jones will catch us." Both were naked from the waist down and still standing. Harrison's hands moved across her body, massaging.

"Hold me," she whispered in his ear. "Hold me and I will take your anger, my love." Maria jumped into his arms, wrapping her legs around him.

He held her by her thighs, bracing his back against a small white pine, while she slowly raised and lowered herself.

""We must be fast, my love. But not so very fast," she said. Then she kissed him hard on his lips, holding his head in her hands.

*

The trip had been wearing for both riders and beasts. Arriving in the seaside pueblo of Guaymas late in the afternoon, Maria immediately found the single hotel.

"Stay with the men and make sure the mules and horses are rested, fed, and watered. And here is money to buy food for the men," she ordered, giving Jose a handful of Mexican silver dollars. "Be ready to leave by sunup."

Daniel and Harrison followed her as she climbed to the veranda of the wood and adobe two-story hotel near the waterfront.

"Look there! Out on the water," Maria said, pointing at a pair of two-masted schooners anchored a hundred yards off shore in the azule waters of the Gulf of California. "Those are our ships. Daniel, tell Mr. Jones that the ships are here," she ordered. "He will know what to do."

Daniel walked rapidly away.

"Here waiting for us, Harry," she said, smiling happily at him. "This is a very good sign."

"They gave the American gun boats the slip, Maria?"

"The cargo came in on an ocean liner. We moved the guns to smaller boats—these sailing ships," she told him as they entered the lobby of the hotel. "The Americans did not see."

"You planned well." Harrison took her arm. Things would work out, he thought.

"The gunrunners are expensive, and very greedy," she said, fretting. "They will take some of our profits."

As they walked together to the front desk, someone called out for Maria. "Fraulein Washington. Welcome!" A light-complected man came face to face with the two. He wore a gray uniform, beautifully tailored to his slim figure.

"Colonel Von Moltke. How nice to see you," Maria replied in a soft, feminine voice. She held out her hand.

The officer delicately lifted her fingers and bowed over them.

"I am most pleased to see you. And on time, too," he said with a German accent. "Ja, and your associate?" He straightened up to look at James.

"This is Mr. Harrison James, colonel." Maria saw a twitch on the German's scarred cheek as he looked directly at Harrison.

"James?" Von Moltke asked as he held out his hand.

Harrison guessed Von Moltke to be about 40. He had a narrow face with sandy brown hair cropped close to the skull. Although blue like his own,, Von Moltke's eyes were more like those of Harrison's mother—hard and pitiless. Two scars slashed across the pale skin of each cheek. A thin, arched nose dominated the skull-like face. The narrowest of mustaches slashed across his upper lip. He was otherwise clean-shaven, and by the sharpest of razors, Harrison noticed. "Bartlett James was my brother," he said, releasing Von Moltke's hand.

"Captain James, sir? Ja, I met your brother." The cold, blue stare held steady. "I was sorry to hear he died. Most unfortunate. A worthy adversary," Von Moltke added.

Harrison nodded in return. The colonel was a German aristocrat, he knew. He had heard the family name mentioned in European political circles. He recalled many Frenchmen still discussing Von Moltke the Elder in reference to their defeat at the hands of the Germans in 1871. For all his perfect manners, there was something frightening, almost grotesque, about Von Moltke the Younger. "Are you related to Helmuth Von Moltke, Chief of Staff of the German Army?" Harrison asked.

The German obviously was surprised that Harrison knew anything about the German Army. "He is my brother, sir. Do you know him?"

"Only of him, sir."

Von Moltke insisted they have tea and relax before any discussion of business. As they sat in the dining room,Von Moltke dominated the conversation. "It has been difficult to train these natives to be good soldiers," he stated with contempt. "They have no appreciation of discipline." He looked at Maria as he spoke.

Harrison looked at Maria for her reaction. He was unprepared when, suddenly, soldiers converged on the table with rifles aimed. Harrison attempted to pull his revolver from its holster, but stopped when he felt the cold barrel of a rifle at the back of his head.

Colonel Von Moltke, watching the two of them, smiled thinly. "Please, Herr James, give me your weapon. And yours, too, Fraulein Washington." He held out his hand.

CHAPTER TWENTY-FOUR

"You will turn over the guns to me, as we agreed," Von Moltke said in a cold, crisp voice. "Please, be comfortable. You are my guests." He removed a pre-rolled cigarette from a silver case and offered Harrison one. "Herr James?"

"I don't indulge, sir," Harrison answered. He was studying the guards.

"Colonel, we will take our payment and go, as we agreed," Maria told him, beginning to stand.

"You will stay, fraulein," Von Moltke ordered icily. "There is a change in plan." The German stared at her. "There will be no payment. Did you think, Fraulein Washington, that General Obregon would allow a half-breed whore to profit from the Mexican Army?"

"If I don't give you the guns, colonel?" she responded with a flash of anger. "You need a password to get them unloaded."

"If you do not, then I will kill your brother," Von Moltke told her calmly. "Your brother and your men are also my guests. See for yourself." He escorted her to the open door of the hotel. Harrison quietly followed the two, with a guard at his heels. Two Mexican soldiers dragged a bound figure out of the doorway of the adobe jail. While one man kept his rifle pointed at Daniel's head, the other threw him into the dusty street. "Those are two of my best men," Von Moltke said distinctly. "But they will not kill him. Instead, I will cut him to pieces with a saber. One piece at a time."

Frightened for Daniel, Maria tried to run into the street, but Harrison grabbed her, holding her tightly.

"Maria," he cautioned.

She caught herself. Fighting to hold back her growing rage and fear, Maria glared at the German officer now standing beside her. "What kind of a man are you?"

"Fraulein, I am a soldier, dealing with bandits." They turned back into the hotel. "Now, we understand each other," Von Moltke told her.

With Mexican soldiers posted at the windows, the three sat in the lobby's wicker chairs waiting for the weapons to be off-loaded from the ships and onto the wagons.

A soldier entered and whispered something into Von Moltke's ear. "Good, good," he said with a smile. The soldier turned and left the room. "It turns out we didn't need your password, fraulein. My men were evidently persuasive enough. The weapons have been loaded into the wagons."

"Was there ever any money to pay for the weapons, colonel?" Maria asked, bitterly.

"Of course," The German replied with contempt in his voice. "However, now it will be appropriated by the German Government for other purposes."

"Colonel, why do you care what goes on here in Mexico? I would think the German Army has more important things to worry about," Harrison said, directing the conversation away from Maria.

"Nein, Herr James. Mexico is an important part of our plans. The Kaiser himself has stated so."

"Plans for what, colonel?"

Von Moltke smiled. "I am rebuilding the Mexican Army. Soon it will be strong enough to finally defeat all the rebel factions. General Obregon will unite Mexico under the banner of El Presidente Carranza."

"How will this help the German Empire, sir?"

"Mr. James, you are an educated man. Consider. A united Mexico will become an important strategic ally of the German Empire."

"With its great oil reserves?" Harrison asked, putting it together.

"Of course, that, too, Mr. James."

"You are wrong, colonel," Maria said flatly. "Not even Carranza would betray Mexico to serve the will of the Germans. Not for the Americans, and not for you."

Harrison frowned at her, willing her to be silent.

Lighting another cigarette, Colonel Von Moltke smiled. "Betray Mexico, señorita? Certainly not. Rather to serve her, by gaining back Texas. Perhaps even more of the former territories taken from her by the Americans."

Both Harrison and Maria understood immediately what Von Moltke meant.

"My intelligence suggests that many along the border would welcome that arrangement," he went on. "Our spies tell us that many areas are ripe for re-conquest, even now." Von Moltke's cigarette smoke hung drifting in the hotel lobby. "Perhaps that was why Pancho Villa invaded and why the American Army chased him," Von Moltke said. He looked at Harrison. "But your army failed to defeat even a bandit. How can you expect to defeat Germany, Mr. James?"

"Tell me about my brother. How did you know him?" Harrison asked, tiring of the subject.

"When we met, Herr James, our countries were not at war, so circumstances were different. I believed there would be war between our countries. Your brother shared that opinion, but we became associates, in a way, here in Mexico," he stated, inhaling lightly on the cigarette. "He was engaged in building spy services, as I was later to discover."

"What do you mean, sir?" Harrison asked, pretending ignorance.

"Captain James was engaged in espionage against the German Empire," Von Moltke answered. Then he added contemptuously, "I see that you yourself have managed to remain disengaged? From the war. And apparently very well off."

"My brother commanded a company of infantry, sir."

"Your brother was like myself," Von Moltke answered. With his expressionless narrow face, he reminded Harrison of one of the large, scaled lizards he had seen on the trip down the coast. "He was doing many things while your American Army blundered through the countryside like a blind elephant."

Harrison quietly listened.

"Your brother was a courageous, intelligent soldier. He even used several of my own employees. He bribed one to obtain the details of a proposed alliance, defensive of course, that the Reich was negotiating secretly with the government of Mexico. Foreign Secretary Zimmermann was most upset that Captain James had discovered its terms."

"Encouraging the Mexicans to invade the United States and retake Texas, New Mexico, and Arizona?" James asked.

"You are too dramatic," Von Moltke snapped. "That was, in reality, only a little incentive that the Secretary offered the Mexicans for signing the agreement." He made a visible effort to calm himself.

"So you see, the Americans already knew the details of our proposed treaty before the English told them. All this, because of your brother." Then Von Moltke smiled his thin smile. "That is another excellent reason for my satisfaction at finding you, Herr James, to be another of my guests."

Harrison observed the last rays of a January sun lengthening across the wood floor. He wondered what would happen next.

Von Moltke smiled at Maria. "It is time to go." He turned to the Mexican guards. "Take the prisoners to the dock."

"My brother?" Maria asked as a Mexican soldier pulled her up and pushed her toward the door.

"For now, he will remain where he is," Von Moltke replied.

The group arrived in time to see the last of the weapons from the two schooners loaded into the heavy wagons. Ten armed Mexican soldiers surrounded laborers conscripted from the town. Maria's men were nowhere to be seen.

"Release the hostages from the ships. Tell their crews they will get their money when all the weapons are loaded," Von Moltke ordered. "Take the whore to the warehouse with the others. Tie her up. Mr. James and her brother will accompany me."

"Wait! Take me as your hostage," Maria pleaded. "Do with me what you will, but let my brother go. He's of no use to you."

"You life is of no value to me," the German said with a scoff. "A whore that not even Villa wants. Anyway fraulein, El Presidente will not hang a woman for spying, and we must hang someone as an example. Politics you understand."

"My brother? He's no spy," Maria said with dread in her voice.

"You are the American spy. Yes, I know this," Von Moltke said. "But he will do. I suggest that you return to the border quickly or your fate will be worse than that worthless brother of yours."

"You bastard son of a snake," she hissed in English. Two soldiers carried her away kicking and screaming. "Bastardo! Hijo del Diablo!"

"Fraulein Washington, I wish you a pleasant evening, and thank you for your assistance to the Mexican Government." He smiled and bowed with elaborate courtesy. Von Moltke then turned to one of his soldiers. "Prepare the hostages for travel, sergeant," he ordered.

"Sí, Colonel," the young man responded.

A third soldier roughly bound Maria's hands with rawhide rope. Then all three dragged her through the wide doorway of an old wooden warehouse standing near the wharf.

"Bastardo," she hissed at the soldier tying her hands. "Hijo de la bruja!"

"Ha, puta," one solder laughed as he threw her forward into the darkness. "Silencia puta!"

The other soldiers closed and bolted the double doors.

In the damp, musty darkness of the wooden building, Maria struggled to her feet, her cheek burning and slightly bruised from hitting the floor. While twisting her wrists in the rope, she called out to each of her men and they all responded, except Mr. Jones. "Señor Jones, donde esta?" she called out. Then, through the cracks in the old wood planks, she saw guards moving about.

"Tranquilo!" one of them called. "Silencio!" He pounded against the wood door with his rifle butt.

"En Engles," she ordered.

"He disappeared just before the soldiers came," José answered. In the shadows, her muchachos gathered around her, including the teamsters. All had been disarmed and were bound. From the wide cracks, slivers of light broke through.

"Untie me, quickly," she ordered José, turning her back to him.

"Señorita Washington, they took our guns and horses," he said as he worked the rope loose with his fingers. "They are many, no? How can we chase them?"

"They will kill Daniel," she said, working Jose's rope loose from behind her. Finally, both were freed. Maria began to pace about the building, thinking. "I know this."

"Señorita, gasolina. Gasolina," one of the teamsters called out from the far side of the building. Everyone immediately stopped what they were doing to smell.

"No!" The men ran to the door and began pounding. "No! No!" they yelled.

*

Seconds later, in the darkness, they heard gunfire, yelling, and then nothing.

"Who's there?" Maria called out. There was no reply.

Then, one of the large doors slowly creaked open. It was Mr. Jones. "They have Daniel, and I do not know about Mr. James," she told him, excited. "I must ride to Villa and warn him. The general will surely kill Daniel, along with the Carrancistas."

Mr. Jones nodded his head. Behind him, three Mexican soldiers lay dead on the ground, their rifles beside them. A torch made of rags lay smoldering on the ground beside one.

"What do you mean, señorita?" José asked, surprised.

"I made a deal with him, José. I told him about the shipment and where it was going. General Villa is waiting in the foothills." She shook her head. "I have no time to explain. We must act quickly. Find Harry. Daniel is with the German and will be caught in the middle of the fighting."

The older man now held her firmly. Her efforts to break free were futile.

"You knew of this, Viejo?" José looked at Mr. Jones for an answer.

The old man again nodded.

"You make deals, señorita," José said angrily, "and with muchachos we cannot trust."

"Did you expect me to allow Obregon and his Germans to destroy the revolution?" she hissed. "Now, I must go."

"No, señorita!" José told her. "It is too dangerous for you. I will go."

Maria nodded, appearing to acquiesce. Hesitating at first, Mr. Jones finally let her go.

Before either man could react, she jerked out the old man's automatic. "Lo siento, amigos. I got us into this. Now, I will get us out of it." Maria held the weapon in the air for everyone to see, then ran toward Mr. Jones' mount just outside the door. It was her own stallion. She smiled at them, took the reins, and swung easily into the saddle. "Wait for me up the coast. You know where," she said, throwing down the saddlebags.

Mr. Jones picked up the bags.

"There is enough money to take care of everyone," she said. "If I do not return in one day, go to the hacienda." She spun the horse and left. Seeing no soldiers, she headed up the street to the hotel to find James.

"What happened to the tall American?" she asked the desk clerk in Spanish.

Finding that her man, too, was taken by the soldiers, she rode off toward the south at a full gallop, keeping the Gulf on her right.

*

The train of seven heavily loaded wagons was escorted by 20 riders. The trip down the coast had been fast, with the road clear all the way. Harrison rode in the lead beside Colonel Von Moltke, his wrists loosely tied in front of him, while Daniel was tightly bound, hands behind his back, in the second wagon. A Mexican soldier sat on each side of him.

On the first day, the group traveled for only several hours, then made camp. But by evening of the third day they had reached Culiacan, a Carranza stronghold. Here, they rested the animals and men to prepare them for the journey through the mountains.

Very little had been said between the two white men during the trip south to Culiacan. After arriving in the dusty little pueblo, the Colonel immediately circled the wagons just outside of town and stationed guards to protect the valuable cargo.

Harrison insisted that both he and Daniel were civilians and noncombatants. Von Moltke ordered that they be treated as criminals. "You do not have proper papers, Herr James. The Mexican Government will determine your fate—with my help," Von Moltke stated when Harrison demanded an explanation. "I suspect that both of you are spies for the Villaistas," he said. "I suggest you prepare a defense." The German smiled.

"What good am I to you, Colonel?" Harrison asked when they arrived in Culiacan. "You know I'm not a spy."

"Herr James, as I said, your presence is a welcome surprise for me personally. I know much about you and your family's influence. Randolph James, Commodity Brokers, is very wealthy, I am told.

But Herr James, I don't care about such things. I will keep you with me as insurance. If I must, I will ransom you for safe passage back to Germany."

"Not all that sure of Germany's victory, colonel?" Harrison said.

"The German Empire will always continue," Von Moltke replied with certainty. "But a soldier's life is not so certain—as your brother discovered."

Harrison glared at the soldier, hating him even more.

"I will keep you safe in a good Mexican prison, Herr James," Von Moltke continued, "because you already know too much and cannot go free. Maybe when the war is over—if the Mexicans don't shoot you—then, perhaps, you can go home to your Chicago." He smiled that evil smile.

"I will escape," Harrison answered. "I will fight you until my last dying breath."

"That, too, can be arranged." The German smiled. "If you try to escape? In that case, you will be turned over to the Mexican government and hung as a spy. I promise you that."

*

James stayed that evening with Von Moltke in a large hacienda on the edge of town, while Daniel, under heavy guard, slept under a wagon.

James and Von Moltke sat in front of a blazing fire following a meal of red beans and rice washed down with tequila. Two guards with rifles stood against the wall behind them.

"Colonel, did you have my brother killed?" Harrison asked directly, the two men sitting in front of a blazing fire, each with a tumbler of tequila in hand.

"Herr James, I will tell you a secret, since it is no longer important to me and my work here in Mexico. When we discovered we had been betrayed, we set a trap. For bait, we used documents that were of no value."

"No good?" James was confused.

"Bait for our little trap."

"To capture my brother?"

"Not your brother," Von Moltke said. "His agent. When the treaty was revealed to the Americans, we figured out that it was your brother who had received the information, but from whom?"

"The woman," James said. "Who told you about Bart's other activities?"

"He had been betrayed."

"By one of your agents?"

"Da, Mr. James. One of our new agents, and very reliable, too."

"Do you pay your agents well to spy on my country, Colonel?"

"That way is the best, I think," Von Moltke replied seriously. "No passion, no politics, just the exchange of money for information. Here in Mexico, where politics change often, that way works best," Von Moltke said. "As an American, I think you understand this."

"You were after just one spy then?" James said, sipping from the tequila. He handed the German the bottle. He refused to pour for him.

"It was only the woman on my staff we worried about. Your brother led us right to her. They were so clever, but not clever enough. She was preparing to tell the Americans what more she learned when we silenced her."

"Who told you?"

Von Moltke smiled. "Herr James, I cannot tell you that, of course. But our agent said to watch Captain James closely. He is much more than an officer of infantry."

"Is he an American?" James asked, persistent.

"You will never know," Von Moltke smiled.

"You must protect your agents, eh?"

"Of course."

James watched him finish off his glass of tequilla. He had a difficult time believing Von Moltke did not order Bart killed. James continued to watch the German with hatred.

"Your brother's actions threatened my mission here in Mexico, and greatly disturbed me."

"So you had him killed?"

"We could not allow our mission to fail."

"You've answered my question, colonel," James said, his voice steady, without emotion. Cold as ice.

"I must tell you, it is good for us that Captain James is dead."

"I must know the name of the man who killed by brother," James said. "Please, tell me. What difference does it make now?"

Von Moltke looked long and hard at James, as if trying to make up his mind. "Before you die, Mr. James, you will learn his identity. But not before."

The Prussian Colonel looked again into the fireplace, staring at the flames. He smiled, but suddenly felt weary. He poured himself another drink, then refilled the American's glass. "Drink up, Mr. James. The next few days will be very difficult for you."

CHAPTER TWENTY-FIVE

The train of wagons resumed its march eastward before dawn the following morning. The day was bright and still. A great cloud of dust from the plodding hooves hung in the air above them. It could be seen for miles. By early afternoon, they had reached the foothills of the Sierra Madre. The terrain became rougher, the road narrower as they began their ascent into the mountains of central Mexico. The train of heavily loaded wagons moved slowly upward. Harrison surveyed the narrow road rising into the distance.

"Who controls this part of the country?" he asked Von Moltke, raising his voice above the noise.

"Herr James, no need to worry. The Mexican Army will protect you," Von Moltke replied confidently, then galloped forward to study the road, leaving his prisoner behind.

Harrison worked at the rope loosely binding his wrists. He turned to look. Daniel was still two wagons back and under heavy guard.

As Harrison tried to free himself, two rifle shots echoed from the overhanging cliffs. The shots were followed rapidly by a full volley. The firing was directed at the front of the column. Men and mules fell, stopping all forward movement.

Finally slipping free of the rope, Harrison rolled from his mount just as a second fusillade of gunfire erupted. He picked himself up quickly from the rocky ground, crouched down low, and ran to the second wagon, reaching its metal step in one determined movement. The guards were taking cover along the road. Harrison pulled Daniel off the wagon, lifting him by his shirt collar. Daniel partially jumped from the seat, his hands still tightly bound. He hit the ground on his shoulder, rolling to break the fall.

As Harrison dived for cover behind Daniel, he saw the first wagon's driver fall to the right and forward, the side of his head disintegrating in a bloody spray. Soldiers, desperately seeking shelter behind the large rocks alongside of the trail, began to return fire against the shadowy targets in the cliffs above them.

"Under the wagon!" Daniel yelled at Harrison as he rolled across the hard ground. Bullets shattered the stones, sending splinters of rock in all directions. Daniel scrambled to get under the wagon.

Harrison managed to pick up a dead soldier's rifle as he, too, crawled under the wagon. They looked at each other.

"Untie me!" the younger man ordered.

Harrison released the young man. To escape, they would need each other.

Heavy firing continued all along the mountain pass. Once over their surprise, the Colonel's Carrancistas put on a vigorous counterattack. Harrison looked for the German. He saw him ten meters up the road, at a bend in the trail. Still mounted, Von Moltke commanded a few soldiers near him. Vigorously waving his arm, he directed them to climb the rocks and meet their attackers. Behind him, further down the road, James saw that the rearguard, although still fighting, was being picked off in ones and twos. Time was running out.

"Follow me," Harrison yelled, grabbing the shorter man by the arm and leading him forward.

"A donde?" Daniel was frightened and confused.

"Get up the road, quickly!" Harrison ordered. The two men ran low to reach a large boulder beside the trail. Dangerously close to a steep ravine, they balanced themselves on a narrow lip of rock. Harrison had picked up another rifle and bandoleers of ammunition lying nearby. Both now armed, they looked up and down the road for an avenue of escape. Harrison knew they had to move, but where?

Behind them, the firing intensified with the Colonel's men now engaged at close quarters with Villa's, who began to pour down the side of the mountain. The wagons were frozen in place, with their teamsters dead or running. The rebels, dressed in colorful cotton and wearing large sombreros, were easily distinguished from Von Moltke's uniformed soldiers. The bearded, and in some cases bare footed, army rushed forward to claim their prize.

The fighting continued ahead of them. The Colonel's men held positions between the attackers and the road. James noticed that the German himself had dismounted to climb the jagged, boulder-strewn mountain.

"Come on!" he yelled to Daniel, seeing an opportunity.

Rifles in hand, they dashed for the bend and two horses without riders. One soldier had remained on the road to hold the mounts. Harrison was almost upon him when the soldier turned. Seeing the tall man racing towards him, the soldier quickly dropped the reins and drew his revolver. Another shot sounded, and the soldier fell to the ground, a single bullet hole in his head. Harrison looked behind him.

"We are even now, gringo," Daniel yelled from a kneeling position five meters back. He worked the rifle bolt to expel the empty casing and insert another cartridge.

"The horses! Before they get away," Harrison shouted, pointing. Reaching the horses, both mounted quickly.

"Up the mountain," Daniel yelled.

*

They rode up the mountain, rounding a bend in the road twenty meters from where the battle raged. Suddenly, three barefooted gunmen stepped onto the road from behind large boulders. They looked like children, still their rifles were pointed directly at Harrison and Daniel.

"Pare," the middle one ordered in a high pitched voice.

The two men reined in their horses to stop.

The young soldier motioned with his rifle for the riders to dismount.

Daniel and Harrison did as ordered. For what seemed like an eternity, they stood facing off with the three young gunmen. No one spoke. Finally, another man stepped onto the road. He was dressed differently from the others, wearing high cavalry boots and a gray suit coat. A pistol was strapped to his side. He wore a fedora with a wide, rounded brim. The hat set back on his head, exposing a full head of dark hair and a high forehead. His face was creased and furrowed from years in the Mexican sun. But it was a very animated face, with clear brown eyes that seemed to miss nothing. Harrison felt his dark eyes on him, like Maria's, taking his measure.

"Oiga, amigos. Where you go?" the man asked, then gave a quick order to his soldiers. They lowered their rifles, but remained in place blocking the road.

Harrison decided the man must be an officer. "You speak English?" Harrison asked. Daniel said nothing.

"Of course. I like gringos, so I learn English," the man said. "Are you the one called Harry?"

"Who's asking, amigo?"

"Perdón a mi. I am not very polite," he said sincerely. There was a shyness about him, stated in the way his dark eyes looked down. "I am called General Francisco Villa." He bowed from the waist. "Now, I ask again. "Are you Harry?" The shyness quickly changed to a cold demand.

The gunfire just behind them continued.

"I'm Harrison James," he replied, suspicious. "Who told you my name?"

"A very beautiful señorita," Villa answered with a smile. "She said I must save you. But I see that it was not necessary." He then looked over to Harrison's mount. "Is that the horse of Von Moltke?"

"I don't know," Harrison said. "It was the first horse I saw."

Villa gave an order to one of his men. He ran to Harrison's mount, removed the saddle bags, then, just as quickly, returned to hand them to the General.

Both Harrison and Daniel still held their rifles, but neither threatened to use it.

"Gracias, muchacho," Villa said, taking the saddle bags. He quickly untied the strap from one of the leather bags. Looking inside, he smiled broadly. "Muy bien, Harry," he said.

"What are you talking about?" Harrison said.

Villa reached in and pulled out a bundle of American currency. "The money for the guns, amigo," he said. "It is here."

At that moment a voice from above them in the rocks called down, "You mean my money, General."

Harrison and Daniel looked up to see Maria standing above them. She made her way to the road. Two more of Villa's men followed her down.

"Maria," Harrison said surprised. "Yes, it's you."

Villa looked up at the young woman coming toward him and roared with laughter. "Of course, señorita. Your money."

When Maria reached the road, she ran to embrace Harrison, then kissed Daniel on the cheek. "You both are alive," she said concerned for them. "Did that evil bastardo hurt you?"

"I'm okay, sister," Daniel said, embarrassed by her fussing.

General Villa watched them with great interest, as if he were jealous of the affection they were receiving. "My sister, Maria. And my ally, amigos," he announced. "Now we can continue to fight for justice."

Another of Villa's men approached from the scene of battle. He carried two rifles. The firing became sporadic. The man, older than the others, spoke quickly to his general, then handed him one of the rifles.

"Good news, amigos," Villa announced to Harrison, Daniel, and Maria. The fight is over. Obregón's men are defeated. And we have an important prisoner." He held the rifle in the air and shouted, "Viva la revolución! Viva México!"

A great cheer went up from around the mountain top.

Villa began to carefully examine the weapon.

Harrison looked Villa's soldiers over. He saw that the men who had come down with Maria weren't much older than the others already on the road, and dressed just as poorly—frayed and patched clothing, simple straw sandals, and several were missing sombreros. But everyone had bandoliers of ammunition crisscrossing their thin chests. They were armed with rifles of various models and makes.

Fearless, Maria walked over to General Villa and spoke to him quietly in Spanish. Harrison and Daniel watched with interest. Villa's soldiers began to spread out across the area of combat, each assigned to different tasks.

"Hermana," Villa said loudly. He looked over to Harrison, smiling. "Your woman is a tough trader, amigo. Esta bien, muchacha," he then said to Maria. "Para frijoles." He held two bundles of currency in his hand. Maria tied up the saddlebags and turned to walk back to Harrison and Daniel.

Villa watched her, then said, "Señorita, next time it must be machine guns. Obregón has too many soldiers. I need machine guns to kill them all."

Maria handed the saddlebags to Daniel. "General, there are no more for sale."

"Steal them, hermana. You must steal them," Villa said.

Harrison knew that he was serious.

One of Villa's soldiers brought his horse from somewhere up the mountain. General Villa mounted the brown stallion in one graceful motion. "Adiós, amigos," he said with a wave. "I hope you find what you are looking for," he called to Harrison.

"General, someday we'll meet again," Harrison said.

"No, gringo, you will never see me again," Villa replied softly. "Siete Leguas, vaya," he said softly, and galloped down toward the wagons.

"Viva la revolución! Viva Villa!" Daniel shouted.

General Villa pulled up, turned in the saddle, to wave his fedora. "Tierra, libertad y equalidad," he shouted back. Another loud cheer was heard across the mountain top.

Harrison watched Pancho Villa ride away toward his spoils. Villa's war for justice, he observed, was now being fought by barefoot boys.

He then looked over to Maria and smiled. *Did she risk her life for Daniel and me, or for the money? I truly believe she did it for us,* he decided.

Another young rebel brought Maria's horse to her. She threw the saddlebags across the saddle and mounted. "We ride," she called to her companions.

"Where to, sister?" Daniel said, also mounting.

"Durango," she answered, then rode off up the mountain. Harrison and Daniel followed.

*

By dusk of that same day, they decided to make camp for the night. They found a level spot off the trail with a stream nearby.

"Where are we anyway?" Harrison asked, resting his head against the saddle. He had found ponchos and a blanket strapped to two of the horses. At that altitude, temperatures fell quickly. He couldn't find any matches to build a fire with.

"Three, maybe four days ride from Durango, I think," Daniel responded. He was intently looking through the saddle bags he carried on his horse.

"Any food in there?" Harrison asked, watching Daniel poke through the bags.

Maria had walked into the bushes to find the stream.

"Nothing to eat, anyway, white man," Daniel said sourly. "I found matches. And cigarettes."

"You can call me Harrison or call me Mr. James, but stop calling me that," Harrison said, looking straight at Daniel. "Give me the matches and I'll build us a fire."

Daniel handed the matches over. "Then I will call you Harry. It is what my hermana calls you, no?"

"That'll work."

Laying the cigarettes aside, Daniel dug deeper into the leather bags. "Harry," he said, smiling. "I think I find something." He pulled out his hand. He was holding several bars of German chocolate and cigarettes. He offered Harrison a chocolate bar, but kept the cigarettes for himself.

"Thanks."

Daniel tore open a pack and lit a German cigarette, but continued searching through the bags. "What is this? A book?" he asked, pulling out the leather bound object.

"Let me see that," Harrison said.

Daniel handed it to him.

"Maybe Von Moltke's," Harrison said, carefully looking at the dark green leather. He opened it. On the first page he saw a map of Mexico. He leafed through the journal to the final entry. "January 28, 1918. Felix has delivered a message from the American soldier." Harrison translated as he read. "Der andere James muss sterben," Von Moltke had written. "The other James must die." That entry was written two days ago.

"The map may be helpful, eh?" Daniel said.

"I think you're right." Harrison was still distracted by the entry.

"Look. Here's Durango." Daniel said. "A train passes through Durango. See?" Daniel pointed at the thin line on the map. "The tracks are not too far from us. The map tells us how close."

A twig snapped in the darkness. They both heard the noise. "Maria?" Harrison called out.

"So, we go to Durango. Then what?" Maria stepped into the small clearing. Starlight glistened off her tears.

"Maria, you're crying," Harrison said, getting up. He caught her in his arms and they embraced. "Why are you crying?"

"Harry, I thought I'd never see you again. Or Daniel," she said, wiping away the tears. "That man—I thought he'd kill you both even before we could rescue you."

"Maria, what you did.... The courage it must have taken to find Villa. Then to get us," Harrison said. He kissed her with more passion then he ever thought he had to give.

"Whew, Harry," Maria replied with a gasp. "You are so.... I cannot find the word."

Daniel watched in silence.

"How did you find us, hermana?" he asked finally.

"I made a deal with General Villa before we left Las Palomas, Daniel," she replied. "For the weapons."

Harrison began collecting firewood. He didn't want to be part of the discussion on her secret plan.

"A deal with Villa?"

"Yes," she said. I could never betray the revolution."

"You didn't tell me?" Daniel said, hurt by her duplicity.

"I couldn't."

"Did you tell him?" he asked, looking at Harrison.

"Yes," Maria said. "Daniel, I'm sorry. My plan had to be a secret."

"But Harry?"

"I forced her to," Harrison added, returning with an arm full of wood. "I discovered the plan by accident," he lied. He began to build a fire, carefully stacking the wood. Then he struck a match to the kindling.

"Now, it is good that I did, or all would have been lost. The German would have killed you both."

"Yes," was all Daniel said. He reached into the saddlebags, pulling out bundles of one hundred dollar bills. He held one up to examine closely in the light of the fire. The heat from its flames was just beginning to touch them. The dry wood crackled and popped as it ignited.

James knew she was right. They would have shot both of us as spies, he thought.

Maria lay down beside Harrison near the fire. He continued to feed small twigs and bark into the flames. She lay her head on his saddle.

"Harry, I want to tell you something," she said softly, rubbing his back gently with her hand.

"Yes, my love," he replied. "What is it?"

"I won't steal machine guns, even for General Villa," Maria said. "Today, I saw that the war cannot go on much longer. Those muchachos, they seemed so young. Younger even than Daniel.... He has run out of soldiers to die for him, I think."

"Maria," Harrison said, turning to see her loveliness in the light of the fire. "I love you. You are wise, as well as beautiful."

She rose up to embrace him.

CHAPTER TWENTY-SIX

The three bought rail passage on the Mexican National Railroad from Durango to Torreón, then to the Villa stronghold of Chihuahua a week later, finally arriving in Juárez as February ended. Maria bought horses and supplies for the ride to Las Palomas and the Washington hacienda.

After days on the trail, the three reserved two rooms in the finest hotel in town, El Palacio del Revolución, before the final ride home. One room was for Harrison and Maria. Daniel was trying to accept his sister's love for the white man, and even grudgingly admired him.

"Be good to my sister, gringo," Daniel said, winking at Maria. "I see you in the morning, and we go home."

"Hermano, stay out of trouble," Maria said sternly. "And no gambling."

When they had retired to their room, Harrison immediately saw that it was more spacious and better furnished than the rooms he'd had in Columbus. There was even a vanity. Maria had undressed quickly and slid into bed beneath silk sheets, exhausted. She watched as Harrison paced slowly around the room, deep in thought. "What is it, my love?"

He looked at her from across the room. "Maria, I have business here in El Paso that I must attend to."

She immediately sat up, her breasts exposed above the sheets. "What kind of business?"

"An old acquaintance. A man who I think has information."

He turned for the door. "I'm sorry, my love, but I must go."

"Go then," she said sadly. "Wait." Naked, she got out of bed and tip-toed across the room.

James could only stand there watching her, drowning in her perfect beauty.

She threw her arms around him, and kissed him passionately on the lips.

"Come back soon, mi corazon."

Harrison opened the door and left, knowing that if he looked back, he wouldn't go.

Maria lay fully awake in their bed, worrying about her gringo.

*

Harrison found Daniel gambling in the casino below. "Here Harry, deals are made and the most beautiful women in Mexico are found," Daniel told him, obviously excited. Harrison, looking around, saw Mexican soldiers, rich ranchers, and Americans at the gaming tables. Much like European casinos, he thought. The perfect place to buy and sell anything.

Harrison watched the flow of the crowd closely, looking for Smith. Two hours later, sitting at a table playing high stakes poker, flanked by Mexicans and Americans, Harrison noticed a man standing to one side. "I fold," he said. He gathered up his winnings, stood, and walked over to the man.

"Jackson Smith? So it is you," Harrison said.

The man was visibly startled upon being recognized. Finally he spoke. "Harrison James. How are you, old boy?" The two men shook hands.

"I heard you were across the border in El Paso, Mr. Smith, working with the U. S. Army? Is that right?"

"That's correct," Smith answered. At El Paso Feed and Grain, we do business with the army and with ranchers. Just came down here for some leisure time. You know how it is, don't you, Mr. James?" Smith said. He looked strained. "Sorry about your brother. A real tragedy, that. Suicide, I heard."

"How did you hear about it?" Harrison asked him.

"I read it in the paper."

"Does your business take you to that army camp over by Columbus?" Harrison asked.

Smith hesitated. "I've been there. I still do business with the Regiments left there."

"What do you sell to them, Mr. Smith?"

"Grain for their horses, mostly," Smith replied. "Not the same type of work that I did when I worked for Randolph James. Much more like your work, I imagine. Still brokering commodities, Mr. James?"

"I gave that up," Harrison responded. "Now I'm investigating the murder of my brother."

"The murder?" Smith said, beginning to edge away. "I have to go, Mr. James. Someone waiting for me. You know how that is."

"Sorry to hear about your warehouse," Harrison said before Smith could move. "I heard it was arson." He leaned closer. "I also heard you're doing business with the Mexican government. Running the embargo and selling arms.... That sort of thing."

Smith stopped immediately. "Who told you that?" he whispered.

"I've gotten to know some of your associates, Smith. They say you sell thousands of dollars worth of munitions to Mexico—to the government, to Villa. Whoever can pay."

"My associates?"

"It's best if I don't give out their names. I'm sure you understand," Harrison told him.

"Of course," Smith said, staring hypnotized at Harrison, as if he were a snake.

"I've also heard you've built quite a reputation for yourself down here."

"Listen, Mr. James. I may have shipped a couple of items across the border. You can't fault a man for picking up some quick cash, can you?"

"I think the word is smuggling," Harrison told him.

"News travels fast out here, doesn't it?" Smith replied, absently placing a bet.

Harrison sipped at his whisky. It burned. Cheap, he thought.

"Mr. James, I heard Maria Washington shipped a cargo of Japanese guns from Asia, ran the blockade, and delivered them to the Germans at Guaymas. They also call that smuggling. But then, it all depends which side of the border you live on, doesn't it?" Smith lost, and a younger Mexican collected his chips.

"Yes. And no," Harrison said thoughtfully. "Take yourself for instance. If your friends across the border found out that you were identified by your enemies on this side of the border, you might find yourself in a bad spot, one that could cost you dearly. Somebody without a friend on either side of the border." He leaned closer still. "And Smith? I think that's already happened."

"The Washingtons are smugglers and murderers. And you're mixed up in it," Smith hissed. He started walking away.

"Wait," Harrison said. "I have to ask you something."

"Yes?" Smith said, reluctantly turning back to face James.

"Do you think you'll live long enough to see how it all comes out?"

Smith said nothing.

"What did you and Bart talk about when you met him in El Paso? That day just before he died."

"I'm a businessman," Smith said. He was sweating. "I don't know what you're talking about."

"You didn't see my brother?" Harrison pressed.

"No, Mr. James, I did not," Smith answered. Again he turned to leave. "If you'll excuse me?"

"You're a liar, Smith. Tell me what I want to know, or I'll tell somebody what you're really up to." Harrison had the other man's arm, pressing tight.

"I don't think you're in any position to have me arrested." Smith tried to pull free, but couldn't.

"One telegram, Smith—that's all it will take. And I didn't say anything about telling the Army."

Smith looked around. He swallowed hard. "Not here. Let's go over to that corner table, pretend like we're gambling."

They walked over to a roulette table and placed bets.

"We met," Smith admitted. "I needed cash and your brother gave it to me in exchange for some information."

"What did you tell him?"

"I told him about a soldier I saw meeting with a German agent here in El Paso. I saw them meet twice last spring after the army gave up on chasing Pancho Villa."

"Why do you think one was a German agent?"

"I knew him. Felix Sommerfield, the reporter. I was told by Villa's brother that he betrayed Villa to German intelligence. I heard later he was on the payroll of a German colonel named Von Moltke."

"How did you know the soldier was spying?" Harrison was still skeptical. "He wouldn't exactly wear a uniform."

"Earlier that day, I saw the same man in officer's uniform at the Sheldon Hotel. Where I stay. So after he met Sommerfield, I had him followed for several days."

"And?"

"My man followed him to Camp Furlong. I found out he was an officer in one of the Negro companies that rioted in Houston last summer."

"Why did you tell Bart?"

"I'm a businessman, Mr. James. Not a traitor," Smith said. "And I needed the money. I knew Bart would have it."

"Does the officer have a name?"

"I don't know it," Smith replied. "Maybe your brother figured it out, checked the dates I gave him against their duty rosters or something."

"Give me those dates, Smith," Harrison said.

"May 28, June 18, and I saw him the last time on January 27."

"Why do you do it?" Harrison asked, genuinely curious.

"For the money," he said easily, then walked away into the crowd.

"I suggest you get out of El Paso real fast, Smith. Or whatever your name is," Harrison said louder than he had wanted, then watched him disappear deeper into the smoke filled room.

Harrison smiled grimly, and strolled back to the table where Daniel was gambling. Duty rosters, he thought. How do I get Snow to assist me? Or maybe Snow is the traitor?

*

Before riding out of town the next morning, Harrison located a Sunday edition of the *El Paso Sun*. The front page headline caught his attention: "German Officer summarily executed by Villa. German and Mexican governments outraged, threaten retaliation." Maria will like this, he thought, reading the article while waiting for her and Daniel.

Casually glancing through the paper, the first American newspaper he had read in weeks, he saw an advertisement. "Good weapons for sale," it exclaimed in bold print.

When the other two arrived leading horses, Harrison showed Daniel the advertisement. "Is this another competitor?" he asked.

Daniel read the address out loud, smiled, and looked at him. "No longer, Harry. The army put him out of business. Now, he sells only to Americans." He prepared to mount. "Hunting rifles and revolvers for shooting rats."

"When he was selling to the Mexicans, where did he buy his weapons?" Harrison was curious.

"He stole most of them from the army," Maria answered, laughing. "That's how they caught him."

"Where do others get their arms?"

"You mean your friend from last night?"

"Yes. My friend."

"He probably has contracts with the U.S. Army," Daniel said. "You should know, Harry. Men like him work with the gunmakers in el Norte. A hundred rifles here or there. Who cares?"

"Should I?" James responded, trying to put the pieces together.

"They are rich white men, like yourself," Daniel said with a smile. "These hombres don't worry about going to jail. Their rich friends fix everything."

"I think you overestimate my own power and influence," Harrison said dryly.

"Sí, if you wish to believe such things." Daniel looked at Harrison, then he sighed. "Before the embargo, anyone could buy weapons—good weapons."

Maria stood in the bright sunshine, paying no attention to them. She lightly stroked the mane of her horse, then inspected the saddle.

"So, how did it work for you and Maria? They met you at the border and made the deal?"

"No, a man in Columbus made the deal for us. Safer that way."

"A middleman?" James asked. Like Randolph James Commodity Brokers, he suddenly realized, disgusted.

Daniel smiled. "Someone who knows everyone, Harry."

James mounted his horse next to Maria. Daniel rode behind the two.

"Maria," James said, waving the newspaper, "Von Moltke is dead."

"Good, Harry," she said. "He deserved to die."

The three spent most of the ride back to the Washington hacienda without talking. The only sound heard was the wind at their backs. The bright sunshine touched James' face. He enjoyed the fragrance of a desert being reborn as they passed through flowering cacti and sage in bloom. The majestic Socorro's towering presence seemed to guard their solitude. Still, watching Maria gallop across a land exploding with color held the greatest beauty in his eyes.

Paris was a lifetime away, and he knew already that he could never return to her as she was. Selling wheat to the hungry for a profit and providing weapons to governments for obliterating their own progeny now seemed not only ugly, but brutally immoral, he thought, now having had the time to consider things. He understood why Maria and Daniel had smuggled guns. He understood their anger and, most importantly perhaps, he saw the pain of a lost birthright that passed from generation to generation. They had acted from a basic need, not only to survive, but to build a better future for their children.

Daniel and he were both riding beside Maria when she suddenly nudged her dark gelding in the flanks. Full of energy, it galloped off, sending up a curl of brown dust to powder the two men. Maria laughed and Harrison resigned himself to watching her fly across the flat landscape ahead of them.

"Let her go, hombre," Daniel said, smiling.

The riders continued west, the red orange ball of the sun beginning its descent into the southwestern sky.

*

They arrived at the Washington hacienda that same evening. Mr. Jones and José ran excitedly to the gate to greet them. Helping them from their horses, they both were speechless. "You are alive?" Jose asked, hugging Maria and slapping Daniel on the back. "You escape from the German, eh?"

"No German could hold us, amigo," Daniel bragged

Mr. Jones shook Harrison's hand in a distracted way. He was watching Maria walk toward the hacienda. She had left her horse for the men to tend. The house that had been shuttered and dark began to light up, window by window, as it again came alive.

"We could not get a message through to you," Harrison told them. "We tried, but the telegraph was down.

"Sí?" José answered. He turned to Daniel. "I cannot believe you are alive, amigo."

"If it wasn't for the gringo and for my sister, I'd be dead," Daniel responded, and then turned to James. "Harry, we talk more about the business. I want that you understand," he said.

Harrison turned to follow Maria.

"Your sister make the deal with Villa, Señor Daniel. Did you know?" he overheard José say.

"I know about it," Daniel answered.

All Harrison could think of was Maria. Entering the large house, he climbed the stairway. He saw a light in her bedroom, and got to her open doorway in time to watch her wrap a large red blanket around herself.

Maria turned and looked at him. Her clothes were scattered about the floor. "Harry," she smiled. "I thought you would hurry.

"Maria," he said softly.

She let the blanket drop to her feet.

Harrison tore off his clothes. Naked, he walked toward her. She did not move. He kissed her hard on the mouth, then bent down to caress her breast. He felt her nipples growing erect from his touch.

He lifted her up in his arms and carried her to the bed.

"Don't leave me tonight," Maria whispered.

There was no more talk.

*

Later, both lay in Maria's European style tub of slowly cooling water, enjoying the peacefulness of the moment.

"Harry, I must dress," she said, preparing to stand.

Before she could move, Harrison grabbed her by her buttocks and pulled her down. She giggled like a small girl, enjoying his tender playfulness.

The two did not leave each other's arms until the water had cooled and darkness had finally settled in. Lying in her bed, they watched the great wheel of stars in the vast expanse of velvet sky shining through the unshuttered window.

"What will we do now?" Maria asked, gently rubbing his chest.

"Find my brother's killer, then settle the matter of Lieutenant Floyd's death. And clear my name," he told her.

"To Columbus. Then I must go with you," she said. "We are together now."

"No, my love," he said, rolling on his side. "Too dangerous for you."

"Take me with you," she said. "I have many contacts there. I can protect you."

"Out of the question," Harrison told her flatly. "You'd be arrested immediately."

Maria saw that she could not change his mind. "I will send Mr. Jones with you." She nodded vigorously. "Mr. Jones will take you into Columbus by a back way, on horseback through the desert. He knows how to avoid the army patrols. He can get you into town without being seen."

"He would agree to this?"

"Oh yes, Harry," Maria told him. "He owes you a debt. You saved his nephew from the hangman."

Harrison nodded. "I could use his help." He got up and began to dress.

"Mr. Jones has a good friend there who will help you and hide you. Grover will also help."

"Yes. Good work, Maria," James said. But he was forming his own plan.

"Harry, please don't do anything foolish." She was watching him closely.

"Don't worry about me, Maria," he said. "When I return, then we can begin our lives together. Paris, New York—wherever you wish to go. We'll travel on that ship."

Harrison could feel Maria's eyes on him in the dark as he quickly dressed. It was time to move.

"Horses?" he asked, finally putting on his hat. "Your fastest."

"Take mine." Maria's brown moist body shimmered in the moonlight as she came toward him, walking through the shadows. She embraced him one last time. "I love you," she whispered. "Come back to me, my love. Without you, I have no life to live."

He smiled at her, tucking another .38 into his belt. "You are my woman, and we will have that life. Together."

"Be careful," Maria said, holding on to what he had just told her.

"When it's safe for Daniel, I'll send for him. To clear him of the murder charges. But he stays here until he receives a message from me. From me only. Tell him that," Harrison said.

"He will do as you say, Harry," Maria whispered. She wiped away tears and clung to him one last time before he left her.

"Good-by, Maria," he said.

"I'll watch for you," Maria said softly. "Always."

*

Harrison and Mr. Jones rode out through the heavy wooden gate and into the darkness. Harrison thought back to what Juan had told him in the desert not very long ago. "There is no justice without respect," he had said. Justice is much more than applying the rule of law, more than proving innocence or punishing the guilty. The world was much more complex than that. Harrison would see that Bart and his killer received the justice they deserved.

CHAPTER TWENTY-SEVEN

Harrison headed north in the moonlight, traveling across the border and into Columbus with Mr. Jones to guide him. They carefully navigated through an arroyo, the place where he had almost died five weeks earlier. Circling Camp Furlong, they entered town through the Mexican neighborhood on the western side and stabled their horses with Mr. Jones' friend, an older Hispanic man hobbling along on a cane.

The man knew exactly what was expected of him. Mr. Jones remained at the stables, but the old man led Harrison with great energy down dusty back streets until they reached the rear entrance to the Hoover. Here the old man left him, and Harrison entered quietly.

The first person he saw in the kitchen of the hotel was the young clerk. "Miguel," Harrison called from the shadows, catching him by surprise.

Upon hearing that voice, Miguel froze, then he slowly turned to see the tall white man standing before him. "Señor James, it is you?"

"I need your assistance," Harrison said quietly.

"Pero, señor...." The young man continued to stare at him.

"You look as if you've seen a ghost."

"I didn't know what happen to you. There was the shooting. The constable, he is killed. An Indian is found there dead beside him. And you, señor, were gone. The policía look for you. Everyone say you and Daniel Washington kill them. But I cannot believe this. Then Sergeant Juan tell me you escape to Mexico."

"I'm back now, Miguel. I need your help."

"I find you a room now," Miguel said, still surprised. "I keep your bags because, Señor James, someday I know you return to us. I will not tell that you are here, señor." Miguel spoke in a low voice.

"Miguel, you are a smart young man," Harrison said. "Will you do something for me?"

"What I can do, señor, I will do for you."

"Thank you," Harrison said. "And I will do something for you when all this is settled. I have many friends in Chicago and New York. Some of them own large hotels and would like to have a good, young desk manager. They pay well."

"Gracious, Señor James. You are very kind." Miguel smiled broadly.

Harrison considered for a moment. "Miguel," he said, "I need to move through town without being noticed. You understand?"

"Sí."

"No one must know I am here," James stated, watching the young man. "No one."

"Sí. No one will know," Miguel said, thinking. "Do not go on Broadway, señor. Too many soldiers. And stay away from the Last Chance. Maybe I go with you"

"No Miguel, but thanks. I must go alone," Harrison said. He turned quickly and headed for the door. Then he stopped. "Miguel, tell your uncle that I will meet him at the Last Chance in twenty minutes. Please do that."

"No señor. I cannot," Miguel replied.

"Why not?"

"Because two days ago he go to El Paso with his esposa and niño," he replied. "I see them get on the train."

"When will he return?"

"Mañana, I think.

*

A few minutes later, taking an alley route, he stood at the double door to the Last Chance Saloon. He saw Paddy Derry behind the mahogany bar. A few men sat at tables, but no one was at the bar. Good, he thought.

"Paddy," Harrison stated directly as he walked briskly across the large room. "Not much business this evening."

"Sunday be bad, gov'nor. No soldiers an' too many temp'rance goils these days," Derry said, coolly. "And it be late."

"You know a lot about what goes on around here, don't you Paddy?"

Derry was immediately on guard. "I be thinkin' you was long gone, lad. You bein' a wanted man." He watched carefully as James stepped up to the mahogany. "What'll it be for ye? Another Blue Ribbon? But no ice left, gov'nor."

"I need some information, Paddy," Harrison said, only inches from the bartender's face. "And a whisky. Your best."

"I be wonderin', here. The deputy, does he know you be back in town, squire?" Paddy backed away to reach for the bottle. He slid a glass across the bar, then poured.

"I'd be very careful about telling him, Paddy. That is, if I were you."

"What ye be wanting here, lad?"

"The deputy's not going to do you any good," Harrison said, flashing his .38 under the jacket. "And keep your hands on the bar."

"Be careful now, lad. Those barkers can go off easy enough," Paddy said nervously.

"I need a couple of questions answered, Paddy," Harrison told him.

"Do ye now? You're always askin' question, boyo, aren't ye?" Derry said. "But ask then." He carefully resumed polishing glassware.

"Tell me about trading with the Mexicans. You know what I mean," Harrison told him.

"Don't be believin' ever'thing ye hear," the bartender said, looking not at Harrison, but across the room.

"Heard you and Lieutenant Floyd had business connections," Harrison said. "And don't look for someone to come through that door to get me. You'll be going first—with a hole in your head."

"I don't know what ye mean, lad. I'm just a honest businessman, so I am, like yourself." But Paddy still didn't look at Harrison.

"You saw Lieutenant Floyd and I leave this saloon the night he was killed." Harrison reached across the bar with his right hand, grabbed Derry by his shirt collar, and pulled him closer, forcing the older man to look at him. "You watched as we left. Only a few minutes later, someone bushwacked us," he said, feeling his anger build. "Derry, I think you know who did it." Harrison hoped he could scare Derry into giving up information.

"That's a black lie, so it is," the bartender told him, breaking out in a sweat. He saw Harrison's rage reflected in his eyes.

"Tell me, you bastard."

Derry was quiet and shaken.

"Tell me," Harrison demanded, now barely able to contain himself. "I'm going to give you until the count of three." He pulled tighter on the man's shirt.

Derry's fleshy face turned beet red. "You be murderin' a innocent man. I swear I know nothin'."

"One!" With his left hand, Harrison slipped the .38 from his belt and held it so Derry could see it. "Two!"

Derry attempted to swallow, but did so only with great difficulty. "I swear to yez I don't know nothin'."

"Three!" James said softly, beginning to bring the .38 up to Derry's chest.

"Be Jasus! Yer a crazy man. Don't kill me, squire." Derry's hands shook.

The two customers in the saloon stood up. They were cowboys who had been content to drink and mind their own business. But now things were going too far. They couldn't see the pistol, but knew there was a problem.

"Leave 'im be or we'll get the law, mister," the tallest said. Neither was armed. "Freddy, git 'im," he said to his partner.

"Okay," Harrison said, letting go of Derry's collar. He stuck the pistol back in his belt. "Sorry boys, just a minor disagreement. We're okay here. Sit down, and Paddy'll bring you another."

"Don't worry none, lads," Paddy said, relieved. "Two beers comin' up." He tapped the beers and walked them to the table. "Thanks lads."

"Who ambushed us, Paddy?" Harrison asked softly when he returned.

"A drunk down on his luck. So I hear from pub talk here, but it be only talk. It were a robbery gone bad, they say."

"Liar." James pressed, but he didn't touch him. "Those boys saved you this time, Paddy. But there's always later."

"The Washingtons. The Washingtons probably done it, yer honor. They're a bad lot jus' 'cross the border from here."

"Hmm, that's interesting now," Harrison said. "They say you know all about it, Derry." He lied.

"That be a lie. And damn that whore, too." Derry's voice shook, but with anger rather than fear.

"The two cowboys finished their beers and got up to leave. "You okay thar, Paddy?" The tall one asked again.

"Don't ye worry 'bout ol' Paddy, lads. Me an' the gov'nor here jus' be havin' a friendly spat."

"Maria? A whore? I ought to shoot you right now."

"I know'd some a them soldier boys be watchin' ye. They think ye got money, so they do," Derry said, changing his story.

"The truth, Paddy," Harrison said coldly. "Why did someone want Floyd dead?"

"The lad not much liked, I hear. He had his enemies. That's what the lads tell me. 'Tis the truth, so it is."

"And?" Harrison pressed.

"He was one a them smugglers we al'ays hearin' 'bout."

"Who shot him?" Harrison asked. "Tell me, Paddy."

"A soldier from the camp. A despic'ble crim'nal he is," Paddy said, squirming. "I can find 'im fur ye, squire."

"You're a damn liar, Paddy," Harrison said.

"That's all I know," Paddy said. "He works for the big boys, he does."

"Paddy, his name," Harrison said, leaning across the bar.

"That's all ye git from me, laddy," Derry asserted. "If ye push me harder I be gittin' the deputy. I swear on mi mudder's grave."

I'll get no information from Derry, Harrison decided.

"Git out a mi establishment now," Paddy ordered, looking down for the shotgun.

"You're hiding something, Derry," Harrison said, prepared to leave. "I'll be back."

"Harry, how 'bout that ride in the country ya promised?" a woman's voice called from above them. "Remember?"

"Harry and Paddy looked up to see Sal coming down the stairs.

"Go home, woman," Derry ordered. "I be closin' now. Ain't no bus'ness anyways."

"I always keep my promise, Sal," Harrison said, watching her. Tonight, she looked her age, rouge smeared, breasts squeezed too tight in the bodice. Walking to the bar, her shoulders sagged slightly, but seeing Harrison, she made an effort, fixing her hair and pushing up on the bodice.

"Pay me ma money, Paddy," she said, standing next to James.

Paddy pulled a wad of bills from under the grimy apron and slapped two in her hand. "Good eve' to ye, woman," he said curtly.

"That's it for all mi work tonight?" Ya cheap bastard. I deserve better fer what I do fer ya."

"That's it, woman. Now git home."

Sal sighed, rolled the bills up and slid them between her breasts. "Good evenin' then." She turned to walk across the almost deserted room. "Best git ya boy in here ta clean, Paddy," she said, running her finger across the table where the two cowboys were sitting. "The place is filthy."

"Don't ye worry none," Paddy answered. "Peck be comin' in the morning."

He must mean Private Peck, Harrison thought. "Wait Sal. I'll escort you to your room," he called out to catch her attention. "Paddy, we'll settle this later," Harrison said softly, only inches from Derry's face.

"That we will, lad," Derry answered. "That we will."

Surprised, Sal stopped and turned. "I'd be honored, Harry," she replied with a smile.

Harrison quickly caught up to her, and together they walked arm in arm out the door. Paddy watched them leave, glaring. She best keep that big mouth shut, if she knows what's good fer her, he thought.

"You won't be sorry, Harry," she said, squeezing his arm.

Harrison pulled a twenty from his trouser pocket and handed it to her.

"I don't want yer money," she said, refusing the bill. "I jus' want a man to be close with tonight, Harry. I'll do whatever ya want."

"Sal," Harry tried to explain, apologetically. "Please understand. We can't be together, tonight. I just need some information. On Derry. Will you help me?"

She reconsidered and took his money. "The cheap son a bitch," she growled. "What ya want to know?"

"I need to know more about other types of work he's involved in," Harrison continued. "Last Fall, you mentioned that he and Floyd worked together. What was that about?"

"Guns, Harry," Sal replied. "They was sellin' guns to the Mex jus' like ever'one else 'round here, I guess."

"Do you think he knows something about Floyd's death?"

"Poor Jimmy," she replied. "He was good ta me, real good."

"I'm trying to find out who murdered him, Sal. And you can help me."

She stopped walking. "Let me think a bit on it." Sal rubbed the side of her temple. A curl fell over her forehead. Derry know'd somethin' 'bout most things happen 'round here.

"Yes?"

"That night, when you boys leave the Last Chance, I seen yas go," Sal said, considering. "Paddy, he seemed mighty int'rested like."

"What do you mean?"

"He watched ya careful," she said. "I know it because I was standin' beside 'im.

"Anything else you can think of?" he pressed. "Anything at all?"

Sal considered, then smiled brightly. "Yeah Harry, one more thing. That evenin', I seen the Injun in the back room. He was talkin' ta Paddy. They didn't know'd it, but I seen 'im. Don't usual see that one come by here, but I know'd 'im 'cause one a the girls services 'im real regular. A dangerous one, he is. Treats Molly real rough."

Carlos. Harrison knew it had to be Carlos.

*

He returned to the hotel and entered through the back door to find the clerk. Miguel was behind the front desk. He paid the cook a dollar to go get him. "Tell Miguel it's Señor James. I need him now. Ahora!" Harrison told the old cook. Five minutes later, Miguel was in the kitchen.

"Sí, señor," he said. "You have problema?"

I need to get into Camp Furlong. I can't get through the gate without your help," Harrison told him.

"The deputy come and ask questions about you, señor," Miguel told him. "I tell him I know nothing."

"Bueno. Gracias, Miguel. Can you go deliver a message to someone out at the camp?" Harrison took a pencil and notebook from his vest, then hastily scribbled a brief message, folded the paper, and handed it to Miguel."Take this to Grover Burns in Second Platoon, M Company, Third Battalion, 24th Infantry, on the far side of the camp. You remember—he was the young Negro with me in January."

Miguel nodded. He motioned for the old cook, who was watching them. The older man spit on the floor. "Jesus," Miguel said. "Camp Furlong, un soldado se llama Grover Burns. Un Negrito." He handed Jesus the folded message.

Jesus looked at the note, scratched his balding head, then he nodded.

Harrison stuck another dollar bill in his hand. "Two more when you return with Private Burns. I'll wait here."

"Sí, señor." Jesus went out the back door.

Within an hour, Jesus entered the kitchen again, with Grover close behind.

"I'm back, Grover, and I need your help." Harrison gave Jesus a five-dollar bill. The cook smiled, then stuck it in his pocket.

"Yes, suh. Anythin' fur you, I reckon."

"I want you to get me into Camp Furlong without anyone seeing me. Tonight," Harrison told him.

"I kin do that, suh."

"Thank you, Grover," Harrison said, shaking his hand.

"We best be careful, suh. The law is lookin' fur ya."

"Let's go," Harrison said.

CHAPTER TWENTY-EIGHT

Slipping down alleys and unlighted streets, they easily avoided detection. Harrison did not see anyone until they reached the Mexican section of Columbus. There, only an old man relieving himself against a wall looked up as the two walked by. At the outskirts of town, Harrison followed Grover down a desert trail that circled the camp from the southeast, avoiding the main gates with their posted MPs.

About 50 yards from the perimeter, they spotted a sprinkling of lights. Before they reached the tents, they heard talking off in the brush.

"Shh, Mista James," Grover said. "Soldiers."

They crept up on the voices.

"I'll talk with 'em first," Grover whispered. "Stay here." He stood and casually walked toward the soldiers.

"Hey boys, watcha doin' out here?" he asked three men. They were soldiers from his battalion.

"Hey, who's you thar?" one called out.

"Burns from L Company, comin' back from town," he said. He saw the bottles.

"We slippin' past the guard, too," the largest man said. He was obviously drunk.

Harrison remained in the shadows, listening. He could see how easy it would be to sneak guns out of the camp and into the desert without being detected.

"Ya got somebody witya thar, Burns?" Another soldier asked. "Maybe a white whore fur us?" They all laughed.

"Jus' Jackson from I Company is all," Grover answered, trying to laugh.

"Well, let's git on outa here then," the larger man ordered. "And we ain't seen ya, neither."

Grover returned to Harrison. "Let's go. Them boys won't bother us none," he said.

They continued along the perimeter until they were only 15 meters from the battalion area. They could easily make out men walking around. "A sentry," Grover whispered, pointing at a soldier with a rifle about 10 meters away, walking towards them. He immediately dropped to the ground. Harrison followed him. They lay behind a clump of mesquite brush. The guard walked by slowly without noticing them.

When the sentry passed out of sight, Grover rose to a kneeling position. "Come on," he said. "We's in the camp. Where ya want ta go?"

"I want to see Major Snow."

Grover frowned. "Suh, you wants to go to jail? But wait here. I gotta talk with the fireguard over thar to get ya through. He's a friend a mine." He pointed to a lighted area. "I be right back." Grover stood and walked casually through the tent area, hands in his pockets.

*

"Major Snow," Harrison whispered, kneeling beside the soldier asleep on the cot. "Wake up, damn it." He shook him.

"What? Who's there?" Snow muttered. He rose up. In the dim light he saw the intruder. "You." Then he stared.

"Get up, Harrison ordered. "We have to talk."

Snow looked beyond Harrison for his military escort, but saw no one. "How did you get in here, sir? Guard!" he called out.

"I'd be quiet if I were you, major," Harrison said, showing him the pistol in his belt. "I think your sentry is over at the latrine."

"What do you want?" Snow blustered.

"There is still the matter of my brother's death," Harrison said quietly. "And I think you know what I'm talking about."

272

"I told you everything I know, Mr. James," the major said, reaching for his trousers. "Now get out."

"Not everything." Harrison replied. "Please, get dressed."

The major quickly threw on his trousers, then a shirt. "Mr. James, I've heard about your exploits. But murder?"

"A misunderstanding, Major. One that will be cleared up soon," Harrison told him. "I now know some things about my brother. And you."

"What?"

"I have something here I want to read to you." James pulled a bundle of papers from inside his coat and carefully unfolded them. "Testimony of Mister R.R. McDaniels, Katy, Texas, given to County District Attorney, John Crooker, on August 27th, 1917." This is testimony I found in San Antonio at the court martial. It was never used, strangely enough."

"San Antonio," Snow said. "I congratulate you on your successful defense of Private Burns. I was happy to see him returned to Camp Furlong."

"Harrison focused on the document, ignoring him. "You remember Mr. McDaniels, don't you, Major?" he asked. "It was his automobile that you hid in during the riots."

"I don't know what you're talking about, Mr. James. I went to get help, risking my own life in the process."

Harrison began reading the testimony:

"...before I could get my car turned around to go back to Houston, Major Snow jumped on my car and begged me to save him. Then he laid down in the back of the car."

Harrison looked directly at the major, but said nothing.

"I committed no crime, Mr. James. The trial made that quite clear." Major Snow's voice was shaking.

"There's more," Harrison said. "Oh Lord, save me; oh God, take me away from here. They are going to kill me." Does that sound familiar?" he asked. He continued further down without waiting for a response. "'I told the druggist to give him something for his nerves,'" Harrison read on. "He gave him spirits of ammonia. The major was scared to death, I guess. He was holding his handkerchief over his head and kept saying, 'Oh Lord, Oh Lord.'"

"What's your point, Mr. James?" Snow asked in a tired, beaten voice.

"My point, Major Snow…." Harrison stated slowly. "My brother knew what you did that night. As Officer of the Day, your actions were reported to him. He probably found your behavior to be, at the least, deeply troubling. Evidence of your behavior presented at the court martial would have ruined your career."

"My actions were not relevant to the guilt or innocence of the Negro mutineers. Is that so difficult to understand?" Snow asked quietly.

Harrison ignored the question. "My brother never reported you, did he?"

"Your brother and I discussed many things before the Adjutant General's staff interviewed us. But you are mistaken if you think my conduct was at issue. Did you read his testimony?"

"I did," James said.

"And?"

"It was not in his deposition presented at the trial," Harrison said. "But there's more, isn't there?

"What do you mean?"

"I mean my brother had also included a statement that you should be removed from command. He was preparing it that night. You knew because he told you that he had to write a statement that you were unfit for command."

"Preposterous, Mr. James," Snow replied.

"When you found his body, you took that statement and destroyed it," Harrison charged. "Yes, Major, I believe you when you state that you did not kill my brother. Still, you took that statement from his desk."

"He blamed me because he could not accept responsibility for his own actions," Snow said. The major ran his hand nervously over the top of his head. "Don't you see? Captain James still could not blame me for all that happened in Houston that night. He, himself, could not escape from its burden. He knew that his refusal to halt the mutineers before they got out of the camp led to the fighting and the deaths. Your brother's failure was as great as my own in the eyes of the Army. Remember, Captain James' career was also on the line." Snow watched the angry James brother. "Your brother felt trapped. He believed he had failed, too. I believe he took his own life," Snow told him sadly. "You cannot seem to accept it, but that is what happened."

"No, sir," Harrison answered. "My brother felt little remorse for his actions. Actually, I believe he was proud of not giving the order to shoot the men."

"Mr. James," Snow began slowly. "I did not steal anything from your brother's tent. I found your brother on the floor. I examined the body and prepared to move him. The desk chair was turned over. I straightened it. There was no reason not to. I saw nothing lying there."

"Disturbing evidence?"

"Evidence of what?" Snow's voice was soft, almost inaudible. He stared at the floor. "I'm sorry. Your brother and I did not like each other. But I respected him, as an officer in the United States Army and as a man." Tears streaked his face. "I came to his tent to tell him I was prepared to resign my command. I had decided earlier that day. I had to tell him that and ask him to not send his statement...for the good of the army." Snow wiped at the tears on his face.

"And yet you're still in command here, major."

"I am resigning my commission. See for yourself. Here's my letter of resignation." Snow handed Harrison a paper.

He read it. It was to be effective as of April 1, 1918. "Major, I believe you. Still, Bart did not take his own life. I think, with your help I can find out who did kill him. I may also find out who's stealing weapons from the army here at Camp Furlong."

"Mr. James, I want to hear what you've learned—your suspicions, but most importantly your evidence." Snow, exhausted and tired of dealing with James, was doubtful.

James explained what he had learned about how guns were smuggled out of the camp, and who he suspected was involved.

"Lieutenant Floyd and Private Peck? You believe they were stealing weapons from the Army?"

"Major, I have only a hunch about Peck," Harrison answered. "If I could speak with him, I'm certain I can get the truth out of him."

"James, it's one o'clock in the morning," Snow said. "I owe you nothing. I should call for the MP's.

"I know you want to get to the bottom of this smuggling. It would look good in your record if you solved the case," Harrison argued. "And major, I don't think you have any other leads to follow. Am I right?"

"That's none of your business."

"Major, I'm certain if we checked the duty rosters we would learn more than just who was stealing guns," Harrison argued.

"We've examined them already," Snow replied. "Do you think we're stupid?"

"You have? Personally?"

"Captain Blaine looked at them in the course of his investigation. He found nothing of value."

"Captain Blaine?"

"He was my investigating officer."

*

The Negro sentries stared after them as they passed through K and M Company areas.

"My brother was still investigating gun smuggling when he died, wasn't he?" Harrison said. The two walked into the L Company area.

"Yes," Snow replied. "Sentry, come here."

A young Negro private came forward, rifle on his shoulders.

"Take us to Private Jeremiah Peck's tent."

"Yeah suh," he said. "Follow me."

Harrison knew he was taking a gamble. They reached the private's tent. It was dark inside.

"Private, roust Peck, and have him come outside."

"Yeah, suh." He entered the tent. "Peck, Peck git up." James and Snow heard. "The Major wants ta talk wid ya. It's important."

"I hear'd ya," Peck mumbled. "Yeah, yeah. I'm gittin' up."

Within several minutes, the sentry returned with Peck in tow.

"Let's talk in the quartermaster's tent. Peck?" Harrison said.

Snow led them inside. He lit the lantern.

A soldier was asleep on the cot.

"Private, wake up," the officer said, shaking him.

"Suh?" he said with a jerk. "What happen, suh?"

"Private, we need some privacy here," Snow said. "Get dressed and leave us for a while."

"Yeah, suh," the young Negro replied, grabbing his trousers and a shirt.

"Don't forget your boots," Snow called after him.

"Yeah, suh," he said, grabbing them on the way out the opening.

"Mr. James and I have several questions to ask you, Private. About the night Captain James died," Snow said. "Sit down."

"Suh?" the private said, nervously. He looked at both white men.

"Sit down," Snow ordered.

"Yeah, suh."

"How long have you worked for Paddy Derry?" Harrison asked.

"Long time, suh. Since we come to this place."

"What do you do for him?"

"Clean up, mostly, suh. I sweep, wipe tables."

"Does he ever ask you about the army camp?"

"Suh?"

"Does he want to know what goes on here?"

"Sometimes, I guess."

"Does he ask you about weapons here? Where they're stored? Kinds? That sort of thing?" Harrison continued.

"I guess I tell 'im some things," Peck answered. "I says, 'Why ya want a know 'bout dat, Mr. Derry?' And he say, 'Soldiers are mi bus'ness.' That's it."

"He knew you were here in the quartermaster's tent and took care of the weapons, didn't he?"

"Yeah, suh."

"Private, you told me in our earlier conversation that you were at your post in the quartermaster's tent the night Captain James was killed," James said. "You stayed here until the major arrived and called for you. You stated that you never walked outside to Captain James' tent. Why did you tell me that?"

"Don't know, suh. I guess I didn' want ya to think I had something to do with the cap'n's dying, suh. That's all. But I did step out by the capt'n's tent ta see what the ruckus was."

"Why would I think that you had something to do with his death?" James asked. "You thought he shot himself.

"Don't know, suh," Peck replied.

"Did you go inside his tent?"

"No, suh. Ever'thing were quiet agin," Peck answered, looking down. "I think it was some Mex shootin' off out on the road. So I goes back to the guns where I was ordered, suh."

"Did you see anyone around the tent, private?" James asked quietly. "Hear anything unusual?" Peck seemed nervous, perhaps hiding something.

"No, suh?"

"You know something more, Peck. Something you're not telling us," Harrison pushed. "What is it? Tell us."

"Only what I tole ya already, suh. Later, I he'rd the major yell fer me. Then I come to the tent and help 'im with the cap'n."

"Is that all you know, Private?" the major asked.

"Yeah, suh. That's all I knows."

"Private, I think you know more," Harrison said. "You were there in the tent, weren't you? Were you talking with my brother that day…before he died?"

The private shifted his feet, looked down at the ground, avoiding eye contact. "No suh, I was workin' in town, suh, at the saloon 'til evenin'. Special work fer Mista Derry."

"I spoke with your boss this evening."

"Derry, suh? Mista Derry?"

"Yes. He told me that you came in early in the morning to clean up. And that you left early. That's what he told me," James said.

"Yeah, suh. Well, suh, that not true. No suh, not true at all. What time Mista Derry say I leave, suh?"

"About 1:00. Ah, 1300 hours, Private." James watched closely for some reaction.

Peck frowned. Then he clenched his fists. "Mista Derry mistaken, suh. He surely be wrong 'bout dat."

The white men were silent. Then James spoke. "You met with Captain James that afternoon when you returned from town. My brother accused you of stealing weapons from the Army, didn't he?" Without allowing the private an opportunity to respond, he continued, louder, "So later that evening, with no one around, you returned to his tent and shot him dead. You knew where he kept his pistol. So when my brother was out—to eat, perhaps—you crept into his tent and took the weapon."

"No suh, I surely didn't. I didn't do it, suh!"

"You're lying, Peck," James said roughly. "And you'll hang."

"Mr. James," the major said. "Private, we checked the duty roster against when the guns came up missing."

Peck was silent.

"Tell the truth, Private. Derry confessed this evening," James lied. "He said you were stealing machine guns from the army. You carried them out the back way along that path behind K. Company. We have his statement."

"Statement, suh?" Peck looked at the major.

Snow did not respond.

"That's right," Harrison said.

"Da lousy white bastard! I know'd it!" Peck exploded. He lunged for the tent flap, but Harrison blocked his way. Harrison got him in a bear hug. Then he took one arm, twisting it up behind his back and holding it tightly.

"You shot my brother in his tent." Harrison whispered in Peck's ear. "You put his own pistol to his head and pulled the trigger."

"Da dirty plug!" Peck hissed angrily. "Derry say he give me five hundred dollars if I kill the cap'n. He say he know'd too much and gonna 'rest me soon as I come back. He tole me to kill 'im an' make it look like a accident." He began to struggle again. "But I couldn't do it. The cap'n help me. I could never shoot 'im. Someone else done it, not me."

"Private," the major said. "Is that the truth?"

"I come back early, 'round 'bout 1300," Peck said.

James loosened his grip on Peck's arms.

"Then what?" Snow asked.

"The cap'n tol' me he wants to talk. I gotta come to his tent. I know'd what he wants, 'cause he was actin' strange and lookin' at the armory records and rosters. 'Bout 1900, I goes to talk wid 'im."

"What happened?" Harrison pressed

"Suh, the cap'n say he know'd what I done. He say he won't turn me in if I tells 'bout the others. I tell 'im what I know'd 'bout the Lieutenant and 'bout Derry. He say if I talk agin 'em, ever'thing be okay. I say okay."

"So you returned to your duties in here?" Harrison asked.

"Yeah, suh."

"What did you see when you heard the gunshot?" Harrison pressed. "You were lying before, weren't you?"

"Yeah, suh, I surely was," Peak said, his head hanging. "I seen Captain Blaine out in the desert where I run ta look. "I say, 'capt'n, who was shootin'?' He say, "Jus' some Mex on the road.'"

"Why didn't you say something earlier about seeing the Captain?" Snow asked.

"Suh, the capt'n say I should be here in ma tent. That I could be court-martialed for leavin' ma post and goin' way out thar," Peck explained.

"Do you know what Captain Blaine was doing out there?" Harrison asked.

"No, suh," Peck answered. "He say he hear'd the gun, too."

"Why didn't you say anything about seeing the captain?" Snow asked.

"The capt'n say I was disobeyin' orders being outside like that," Peck said. "He say if I git back thar he wouldn't tell no body. I worried 'bout gittin' inta bad trouble if the capt'n know'd it."

"So you kept silent?" Snow said.

"No, suh. Nobody asks me 'bout it 'till Mista James come ta camp wid all his questions."

"And I have one more question for you, Peck," Harrison said. "Did you issue my brother his weapon a couple of days before he died?"

"No, suh."

"Where you in this tent when he got his weapon?"

"No, suh," Peck replied. "Officers git their pistols fer themselves. They don't need no one here. They jus' git 'em and sign."

"They can enter the tent and get them whenever they want?"

"Yeah, suh."

"Did you see Captain James with his pistol anytime during the several days before he was killed?" Harrison asked.

"No, suh. I surely didn't."

"Can I see the log where the officers must sign. I want to see it for the week before Bart was killed."

*

Harrison and Major Snow held Private Peck until the military police arrived.

Harrison watched silently while they took him away.

CHAPTER TWENTY-NINE

Harrison and Major Snow returned to the administrative tent to locate the duty rosters for May 28th, June 18th, and January 27th, 1918, the dates Smith had given him. They quickly realized that the records for the first two dates were missing. No officer rosters at all. Of course, Harrison thought. I should have known the killer would have destroyed them. Probably after taking them from Bart's desk.

For the latter date, the records were complete. In the dim lantern light, the two men poured over them, locating each officer on the roster, except one—Blaine.

"Then he wasn't present for duty," Harrison said to Snow. "We have him."

"Not enough," Snow replied. "We need more evidence before I can act against him, James."

"What else is there?" Harrison asked.

Snow considered. On June 17th or 18th we had a staff meeting called by the Colonel. Yes, I remember that clearly now," Snow said. "The Colonel wanted all officers present for the meeting. It was to finalize plans for our movement to Houston. I'll check those attendance records." He got up, walked over to another filing cabinet, and slid it open. "Bring the lantern over here so I can see," he ordered.

Harrison carried the light over and held it above Snow, while the officer quickly but thoroughly ran through the dozens of files.

"Here it is," he said, pulling out the manila file. "June 18th." He browsed through it. "Attending.... Just as I thought. Blaine is missing. He did not attend that meeting which probably means he was not in camp at that time."

"That's good enough for me," Harrison said.

*

Harrison checked the .38 into his belt as he left the stable. He had returned from Camp Furlong an hour earlier. He had what he needed. He walked through the center of town and into the Hoover Hotel.

"Mr. James," Captain Blaine said as they met in the middle of the mostly deserted lobby. "What is it you have to talk about this early in the morning? Major Snow said it was urgent."

"I'm still looking into my brother's murder," Harrison said, never taking his eyes from the other man. "There are a couple of things you can clear up for me."

"If I can." Blaine smiled. "I've taken over a lot of your brother's work here, continuing his investigation. So be quick. I'm very busy."

"Which investigation is that, Captain?" James asked quietly. "The one involving gun smugglers, or the other one?"

"The other?" Blaine asked, seeming puzzled. "Which was that?"

"I think you know, sir. The one involving spying for America's enemy—Germany." Not getting any reaction, Harrison continued, "My brother had been hunting spies since the campaign against Pancho Villa." He paused. "Is that when you began selling military information to Mexican generals—Carranza, Obregon, and even Villa?"

A town deputy, Major Snow and two military policemen entered the lobby through a rear door, standing unseen behind Captain Blaine. The two Negro MPs were armed with .45s. All four were listening.

"Go to hell, James," Blaine shot back. "I'm a United States Army Officer!"

"I think you even sold information to Villa when you were chasing him. It didn't matter, did it? As long as you got paid for it," Harrison went on.

"I don't know what you're talking about," Blaine replied.

"We have proof that you were traveling to El Paso to sell information to the Germans."

"You're insane," he said. "You don't have anything on me. I think you're bluffing."

Harrison reached into his coat pocket to retrieve documents. "Duty rosters when you were absent, eye witness statements, and this, Blaine." He held up the file of the meeting Blaine had missed. "Missing meetings, Blaine, to spy for Germany?"

"What?" he stuttered, shocked. "Impossible. I destroyed…."

"You destroyed them?" Harrison repeated. "After you murdered my brother you destroyed all the records. Is that it?" He smiled.

Blaine was suddenly quiet. He realized what he had just said.

"We know what you did, Blaine," Harrison said.

"Prove it, Mr. James," Blaine hissed back at him.

"When you sold information to the German…. That's when Bart picked up your trail, wasn't it? He learned about you from his own spy inside Von Moltke's household." James felt his own anger rising. "Later, you found out Bart was on to you. Von Moltke may have told you, or maybe you realized he had you when you saw him going through the duty rosters. Either way, that's when you killed him. You didn't have much choice, did you, Blaine?" Harrison pressed. "You killed a brother officer and you betrayed your country. For money."

"I have no idea what you mean," Blaine answered, seeming indignant. But Harrison detected the hint of fear in his voice.

"Bart had enough evidence to arrest you," Harrison went on. "If we searched your quarters we might find something."

"Ridiculous," Blaine said. "I will not stand here and listen to your accusations." He turned to leave.

"Not yet, Blaine," Harrison said, grabbing his arm and holding it tightly. "Let me tell you the rest. You planned everything from earlier that day. You saw Bart looking at the duty rosters a day earlier. You waited for an opportunity. It was presented to you when Floyd and the other officers went to town. You knew they would be there late playing poker. That was your chance. After it was dark, you went to L Company. The area was empty. You entered Bart's tent."

"That's preposterous. He killed himself with his own weapon," Blaine retorted. "The army's investigation proved that."

"Your investigation," Harrison answered. "And you were able to cover up your murder nicely. That is, except for running into Peck. He was ordered to duty inside the quartermaster's tent. But Peck surprised you, didn't he? Outside Bart's tent?"

"I don't know what you're talking about."

"You went to the quartermaster's tent the day before my brother's death. As an officer, you signed out a weapon on your own—but it was Bart's weapon. You used his signature. The young soldier on duty was probably distracted. He obviously didn't notice the switch."

"Go to hell," Blaine hissed angrily.

"That night, with no one in the area except Peck, who was supposed to be guarding the weapons inside the quartermaster's tent, you entered Bart's tent, shot him at point blank range, then took the rosters. You placed Bart's pistol in his hand, trying to make murder look like suicide."

"That's quite a story, James," Blaine shot back. "But it's all lies."

"Blaine, you should have taken care to learn my brother's signature before attempting forgery." Harrison pulled out a letter with Bart's signature on the bottom. "Bart signed his name "Bartlett R. James," not "Bart R. James." See the difference?" Harrison held the letter, then the gun roster book in front of Blaine.

Blaine partially turned before Harrison, dropping the roster, grabbed his arm again. This time he held it tightly.

"Let go of me," Blaine demanded. He reached up to pull James' hand away. "I order you to remove your hand," he said.

Harrison realized that the captain was unarmed. "Gambling and whoring are expensive, aren't they? Especially on a captain's pay. You needed money to pay off your debts, and then you wanted more."

"You don't know what you're talking about. Ask the other officers. They don't see me gambling in town."

"No, they don't," Harrison replied. "You do your gambling in Juarez. It wouldn't be difficult to find witnesses who saw you there, often at the Sheldon Hotel in El Paso."

"There is no law against going to El Paso, Mr. James."

"I know of one witness who will testify to seeing you there, Captain, with a Mr. Felix Sommerfield."

Blaine was silent.

"You met him on at least three separate occasions—May 28th, June 18th, and January 27th—a month ago. Days the roster shows you were off duty." Harrison still held Blaine's arm tightly. "The Bureau of Investigation will verify that this Sommerfield is a known German agent." He leaned closer. "Even the two troopers you used to break into my room said they regularly saw you on the train. That's how you met them—those train trips to El Paso."

Blaine tugged against James' arm, finally forcing himself free.

"You're going to hang, Blaine. For treason and murder," Harrison said finally.

Blaine turned to run. He found Major Snow blocking his path.

"Arrest Captain Blaine," Snow ordered the two military policemen still standing beside him.

"I'll want him, too, Major," the deputy constable added. He was a younger, Hispanic man, thin as a rail, with piercing brown eyes. The revolver strapped to his side appeared over-size on his small hips. But, Harrison learned quickly, he spoke with authority and self-confidence.

The deputy turned to Harrison. "I'm going to give you a couple of days free on the streets, señor. See what you come up with about the killing of Constable Arnold." He paused. "But only a couple of days. And stay close."

CHAPTER THIRTY

Harrison spent the early morning writing up his statement for the deputy. He was exhausted. But he knew he had one more task before he could return to Las Palomas and Maria—find Constable Arnold's killer. He needed the help of Sergeant Parilla. Then I'll send for Daniel, he decided, returning to his room in the Hoover.

Harrison poured water from the pitcher into the ceramic basin, splashed off his face, shaved, then he changed into his last clean shirt. It was white silk. Somehow that seemed appropriate. Coming back down the stairs, he heard someone call his name.

"Señor," a Hispanic voice said in the lobby. "Coffee?"

"That would be good," James responded, turning to see Miguel's smiling face.

Miguel handed him a cup of steaming coffee. "A dangerous night?" he asked.

"It could have been," James said.

"I worry where you go," Miguel said. "But the deputy no longer look for you. I hear this."

"That's correct," Harrison said, finishing the coffee and returning the cup. "Has your uncle returned, Miguel? It's important that I speak with him."

"I think he come home muy temprano on the train."

"Good," Harrison replied. "Hasta luego." He left the hotel. Crossing the dusty street, he made for a narrow alley.

A young soldier in a crumpled uniform with the beginnings of a beard darkening his face saw the tall man crossing the street. "I gotta tell Derry. There's money in this'n," the soldier mumbled, staggering slightly as he rose from the straw, his head pounding. He continued to watch through a wide crack between the clapboard sidings as Harrison made his way up the dusty alley toward the

Mexican neighborhood. Then he straightened his uniform and reached for his hat and revolver belt.

Harrison reached Parilla's house around 9:00. He knocked softly on the old wood door. "Hola," he called in Spanish. "Is anyone here?"

"Venga, Harry," a voice replied. "Please, come in."

Harrison entered to find Juan sitting at the small table, a bottle of tequila and two glasses before him. The sun was shining brightly through the single window facing east, lighting the center of the room. Juan was dressed in army trousers, but without a shirt or boots on. He was alone. For the first time, Harrison noticed the tattoo on his arm. It was an eagle.

"Buenas dias," the sergeant said. "Please, sit and drink with me. Although he looked slightly disheveled, Juan's voice was clear and sharp.

Harrison sat and poured himself a drink from the bottle. Juan had obviously been waiting for him.

"La revolución!" Juan said quietly yet forcefully, holding up his glass. He then tossed the drink down in one gulp, immediately pouring himself another.

"To the Revolution," Harrison agreed, taking only a small sip from his glass.

"Harry," Juan said, "I hear you want to talk with me."

"I have a couple of questions, Juan," Harrison said. "And I need your help."

"Dígame, Harry."

"Juan, when did you get to the constable's office the night he was killed?

"I get there right after you, Harry. You go too early, amigo, so I am late to warn you to stay away, eh?"

"I received a message from Arnold to go to his office."

"But too early, I think. It was, how you say it, you were not to go there at that time when Daniel has business there also."

"Did you ever think that maybe the constable had no idea that Daniel was coming to his office?" Harrison asked.

"No comprendo," Juan replied.

"A trap set by the Indian, Carlos, to kill the constable and blame it on Daniel. Or to kill Daniel also. I don't know."

"I think you are too smart," Juan said with a sigh. "Harry, sometimes it is better to mind your own business. You do not know this," Juan said, frustrated. "Everywhere you go you find dangerous business. I try all the time to keep you alive. You are a very lucky man, amigo."

"What do you mean?"

"You ask many questions to the wrong people, Harry. They want to kill you. But here you are, still alive."

"You know about those people, don't you?" Harrison asked.

"I know about some of them. It is a very big business, smuggling." Juan sighed long and deep, then finished the remaining tequila in his glass. "I try only to mind my business, like I tell you, amigo."

"I have to find who killed Constable Arnold," Harrison told him. "Or Daniel and I will hang for it."

"I think Carlos kill him," Juan said.

"I need to know who hired Carlos. Carlos was only a pistolero. Was it Derry?"

"There. More trouble for you," Juan said.

"But that's why I'm here." James told him. He looked at Juan patiently, waiting for him to speak.

"Daniel could not kill the constable that way. That's why it was Carlos. As you say, Carlos is a killer. I know this. You must tell the deputy, Harry. So Daniel does not hang."

"I will," Harrison agreed. "But who paid him to do it?"

"It could be many people," Juan said slowly.

Harrison studied him, considering his answer. "Were you part of it?" he asked finally.

"You think that, Harry? You come to take me?" Juan reached into his coat and pulled out James' Colt automatic. "Here, señor. This belongs to you." He set it on the table.

Cautiously, Harrison took the weapon, quickly looked it over, and then removed the magazine. It was empty. He dropped it into his coat pocket. "Where did you get this?" he asked. But he already knew.

"I find it in the desert that night," Juan told him. "I look for you. I find only the pistola." He pulled an Army .45 from his belt and pointed it at James. "This one is loaded. So please, put your other weapon on the table where I can see it."

Harrison slowly placed the .38 on the table. "As a soldier, you must help me turn the murderers over to the law."

Juan laughed heartily, surprising James. "Laws are paper with lots of words. They can be twisted by anyone with a sharp tongue. I know. I see this. I saw how the law worked in Houston."

"But it can work, Juan. You have to believe that it can."

"Do you believe that, amigo?" he asked, looking directly at James.

The two men faced off. Neither flinched.

"Remember our talk out in the desert after we see La Senorita?"

"I remember, Juan," Harrison said.

"Now I ask you to respect what I do. Me comprende?"

"You ask for my respect?" James said, surprised. "A long time ago, you said you didn't know why President Wilson chased Villa. Well, perhaps he did it to bring him to justice. Justice for the families of the innocent people Villa killed in New Mexico. Isn't that possible?" he asked.

"Was that justice, Harry? Or was it revenge?"

Derry entered the house before he could respond.

James looked to Juan, then back to the bartender. "Derry," he said.

"Aye, lad. Ye wouldn't take my advice," he said.

"Maybe I should have," Harrison said grimly.

"Too late for you, me foin bucko." Derry grinned.

"Amigo, you know too much now," Juan said.

"Shoot the bastard, Parilla," Derry growled at Juan. "A thousand dollars to shoot 'im."

James did not take his eyes off the .45 pointed at his chest. "Why Juan?" he asked. "Where's your respect for me?"

"I'm a good soldier," Juan answered. "But, señor, I must feed my family, buy shoes for mi Juanito. The Army, it does not pay so well. Señor Derry say he will pay me," Juan said, looking hard at Harrison. "Remember what we talk about the first day we meet? The enemy of my enemy is my friend."

"What kind of work did Floyd do for you, Derry?" Harrison wanted to know.

"The lad sold information, he did. He tells me that 10 Army machine guns be sellin'. Then I be meetin' with the young Peck. A good thief that un. Brownings. So I be hirin' 'im," Derry said with a smile.

"Did my brother find out about this business of Floyd's?"

Juan smiled. "El Capitan knew about it."

"But he never caught him, did he?" James said.

"No, he never catch him."

"Did he kill Floyd?" Harrison pointed at Derry. "And the constable?"

"You should ask Señor Derry, amigo," Juan said, looking to the bartender. "Like I tell you already, I do not know everything. Too many hombres that want to kill each other, eh? That is part of the business of smuggling."

"Help me bring him to justice."

"Justice?" Juan leaned forward, suddenly intent. "We talk already about justice. The white man wants revenge. He wants to punish, not to find justice."

"Grover Burns found it, Juan," James told him.

"Señor Derry, tell him what he wants to know," Juan said, still pointing his automatic at Harrison.

"'Twas in me own best int'rests that Floyd be killed," Paddy said. "Poor lad. He was greedy."

"Was it also in your best interest to kill the constable?"

"Sure, that was na me. An important man in El Paso done it."

"A big smuggler in El Paso?" Harrison asked. The pieces finally fell into place. "Jackson Smith is his name?"

"Aye, 'tis," Derry said, proud to show how much he knew. "The Injun needed help settin' things up, so I fixed his game, I did. An' he paid me good."

"Why kill the constable?"

"The constable was on ta 'im," Derry said. "An' the constable weren't a constable at all, see? He worked for the Bureau of Investigation. They figured 'twas too dangerous to let 'im go on breathing."

"Why involve Daniel Washington in the shooting?" James asked.

"Smith wanted to blame the shootin' on 'im and his sister. They'd hunt the woman down, too, he figured. Then he'd take over their weapons deal." Derry sighed. "Ever'body wants to git rich. But 'twas Smith's idea to support both generals. He be a man ta hedge his bets. Then the constable figured out Smith's game, boyo," he added, grinning. "Smith's ideas be too bloody big fur 'im, now."

"What's your game, Paddy."

"Oh aye. Ye can die knowin'," he replied. "Smith be people not like ma self. Sure, I like the money. But I do na want the bloody

English to win the war in Europe. I hate the Limey bastards. I be jus' a small business man now. But others who believe the same, they be powerful an' have money. They knows that if the Americans be fightin' the Mex here, it'll take 'em longer to git ta France. Jus' a couple a months an' maybe the English get whipped good. Ye git ma meanin', bucko?" Paddy asked.

"I think I understand what side you're on," James said slowly.

"But seein' it way too late," Derry grinned. He looked at Juan. "Now kill 'im."

Juan sat motionless. "Remember what I tell you earlier, Harry," he said.

"Shoot 'im, ye bloody fool!"

Juan ignored him.

Paddy looked over to Juan. Harrison sat still. He felt beads of perspiration break out on his face. He inhaled deeply, preparing to make some move. He measured the distance to his loaded gun, still lying on the table.

"I have killed many men, Señor Derry. But I am not a murderer," Juan said calmly.

"Shoot 'im. Like we agreed," Derry ordered. "Or I be givin' the green ta another man. One wid some guts in 'im."

"Juan, I mean to take this man in," Harrison said. "He's responsible for killing one man and helping kill another."

"For us, Harry, justice comes from this." He held up the weapon. "But it is to survive only." He looked at Harrison. "You and I, amigo, we are not so different."

"Aren't we?"

"I think I let you do it your way." Juan motioned for James to pick up his .38. He lowered his .45.

"No," Derry yelled. He lunged for the revolver.

James snatched it before the other man could.

The bartender went for Harrison's throat.

The adobe room seemed to erupt as the .38 caliber exploded. The bartender, only inches from James' face, was shot in the chest. The force of impact threw the heavy man backward against the door. Blood splattered across the adobe wall.

Numb, Harrison slowly got up from the table, gun in hand. He stood staring down at Derry.

Powder smoke hung in the air, burning their eyes and nostrils.

Juan stood up. "Put your pistola away. It is done," he said softly. "Justice has been served, no?" He holstered his own automatic.

James stuck the .38 back into his belt, his ears ringing.

"Amigo, it is over for you," Juan repeated. "Now you go back to your world."

"I'll bring the deputy here," Harrison said. He walked out the door and down the street. On the way, he passed Charlie and Jonesy. Standing in the shelter of an old porch, they watched him pass, their heads turning slowly, mouths wide open.

*

Harrison went immediately to the constable's office and turned himself in to the deputy. They returned to the adobe house where Juan waited. The door was wide open. He sat at the table dressed in his Army uniform.

It was midday before the deputy completed his investigation. Two of his men took the corpse away, wrapped in an old blanket. Harrison and Juan told the deputy that Harrison had shot Derry in self-defense. Harrison was not charged with any offense. He explained that, because of their smuggling activities, Paddy Derry and Jackson Smith had hired an associate to kill Lieutenant Floyd and the constable. There was no mention of Juan's knowledge of smuggling. Their statements cleared Daniel of murder charges.

The deputy telegraphed the Police Department in El Paso. A warrant was issued immediately to arrest Jackson Smith.

When finally the deputy was convinced he had the truth, he released them. "Stay around until the investigation is closed," he said to both men. "There may be a trial."

"I must travel to Palomas on personal business," Harrison told him. "It's important."

Juan smiled.

"If you cross the border, you must post a thousand dollar bond, Señor James," the deputy replied.

"I will wire my bank in Chicago immediately. But I can assure you, I'm good for it,"

*

Later that evening, after receiving his reply from Chicago, Harrison promptly posted his bond. A short time later, he stood in the wide doorway to the stables with the old man and Mr. Jones.

"The horses are ready, Señor Harry," the old man said simply.

"Thank you," Harrison answered, handing him two hundred-dollar bills. "For your troubles, señor." He stepped into the saddle and, with the silent old black man beside him, headed south again toward the border. Riding down Broadway, they rode toward the Last Chance Saloon.

Harrison pulled up on the reins as they passed the saloon. Surprised, Mr. Jones also stopped. A blond woman out front was painting on the window. They watched her write "Sal's" in front of "Last" in large black letters.

"Looks good, Sal," Harrison called. "Damn good."

The woman turned, still holding the large paint brush, and smiled back at the riders. "Thanks, Harry. The place'll be all mine someday."

*

Riding the stallion through the open wood gates, Harrison saw the only person in the world who mattered to him. Maria stood on the veranda, waving. Before his mount had stopped, he was out of the saddle and racing toward her. "Maria, Maria," he called. They embraced.

"Oh Harry, my love," she laughed through her tears, "I was so worried that I would have to go to London and Paris alone."

Then they both began laughing.

*

Later that evening, in the solitude of Maria's great study, James wrote:

> Mother, I have reached the end of my investigation. I proved Bartlett's integrity, dedication to duty, and his love for the United States Army. I learned that he was a man highly respected by his friends and his enemies. He was a man of great courage and loyalty, and a man who believed in justice. I found his murderer, and attended to the situation. My mission is now completed.

> Goodbye,
> Harrison

POSTSCRIPT

Defeated again, his few remaining soldiers demoralized, Pancho Villa finally was forced to make peace with the Mexican Government in 1920. He retired to his Rancho Canutillo in Durango State. The political violence in Mexico, however, continued. On July 20, 1923, Francisco "Pancho" Villa died in a bloody assassination. The identity of his killer was never discovered, although most people suspected that General Obregón was behind it.

The 24th Infantry's colored battalion stayed in Camp Furlong for the duration of the war. Major Kneeland Snow resigned as its commanding officer and returned to civilian life. Private Jeremiah Peck, arrested for theft of government property, never went to trial. On the morning he was to be shipped out to Fort Sam Houston, Private Peck was found dead in his cell, hanging by a knotted bed sheet from the bars of his narrow window. The coroner immediately ruled it a suicide. Harrison, who heard about it sometime later, knew the "suicide" was very convenient. Peck never had an opportunity to implicate any others in his crimes.

Captain Blaine was court-martialed. He pled innocent to both charges against him. But, after considerable deliberation, the panel of presiding officers determined that there was sufficient evidence to convict him of espionage in wartime and murder. The earlier ruling that Captain Bartlett James had committed suicide was overturned.

Having attended the court martial proceedings, James returned six months later from Las Palomas for the hanging. The evening before Blaine was scheduled to be executed for spying, he asked for James to see him in his cell.

James stood in front of the dark steel door looking through the small opening at the condemned man. Blaine stood and walked slowly to the door. "I killed your brother," he confessed without remorse. "I had no choice." Blaine looked blankly through the small opening at James. He then turned to slowly walk back to the cot.

"I look forward to tomorrow, Blaine," was all Harrison said, his voice cold as ice. Then he left. Blaine was hanged at Fort Sam Houston on December 6, 1918, after all appeals had been exhausted. The execution took place on the same gallows as that used to hang the Negro mutineers a year earlier.

Harrison asked himself if Blaine's execution was a measure of justice for Bart. He was troubled by the question, until he saw that Blaine was also dead. That would have to be enough.

*

Eventually, the white cavalry units at Camp Furlong were ordered to France. Both Charlie and Jonesy, now transferred to the infantry, saw action during the Allies' 1918 summer offensive spearheaded by General Blackjack Pershing's American Expeditionary Force. The Americans' long-awaited offensive succeeded in driving the Germans back, accomplishing the first major breakthrough on the Western Front since 1914.

For his courage in killing and capturing several enemy soldiers on the Marne River, Charlie was decorated. One week after receiving his medal for valor, he fell to a German mustard gas attack. The poison severely damaged his lungs. He spent the remainder of his life in a veterans' home in Lexington, Kentucky.

Jonesy fought on through the long summer and into the late fall of 1918. Four days before the Armistice was signed, he was killed by a sniper's bullet to the head.

Juan Parilla never left Camp Furlong, finally retiring from the United States Army on January 1, 1919. With the horrible destruction of the Revolution finally drawing to a close, he took his family to Mexico. Joining with Daniel, Mr. Jones, and Grover, they bought more land and became cattle ranchers. By 1922 the Washington rancho had grown to become one of the largest in Chihuahua State.

Not content to live the less exciting and more sedentary lifestyle of a rancher, Daniel left in 1920 for New Orleans. Several years after Daniel's departure, receiving no word of his whereabouts, Juan went to look for him. He searched the gaming halls and pleasure establishments of black and white New Orleans. He engaged the efforts of the city police, but still found nothing. Daniel had simply disappeared. Finally, in late 1923, Juan returned home. Daniel was never heard from again.

Jackson Smith attempted to flee to Mexico, but he did not leave quickly enough. Bureau of Investigation agents intercepted him at the border. The charge of murdering Constable Amos Arnold was dropped. There were no witnesses or evidence to prove he had hired Carlos. Smith, real name Andrew Cobb, agreed to testify that he saw Blaine meeting with a German agent in El Paso on three separate occasions. In July 1918, Smith was convicted of violating the American embargo against selling weapons to the Mexican belligerents. Throughout his trial, he refused to reveal who he worked for. After serving six months of a five year sentence, Smith was released from prison.

But justice often works in its own way and time. In October 1929, Smith took his own life by jumping from the 15th floor window of the Chrysler Building in New York City, having lost everything in the stock market crash.

Harrison's mother died rich but alone in Miami Beach in 1934. She refused to speak with her son, and saw him only once more before her death. Her faithful servant, Jonathan, had died quietly in his sleep in 1920. Harrison returned from Europe alone to attend both funerals.

With the coming of 1919 and peace, Harrison and Maria left the Washington hacienda, first for New York, and then Paris. They avoided Chicago. Even before leaving the hacienda, Harrison ordered that his mother be removed in all capacity from Randolph James. He then turned over his duties as President to a trusted aide, one who believed in the law. Content to travel the world with his bride, he never again involved himself in the business. Following the stock market crash of 1929, the two, with their small children, returned to Las Palomas to live.

Every year at Christmas while traveling, Harrison and Maria sent a special gift to Juan. The accompanying note always read simply: "Still searching for Pancho Villa." Juan understood.

THE END